SCANDAL POINT

FAHAD SAMAR

HarperCollins *Publishers* India

First published in 2013 by
HarperCollins *Publishers* India

Building 10, Tower A, 4th Floor, DLF Cyber City, Phase II,
Gurugram Haryana – 122002, India
www.harpercollins.co.in

ISBN: 978-93-5116-025-0

2 4 6 8 10 9 7 5 3 1

This is a work of fiction and all characters and incidents described in this book are the product of the author's imagination. Any resemblance to actual persons, living or dead, is entirely coincidental.

Typeset in 11/14 Dante MT
by Jojy Philip, New Delhi 110 015

Printed and bound at
MicroPrints India, New Delhi

SCANDAL POINT

Fahad Samar studied at Bombay International School and at St. Xavier's College, Mumbai from where he graduated with a degree in English Literature. He began his career as a film-maker with Merchant-Ivory Productions in 1987.

In 1993, Fahad established his company, Bombay Talkie and has since written, directed and produced scores of commercials, documentaries, corporate films and TV shows.

A pioneer in youth culture programming in India, he has directed cult TV shows like *BPL OYE!*, *Superhit Muqabla* and *The Poppadum Show*.

Fahad is a well-known social commentator and has contributed columns regularly to the *Mumbai Mirror*, *DNA* and the *Indian Express* over the past ten years. He also writes on food, wine and travel for *Upper Crust* magazine. Fahad's articles and essays have appeared in *Elle*, *Harper's Bazaar* and *Conde Nast Traveller* among other publications.

He lives in Mumbai with his wife, Simone Singh.

For Simone,
whose soul selects her own society

ONE

A savage lust for scandal consumes us. We have devolved into vampires that feed on the depravity of others. The media daily serves up juicy nuggets of sleaze and sensationalism so our voracious appetite may be gratified. Tiring quickly of one fable of iniquity, we rabidly move on to the next, hoping that the new tawdry tale will prove spicier, filthier than yesterday's.

Ricky Kumar closed his eyes and braced himself as the burly Goan attendant perfunctorily lubricated his sphincter and proceeded to slide a plastic nozzle six inches up his rectum. With the flick of a switch, gallons of cold water surged up Ricky's bum and gurgled about his intestines. Propped up on the clinic bed, his legs spread, Ricky squirmed as more and more water flooded his colon. Just when he was sure he was about to explode, a sudden reflex forced him to expunge the unbearable build-up inside. The relief that Ricky experienced was, however, temporary as within moments, the process was being repeated.

It was fifteen years since Ricky had last had anything

shoved up his anus, but the memory of the brutal buggering he'd received from the senior boys at Eton remained fresh. He had called his mother in Mumbai, sobbing uncontrollably, too ashamed to reveal the real reason why he wanted to return home less than a week after excitedly entering boarding school in England.

Ricky's father, Kapil Kumar, then one of the shiniest stars in the Hindi film firmament, was livid when his wife Manju called and insisted he leave his movie shoot in Switzerland to go collect his homesick son. Kapil 'King Cock' Kumar, as he had been reverently christened by his cronies, had only just succeeded in bedding Ragini, the voluptuous nineteen-year-old starlet cast opposite him in the bloody romantic revenge saga, *Khoon, Khoon, Khoon*. Ragini's mother had been convinced that a liaison with the senior actor would do wonders for her daughter's fledgling career and had tactfully stayed behind in Geneva at the producer's behest and expense while her daughter carried on to film and fornicate in Gstaad.

Safe at home in Mumbai, young Ricky resumed school in Bandra, the posh suburb where most movie stars reside in high-walled bungalows, shielded from sight and the stench of the city. Ricky grew up surrounded by fellow filmi brats, the progeny of actors, directors, producers, scriptwriters and other stalwarts of the Hindi movie industry. There were no permanent friends or foes in this loose-knit community and even as they bitched out and back-stabbed one another, their kids invariably attended the same schools, frequented each other's birthday, Diwali and Christmas parties and fell in and out of love with one another.

Rhea, the petite, pixie-like daughter of Kaamiya and Kantilal Zaveri, was one such creature who had made Ricky's pubescent heart flutter. Rhea's mother, the sultry Kaamiya, had been a B-list actress for years, struggling to gain a foothold in the film industry, working first as a background dancer and then as the heroine's best friend, till she finally got her big break. The film that eventually catapulted her to stardom was produced by a smuggler turned social worker, Sultan Habib. Rumour had it that Kaamiya had been his mistress for several years, until Antwerp-based diamond merchant Kantilal Zaveri fell vigorously in love and married her overnight, to general consternation. At the time, it was inconceivable that a conservative Gujarati Jain billionaire should propose to a Punjabi Hindi film heroine, particularly one with such a gloriously Technicolor past. But mild-mannered Kanti was quite prepared to overlook Kaamiya's dubious antecedents if she was willing to forego the glamour of tinsel town and live a life of opulent anonymity in Antwerp.

Kaamiya, for her part, was only too glad to escape Mumbai and the sweaty clutches of her benefactor, who had already filled his permissible quota of four wives and wasn't likely to wed in the foreseeable future. Besides, marriage to such a wealthy businessman garnered Kaamiya a modicum of respectability, if not actual respect, in the eyes of the Indian upper crust, which had long delighted in looking down upon this arriviste actress.

Shortly after, Kaamiya presented Kantilal with a sparkling little jewel in the form of their daughter Rhea. This beautiful, bright girl was educated at Wycombe Abbey and later at the Sorbonne. Her parents, fiercely proud of their roots, ensured that Rhea vacationed annually in Mumbai and attended classical dance and cookery classes. She would stay with the Kumars, her local guardians, and each year little Ricky would anxiously await her visit.

Born a year before Ricky, Rhea was extremely fond and protective of the shy, sensitive boy who was fast blooming into an exceedingly good-looking young man. And over the years, as the hormones began to rage, Ricky started developing feelings for Rhea that were decidedly non-platonic.

Three long beeps signalled the end of the hour-long colon cleansing session and the Goan attendant returned to disengage Ricky from the pipe up his posterior. Disoriented by the intense intestinal irrigation, Ricky walked tentatively in his rubber flip-flops along the gravel path that led from the treatment centre to his living quarters. The sun was beginning to set at the Suryanamaskar Wellness Spa and flocks of egrets flew in tandem overhead to roost in the banyan trees that dotted the verdant island of Divar. Entering the red-roofed Mediterranean-style villa that had been home these past ten days, Ricky flopped face down on the soft bed only to realize he had squashed the pack of puffed rice in the pocket of his spa robe. The lady at the treatment centre had instructed him to consume it within half an hour of his session with plenty of water. The thought of ingesting more fluids via any orifice revulsed Ricky, but he dutifully sat up and munched the mangled contents of the plastic pack.

'I really hope Papa is doing something to get me out of here as soon as possible,' he thought, as he poured himself a tumbler of tepid water.

There was a knock and a high-pitched, cheery voice called, 'Hiya Ricky, you there?'

Ricky slipped on a pair of shorts and a snug tee and opened the door to Amanda, a thirty-something, perky Englishwoman who flounced into the room and planted an extravagant kiss on his cheek.

'So, my young chum. How was it?'

'Well, not as bad as I had expected, but it's still seriously invasive stuff, you know. Frankly, I'm feeling quite violated.'

Amanda let out a guffaw as she amiably patted his buttocks. 'Look on the bright side, love. A couple more sessions and your sins will be flushed away, literally.'

Ricky grimaced. The prospect of two more colonics was daunting. He quickly changed the subject. 'So, what time do you check out tomorrow morning?'

'I leave at eight. My flight to Mumbai is at eleven. That should give me enough time, right?'

'Yup, plenty. Ram Singh will meet you at the airport. He'll have a placard with your name on it. My mum's expecting you for lunch, so don't eat crap on the plane, all right?'

'Oh, bless you! I can't believe I get to stay in your tony mansion in Mumbai while you're stuck here for another three weeks! You are so sweet, you darling, darling boy. Really, everything they say about Indian warmth and generosity ...'

With that, Amanda leaned over and gave Ricky another sloppy kiss. He blushed, embarrassed by her outpouring of affection and gratitude. Ricky had met Amanda a week ago at the spa and had been drawn to the plain, pleasantly plump Londoner who disarmed everyone with her big smile and easy manner. She was at least ten years older than him and the absolute lack of physical attraction resulted in them quickly becoming friends.

Barely four days after checking in, the tedium of the spa routine had begun to take its toll on Ricky. Rising at five to practise yoga, undergoing various gross Ayurvedic treatments, enduring banal counselling sessions and bland vegetarian meals was certainly not his idea of quality time in Goa, the party capital of India. But the extraordinary developments over the last couple of weeks had necessitated his staying at least a month at this secluded island spa until things cooled down in Mumbai. Amanda's arrival had helped take Ricky's mind off his problems and eased the drudgery. He had been more than happy to extend his hospitality to the giddy Brit on her travels through India.

As they hugged goodbye, Amanda whispered, 'You'll be fine, Ricky, I know you will. You've been so brave through all of this. Just stick it out a little longer, ducky. I may be the queen of clichés, but trust me: this too shall pass.'

Ricky smiled, fighting back tears. 'Thanks. I'm going to miss you, Mandy. Have a safe trip and enjoy Mumbai. Give my parents my love and, whatever you do, please don't tell my dad about the colonics. He won't ever let me hear the end of it.'

Amanda laughed and winked. 'You obviously mean the rear end of it!'

A fortnight before Ricky Kumar went into exile in Goa ...

Gautam Goyal was the first passenger to disembark from the British Airways flight that touched down at midnight in Mumbai. He was received at the gate and whisked through immigration and customs by his father's earnest office manager.

'A warm hello and even more warm welcome to Mumbai, Gautam baba! Myself, Waman Dixit. You may remember? How is daddyji and Rani beti? How do you like our new airport? Fancy, nah? Not like before, stinking, smelling. I think so you must be last visiting Mumbai minimum five, six years ago, hai na?'

'For fuck's sake, spare me the small talk, dick shit! It's almost one in the bloody morning, so why don't you bugger off home and let me do the same!'

As Gautam got into the waiting Mercedes and commanded the chauffeur to drive off, a red-faced Waman Dixit suddenly remembered something. He hobbled after Gautam's car and rapped urgently on the rear window.

'So sorry, sir. Your daddyji said to give you this iPhone mobile phone card. With STD, ISD fully activated.'

Letting loose a barrage of the choicest Hindi expletives, Gautam yanked the nano sim card from the obsequious manager and sped into the night. Hurt and humiliated, Waman Dixit berated himself for attempting to make polite conversation with the obnoxious son of Sir Dharmesh Goyal. 'The father is such a top-class man. Always asking about the family when he comes to Mumbai. Personally distributing mithai boxes and giving big, big bonuses to the entire staff. But this fully faltu fucker of a son is a typical badey baap ki bigdi aulad. A good-for-nothing loafer with no job, no values, no respect for money and definitely no respect for elders. What a total maadarchod mulga!'

Dixit would have derived some solace in knowing he was not the only victim of Gautam's vicious mood swings. Growing up in London, the good-looking playboy son of Sir Dharmesh had been known as a bit of a lad, but now he was becoming increasingly notorious for his bizarre behaviour and crazy antics on the London social scene. The trashing of the suite at the Dorchester, the peeing in the pool after a stag party in Kensington, the stripping and subsequent table-top dance at Stringfellows: these were only a few of the wild stories starring Gautam that had been chronicled in the British tabloids.

Once ensconced in the plush Walkeshwar penthouse, overlooking the incandescent panorama of the Queen's Necklace, Gautam pulled out the bottle of Lagavulin he had picked up at Heathrow and ordered the sleepy young maid to bring him some bottled water and a lowball glass. A few minutes later, the doorbell rang and she nervously ushered a hulking Nigerian into the sprawling living room where Gautam sat drinking.

'Hello, brother, how you doing tonight?'

'It's all good, mate. Did you manage some Colombian? I don't want any local shit, all right?'

'No worries, brother. Salim said only the best for you.' Saying this, the dealer pulled out a small sachet from an inner trouser pocket and handed it over.

The maid furtively peeked from the kitchen door as the Nigerian counted more cash than she made in a month. She wondered what in Ganeshji's name was going on at three in the morning between her young sahab and this African giant.

The next afternoon, Gautam awoke from his stupor to a phone call from his father in London. Knowing full well that avoiding it would prove detrimental to his carefully thought out plan, he groggily answered, 'Good morning, Papa.'

'Hello, betaji—still sleeping? Jetlagged, haan? Did Dixit receive you properly—no problems, na?'

'Everything's fine, Papa.'

'Achcha, now listen. Dr Behramjee is expecting you tomorrow at ten sharp at his clinic. Be on time and listen to everything he says. He completely cured that Bhatia boy last year who was a complete gone case. You also will be cured, betaji—just do exactly as the doctor says. Promise me, Gautam?'

'Don't worry, Papa. I gave you my word. I'll meet the doc tomorrow and update you, okay?'

'Okay, betaji, be on your best behaviour, haan. I love you. Don't let me down.'

Sir Dharmesh disconnected and recited a mantra exhorting

divine assistance to exorcise the demonic drug that had taken possession of his only son.

The little curry house Sir Dharmesh and his wife Sakshi had started together in Wembley four decades ago had expanded into a wildly successful chain of upscale restaurants, bringing Indian gastronomy to patrons around the world. In fact, so popular was the Masala Magic franchise that the Goyals had opened two lucrative branches in Delhi and Mumbai, selling local cuisine at international prices.

Thirty-five years ago, Sakshi Goyal had given birth to Rani, who was undeniably the queen of her parents' hearts. But a daughter is 'paraaya dhan', someone else's wealth that would one day have to be given away along with a hefty sum in dowry. And so, the Goyals yearned for a son who would not only inherit the family business but also ensure substantial cash inflow by bringing home a wealthy bride. For five years, the couple had experimented with varied herbal concoctions and Kama Sutra positions that promised to yield a male heir. In the interim, Sakshi endured two back-alley abortions since on both occasions, to her husband's chagrin, she had erroneously conceived a girl in her womb. Her insides were shredded and doctors warned that another pregnancy could prove fatal. Undaunted, the third-time-lucky Sakshi ultimately bore Gautam and then died from complications at childbirth. Dharmesh Goyal, elated that he finally had a son, attributed this to God's will and stoically accepted his wife's death as collateral damage in pursuit of a higher good.

Little Gautam grew up with an overwhelming sense of guilt. A sullen child raised by a succession of nannies, he expressed his juvenile angst by becoming a delinquent and fell in with a rough crowd that introduced him, at an early age, to the numbing charm of substance abuse. Sir Dharmesh, busy building his culinary empire, tried to compensate for the void in his son's life by indulging his every whim.

'But despite my very best efforts, poor Gautam has been corrupted by his devilish gora friends,' he lamented. 'My family has paid a heavy price for living in the West. It will be better to send Gautam away to India where he will be free from all the evil influences of this damned city. His body and soul will be cleaned in the land of his glorious ancestors and he will come back a new and improved man. And if he doesn't, well then, he will see a side of me that will make him wish he had never been born.'

Ricky Kumar lay motionless on a thin coir mattress as warm, fragrant Ayurvedic oil was poured steadily over his forehead from a brass pot placed four inches above. It was a week since Amanda had left the Suryanamaskar Spa and Ricky was feeling rather sorry that he had another fortnight of purgatory and purgatives to endure. However, the forty-minute Shirodhara treatment, developed by the ancients to soothe the nervous system, was relaxing and Ricky found his thoughts wafting to the time his beloved Rhea had first confessed her feelings for him.

A nervous, excited Ricky had gone to the airport to receive Rhea, who was scheduled to arrive for her annual winter vacation, and she had enveloped him in a tight embrace that seemed to last forever. When they finally separated, it was obvious that something had changed irrevocably in their relationship. Rhea had initiated the flirty, innuendo-filled emails three months ago and Ricky couldn't quite believe the girl of his dreams was hinting she might be seeing him as something more than a childhood chum. His heart began beating even faster when, in the back of the car, Rhea quietly extricated her hand from his and placed it on his thigh, squeezing gently with a naughty smile and a wink of those intoxicating eyes.

Rhea Zaveri had inherited her mother Kaamiya's smouldering good looks and from her father mercifully his good sense and pleasant demeanour. Kantilal Zaveri, to his credit, was acutely aware he was no Adonis and pragmatic enough to realize it was primarily his wealth that had made the glamorous Kaamiya so amenable to marrying him.

'But my daughter is blessed with both money and beauty. And a girl like her will be unencumbered by material constraints, free to love and marry the man of her dreams.' Or so Kantilal believed.

Ricky, on his part, was indebted to his parents, not only for providing him with a privileged childhood, but also for planning to launch what would undoubtedly be a glittering career for him as a Bollywood star. About a year ago, Kapil Kumar had recruited a personal trainer from Melbourne to transform his wispy, under-confident son into a rugged, self-assured young man. Eleven months of vigorous workouts, protein shakes, vitamin supplements and innumerable ab crunches had produced remarkable results. Young Ricky Kumar was now setting female hearts aflutter with his chiselled good looks, buff physique and impeccable manners. His photographs had begun appearing in all the glossies and the Internet was abuzz with the news that he was destined to be the next big thing in Bollywood. After months of media speculation, Kapil Kumar addressed a packed press conference and announced, with characteristic aplomb, that he would write, direct, produce and present a lavish blockbuster to launch his son as a Hindi film hero.

It was small wonder then, that Rhea suddenly found Ricky utterly irresistible and resolved to stake her claim to the delectable hunk before anyone else snapped him up.

Dr Kaizad Behramjee stood at precisely five feet in his three-inch platform heels but cut a formidable figure with his patients. His ancestral property, located in affluent Breach Candy, had been converted into a drug rehabilitation centre where addicts could check in to detox and convalesce for as long as they required. Baronet Sohrabjee Behramjee, his illustrious great-grandfather, had amassed a vast fortune trading opium during the era of the British Raj and perhaps the guilt of coming from a family of glorified dope dealers had spurred the good doctor on his mission to cleanse the planet of this scourge.

Behramjee Manor seemed an anachronism, a sprawling Indo-Gothic edifice built at the turn of the previous century, standing unchanged in proud defiance of the mutating Mumbai skyline. Kaizad Behramjee had refused to part with this coveted piece of real estate despite threats from land-sharks, politicians and distant relatives keen on grabbing their slice of his considerable fortune.

Gautam Goyal sized up the diminutive doctor within minutes of meeting him. He realized that Behramjee had even more family money than he did, so a bribe wasn't going to work. Nor was the attempt to bargain making much headway.

'That's quite ridiculous, young man! You can't seriously expect to live in your own house and come here for treatment every day. No, no—I need you here round the clock. That is the only way we can ensure a drug-free environment, you understand. Now go. You must check in tomorrow morning by nine and we will embark on a wonderful journey on the road to full recovery. Good luck, Mr Goyal!'

Gautam realized that he would have to first convince everyone he was sincere about getting clean and then find a way of ensuring a steady flow of snow into the sanatorium.

The next morning, he dutifully arrived at Behramjee Manor and was shown to his room by the matron, Sister Fonseca. 'I do hope you have not carried any alcohol, narcotics or other such prohibited items in your luggage or on your person, sir.'

Gautam smiled sweetly. 'Absolutely not. I am here to begin my journey on the road to full recovery, Matron.'

'Very good, sir. Nonetheless, our check-in policy requires us to be extremely thorough. Kindly unlock your bags and change into the clothes hanging in the bathroom.'

Gautam managed to hold a smile although he was beginning to get annoyed by the affected tone of this skinny, supercilious bitch. Returning in the pale blue pyjama suit issued to inmates, Gautam found the matron and two ward boys inspecting each item of his belongings. They were obviously familiar with every trick in the book and he was glad he hadn't made the mistake of trying to smuggle coke in his luggage. The matron held up his iPhone and declared it was being confiscated, as was his iPad.

'You're welcome to take my phone, but why this?' protested Gautam. 'It's got all my books stored on it. Surely I'm allowed to read in my spare time? What harm can an iPad possibly do? If you like, I can request Dr Behramjee for permission.'

The matron's eyes narrowed. She did not like her authority being questioned, nor did she want to betray her ignorance about these newfangled devices. Gautam was apparently the son of a particularly rich man, so she was prepared to grant him this small concession. 'That's all right, sir. You can keep it.'

Gautam beamed. 'Thank you very much, Matron. Is there anything else?'

'Yes sir, kindly remove your pyjamas and lie face down on the bed.'

The grin on Gautam's face vanished the instant he saw the matron snapping on a pair of latex gloves. Fifteen minutes later, he lay on the four-poster bed, staring at the peeling plaster-of-Paris moulding on the ceiling of his cavernous room, convinced that Sister Fonseca had enjoyed probing deeper than was strictly necessary in her mission to check for concealed contraband.

Sheena Kansal spotted Gautam Goyal strolling in the sanatorium garden that morning and recognized him from the time they had first met one evening at Tramps. Two summers ago, Sheena had been holidaying in London with her gang of Delhi rich kids who partied with the local Brit-Asian brats, mainly because they provided them access to all the private nightclubs and hippest bars and restaurants in town. The Indian contingent reciprocated this hospitality in December, when the Londoners came down in droves to attend family functions or to escape the miserable English winter.

Gautam had barely noticed or spoken with Sheena that evening but had politely asked if she wanted to join the small group of stragglers headed to his place after the frenetic night of clubbing and drinking. Back at his luxurious pad in Belgravia, he had proffered a line of coke and graciously pretended not to notice when Sheena took an extraordinarily long time in the loo, throwing her guts up after downing way too many Patron shots.

Having spent most of her adolescent years drinking, snorting and passing out, Sheena had recently come to realize that she needed to haul herself from the pathetic morass that had become her life. After their parents' divorce more than a decade ago, Sheena and her younger sister Mini had found themselves suddenly unloved and unsupervised. Their politician father Jagjit Kansal was occupied with defending his good name against a barrage of baseless allegations of rampant corruption and misuse of public office. Their mother Nina, a former Miss India second runner-up, had grown deeply insecure after becoming a divorcee with two teenage daughters and was a favoured topic on the Delhi cocktail circuit, given her penchant for cosmetic surgery, cleavage flaunting couture and a propensity to sleep with most of the eligible young men her daughters brought home.

After an excessively wild weekend, which had resulted in stomach pumping in the emergency room and a three-day stint in hospital, Sheena had finally had her moment of epiphany. Realizing she could no longer continue to use her parents' divorce as a rationale for her own dysfunctionality, she decided to leave Delhi and place herself in Dr Behramjee's care.

At lunch, Sheena looked around the large community dining hall, but Gautam was nowhere in sight. She sat by herself at a table overlooking the courtyard and admired the bougainvillea bushes, ablaze with delicate orange, mauve and crimson blossoms, wondering why he hadn't joined the rest of the inmates. Then she spotted him in the distance, aimlessly pacing about the courtyard. She wondered if she should wave, but he wasn't looking in her direction. Gautam ambled up to the bougainvillea and inspected them for a bit. He then pulled out his penis from his pyjamas and breezily urinated on the fluttering flowers until they wilted under the torrent. Sheena was both embarrassed and amused by his blithe disregard for propriety as well as the healthy size of his willy. Gautam shook himself dry and looked up to see a young woman gazing at him from a window in the main building, giggling uncontrollably. Adjusting his pyjama flap, he cheekily waved at her and was delighted when she waved back.

'Well, hello!' he thought to himself. 'This is a bit of luck. Fancy finding some fanny in this godforsaken dump. And she's obviously a fellow druggie so she won't be like those prissy desi girls who all pretend they don't dope and haven't ever been laid. Bloody hypocrites!'

Gautam was even more pleased when Sheena introduced herself as someone he had apparently met and left with a favourable impression, since such instances were getting increasingly rare. Truth be told, he had no recollection of this tall girl with horsy features who spoke remarkably fast and seemed a bit too bony for his liking but what the heck; under these circumstances, she was perfectly shag-worthy and might even prove a highly useful partner in crime.

Ricky Kumar switched on his laptop and carried it slowly around his villa, trying to locate the best possible Internet reception. The telecom revolution may have swept India, but it seemed to Ricky it had bypassed Divar, where he was forced to undertake this exasperating ritual every day. Relieved when he finally detected a few signal bars, Ricky Googled himself and surfed the web in an attempt to find out what the outside world was saying about him.

Clicking on a link to the *Indian Post*, the country's leading newspaper, he was ecstatic to see that the front page of the entertainment supplement had a massive photo of him with the headline, 'Come back, Ricky. All is forgiven.' The sexy picture they had used was from a recent photo shoot, completed days before he so hastily fled Mumbai. There he was, in full, muscular, bronzed glory, sprawled almost naked on a beach, wearing nothing but a skimpy red Speedo brief. The accompanying article hailed him, without any irony, as an Indian Greek god and beseeched him to return to Mumbai and rightfully don the mantle of the next Bollyood superstar. There were quotes from assorted quasi-celebrities and gushing fans stating that since Ricky had proved himself contrite, it was time the Indian public forgave him his one misdemeanour. Ricky was moved by these words of high praise and found himself tearing up.

Just then, the phone rang; it was his mother. 'Hello, Ricky beta. How are you, my jaan?'

'I'm fine, Mamma. I read the *Indian Post* online. They've said some wonderful things about me. Very positive piece!'

'Yes—this is all Babaji's blessing. I hope you are saying your prayers every day and also eating properly.'

'Yes, Mamma,' said Ricky, lying about the praying to Babaji bit.

'I love you, jaanoo. I know you will come home soon. Babaji came to me in a dream last night and ...'

Before she could quite finish, her husband grabbed the phone. 'Arrey, enough of this Babaji bullshit so early in the morning! Hello, Ricky boy, so you already read the article in the *Post*, ya? Amazing, this Internet technology. It's all zip zap zoom these days. This is it, Ricky boy—the tide is turning. Arrey, what did I tell you—public memory is short—shorter than even an item girl's mini-skirt. One minute it's there, the next minute it's gone. Whooosshh! Achcha, listen, if you are planning to send any more goris from Goa to our house, at least send someone sexier than that Amanda. So much bloody meat on her, but in all the wrong places. I think I have bigger boobs than her!'

As Kapil Kumar burst into peals of raucous laughter, Ricky blushed. He had never got used to his father's bawdy, sexist sense of humour, particularly because he sensed that it annoyed his mother.

'I'll keep that in mind, Papa. Papa, any news of Rhea? She hasn't responded to my messages or emails. I hope she's all right.'

'Arrey, don't worry about her, Ricky boy!' Kapil Kumar boomed. 'You just forget about Rhea and concentrate on your career. This year itself I promise I will make you into a superstar. A mega fucking super-duper star! Love you, Ricky boy. Mwah!'

'Love you too, Papa. But please don't tell me to forget Rhea. You know I could never do that. Bye, Papa.'

Kapil Kumar hung up and turned to his wife, shaking his head in dismay. 'Manju, we may have managed to toughen up Ricky's body but inside he remains that same puny little fellow.'

Manju burst into tears. 'Do something, Kapil, I can't bear to see Ricky in so much pain. I can't ...'

The ageing actor put an arm around his distraught wife. 'You know I'm doing the best I can, Manju. I've paid those publicists through my bloody nose to plant today's story. Now you please stop crying and go pray to Babaji that one day, very soon, we can announce the return of our bhola bachcha.'

'Everything they say about cold turkey is true, Gautam. It really kicks your ass, man. Your body and your mind experience like all kinds of crazy shit. You want to die. Like totally just die!

But you know what? In the end, it's so completely worth it. Because this is it, man. This is the chance to finally get clean. Just get it all out of your system. You get it, right? You get what I'm saying, right?'

Gautam was not interested in getting it. Sheena was a cool bird, but wow, did she have a manic motor mouth. Gautam had no desire to endure the trauma of withdrawal symptoms, no matter how rewarding the result promised to be. He had deftly hoodwinked the matron into letting him keep his iPad, gambling that she wouldn't discover it was loaded with the local phone card his father's office had arranged for him. Using the Skype application on this device, Gautam could now make video calls to Caesar, the Nigerian drug dealer with whom he had pre-arranged a way to procure his daily fix.

As Sheena sat cross-legged on his bed, babbling about how she intended to pursue a career as an artist, Gautam interjected, 'Listen, Sheena, I'm planning to jump the wall tonight. I'm meeting a pusher round the corner from here. He's going to score me some Charlie. Do you want any?'

Sheena was aghast. 'Are you crazy? We're here to get clean, man. Don't do this shit. You'll get into serious trouble and your dad will be really pissed if he finds out!'

'Relax, I've got this figured out. If you don't want any, that's fine. I respect your decision. But I'm going over tonight. Just don't say a word, okay?'

Sheena nodded. She'd always had a thing for bad boys and Gautam was so her type—handsome, athletic, wild, well endowed. Sheena was fast falling for him, but she knew she shouldn't succumb to temptation, even if it meant annoying him. 'I'm sorry, but I really can't blow this chance, Gautam. I'm here because I know I've hit rock bottom. I sincerely hope you change your mind.' Saying this, Sheena drew closer and surprised Gautam by tenderly kissing him on the lips. With an embarrassed smile, she got up to leave, but Gautam grabbed her hand and pulled her back, onto his bed.

It was early December and Mumbai was experiencing the beginnings of 'winter', when the temperature finally drops below hot and humid and hovers at barely pleasant. The wealthier denizens of the city strutted about in contraband shahtoosh shawls and designer woollens, chuffed at the opportunity to flaunt their mothballed glad rags. The less affluent draped themselves in brightly dyed faux Pashminas and argyle knitwear from Ludhiana. The poor huddled around small fires, shivering and burning rubbish collected from the streets during the day.

The night after Rhea landed in Mumbai, Ricky drove her across town to attend the opening of a new nightclub in Colaba, located in a by-lane behind the Taj Mahal Hotel. The gaggle of paparazzi went amok the moment Ricky drew up in his BMW and handed the keys to the valet. Rhea was amazed by the sudden media obsession with Ricky who, until last year, had been just another star son nobody looked at twice. But the hype around him was now so intense that he had become a bona fide Bollywood hero without even having a film to his credit.

Rhea basked in the heady glow of the reflected limelight, realizing she was on the arm of the hottest eye-candy in town, as Ricky held his dazzling smile for the phalanx of photographers for an interminable five minutes. He squeezed Rhea's hand as though to reassure her that she was his girl now and he was going to take her along on this thrilling roller-coaster ride.

Inside the pulsating nightclub, done up in hues of purple and mauve, Ricky was engulfed by a wave of Mumbai's beautiful people, all of whom wanted to be his best friend. Designers implored him to walk the ramp as their showstopper during Fashion Week, south Mumbai socialites requested him to be the chief guest at their charity events, fashion editors entreated him to grace the covers of their magazines and industrialists desperately sought to lock him into long-term endorsement deals before his market value sky-rocketed. Ricky air-kissed each of them with good grace, making sure to introduce Rhea as his special friend.

Later, when the DJ played a re-mixed version of an old Bollywood chartbuster, Ricky spontaneously dragged Rhea onto the dance floor. The crowd cheered lustily as he began to gyrate around her, perfectly lip-syncing the words of the iconic anthem to young love. Despite having grown up in Antwerp, Rhea had watched this particular song dozens of times on DVD, never imagining that one day she would be dancing with Ricky to the same duet that had been immortalized on screen by his father and her mother, twenty-five years ago. She matched Ricky uninhibitedly, move for move, countering his pelvic thrusts with exaggerated bosom heaves in mock homage to the raunchy choreography of the eighties classic.

Five handpicked television crews had been permitted inside to film Mumbai's glitterati letting their carefully coiffured hair down. The feisty videographers jostled each other and the guests to get the very best angles of Ricky and Rhea strutting their stuff. Until one solitaire-studded socialite suffered an elbow to the eye and the management was forced to eject the recalcitrant media.

The assembled hotties shot Rhea dirty glances and bitched her out in the women's loo, sneering at how short she was and how unimaginatively dressed in top-to-toe Chanel. Rhea herself drank it all in—the excitement, the glamour, the jealousy, the champagne. Ricky, however, had become a teetotaller this past year, refusing to ingest the empty calories provided by alcohol and preferring to occasionally indulge in some dessert instead.

As they exited the club a little after one-thirty in the morning, a tipsy Rhea giggled to herself. 'I don't mind if Ricky wants to abstain from alcohol, but I certainly hope he has a healthy appetite for sex!'

Dharmesh Goyal hadn't succeeded in building a culinary empire spanning three continents and ten cities by being a gullible old fool. He was elated when Gautam agreed to enter rehab but knew his beloved son was blessed with an extraordinary ability to deceive those around him. Therefore, through the good offices of his loyal manager Waman Dixit, Sir Dharmesh had engaged the services of a private investigator to monitor Gautam's every move in Mumbai.

Detective Virendra Dhadda or VD, as he insisted his clients call him, hailed from the hinterland and had tenaciously worked his way up in the shadowy world of snooping and sleuthing. He was now firmly established as one of Mumbai's leading private dicks. VD had been provided a clear brief by Waman Dixit. He was to report any suspicious activity Gautam indulged in and eavesdrop on all calls received and made from his phone. Following VD's instructions, Sir Dharmesh had discreetly cloned a copy of Gautam's UK mobile phone card and couriered it to his manager in Mumbai. Dixit, in turn, had similarly cloned a local phone card and handed the original to Gautam at the airport.

It was around noon that Waman Dixit received an urgent email from the diligent detective.

Respected Shri Waman Rao Dixit,

The video calls I have intercepted between Shri Gautam Goyal (UK national, Age 30 years) and one Scissor (Negro national, Age Unknown years) indicates that these two parties are intending to rendezvoos at Scandal Point, Breach Candy, Mumbai 400006 at sharp 2 AM tonight to indulge in a nefarious narcotic transaction. Please advice further cause of action.

Thanking you,
Yours sincerely,
VD.

Waman Dixit smirked. Wah, wah! Within two hours of landing in Mumbai, the chutiya charsi had already bought drugs from some kaaliya and was now shamelessly planning to buy more, less than twenty-four hours after checking into the Bawaji's clinic? 'Just you wait, besharam bhadwa', he thought, 'I will teach you a lesson you will never forget!'

The vindictive manager picked up the phone and dialled his old friend, Senior Inspector Madhukar Bobde of the Mumbai police, informing him that a major drug deal would be going down that night at Scandal Point, the secluded spot frequented by young lovers looking for a little privacy in the midst of bustling Breach Candy.

At a quarter to two in the morning, Gautam crept out of his room and stealthily made his way across the expansive courtyard to one of the high walls that enclosed Behramjee Manor. He had carefully surveyed the premises that afternoon and surmised his best bet would be to climb the large mango tree in the far corner. Its sturdy branches extended well beyond the compound walls and he could clamber back in undetected by ascending the external stone walls and climbing down the tree again.

The solitary watchman at the padlocked entrance was snoring so volubly that Gautam was half-tempted to sneak over the massive cast-iron gates instead, but he refrained. He started up the tree but had barely climbed six feet when, suddenly, an alarm clanged violently and the entire courtyard was instantly illuminated by powerful floodlights.

A startled Gautam scrambled down and decided to make a run for it, hoping to get back to his room undetected before the staff awoke, but it was too late. The perspicacious Dr Behramjee had suspected, from the moment he laid eyes on his cocky new patient, that Gautam was a duplicitous brat. Concealed in the shadows of the courtyard, he had, therefore, been patiently lying in wait for the young man to make his move.

Observing Gautam desperately bolt across the sanatorium grounds, Dr Behramjee smiled in quiet satisfaction and let loose the drooling Doberman straining at its leash. It was vital that fresh inmates be disciplined for their own good. And to achieve this objective, the noble doctor was willing to permit his precious pet the liberty of taking a sizeable bite of Gautam's perfectly toned bottom.

As Ricky drove down the asphalted crescent of Marine Drive towards suburban Bandra, a frisky, inebriated Rhea leaned over and started nuzzling the handsome actor's neck, even as her hand wandered between his thighs. She playfully nibbled a sensitive ear lobe and sensuously massaged his crotch.

When her tongue wandered deep within his ear, an electrified Ricky realized he couldn't possibly wait another half hour to get home. He veered off Peddar Road towards Kemps Corner and drove straight to Breach Candy, expertly manoeuvring his car with one hand as the other clumsily tried to undo Rhea's silk blouse.

Pulling into Scandal Point, the deserted lover's lane at the water's edge, he switched off the engine and cupped Rhea's elfin face in his hands. This was a scenario he had fantasized about since the age of thirteen and Ricky Kumar wanted to savour the moment, when finally, after all these years, he would consummate his love for the beauteous Rhea Zaveri.

Detective Virendra Dhadda, who had been anxiously lying in wait at Scandal Point for Gautam Goyal and Caesar Adebayo, was intrigued by the BMW that had just drawn into the quiet cul-de-sac. VD, wearing a sweater, muffler and woollen monkey cap in an effort to keep himself snug, squinted through the long infra-red lens of his camera to get a closer look at the occupants of the vehicle and almost fell off his perch in the peepal tree when he caught sight of the driver. He recognized the nation's new heart-throb, obviously here with a girlfriend, whose head was currently in his lap. When VD adjusted the focus on his lens, he was flabbergasted to find the girl was not, in fact, resting but performing vigorous oral sex on the rising Bollywood star. The private dick swung his zoom lens into action and shot off a long burst of images at high speed. These sensational pictures would undoubtedly fetch a huge price and VD knew that even though it was Ricky Kumar getting lucky with some young lady that night, it was he who would eventually bhangra all the way to the bank with old Dame Fortune.

Senior Inspector Madhukar Bobde also lay in wait for Gautam Goyal at Scandal Point that fateful night. At fifty-five,

Bobde was fast approaching the age of retirement but had carefully put away a tidy nest egg by following a healthy policy of live and let live with the criminals he encountered on the job. The rotund cop was looking forward to enjoying the fruits of his labour and living off the profits of the brothel he had opened two years ago in collusion with a local corporator.

Bobde's only tragic flaw was his obsession with seeing his portly mug splashed across the papers. He couldn't help giving self-aggrandizing interviews to journalists in spite of being repeatedly reprimanded by his seniors. So, when Waman Dixit called to inform him of an impending drug deal involving the celebrity son of an NRI billionaire, Bobde had licked his chops and immediately invited a few members of the local media to accompany him on his new crusade against narcotics.

At two in the morning, exactly as Dixit had said he would, the gargantuan Caesar Adebayo putt-putted up on his moped and waited for his customer to arrive. Two minutes later, Ricky Kumar emerged from his BMW to take a leak in the bushes after receiving a truly memorable blowjob.

In the dark, the tall, muscular Ricky could quite easily be mistaken for Gautam Goyal and it was, therefore, perfectly understandable that the drug peddler should lumber up behind him and whisper in his ear. 'Hello brother. Finish pissing and give me the cash. I have your shit with me.'

Ricky, who was in mid-flow, turned around and recoiled in horror at the sight of this behemoth who was demanding money in exchange for excreta. This was the cue the police posse and accompanying members of the media had been waiting for. They gunned their engines and with headlights ablaze, charged down the narrow dirt road to arrest Caesar Adebayo and Ricky Kumar. It took considerable effort by four members of the local constabulary to subdue the massive

Nigerian national and succeed in locking a pair of handcuffs around his thick wrists.

Perched in the peepal tree, detective Dhadda continued to click away furiously, marvelling at the extraordinary turn of events.

Caesar Adebayo had come to Mumbai four years ago to study Anthropology but soon came to realize he was himself being viewed as something of an evolutionary wonder by the local populace.

Caesar arrived from Lagos expecting to be treated as an equal in the world's largest democracy but was quickly disillusioned. Brown-skinned locals thought nothing of cheerily addressing him as 'kaala bandar' or black monkey. He had been expelled from Mumbai University two years ago, after a raid by the hostel warden yielded a stash of ganja belonging to his Russian roommate. The authorities refused to entertain the absurd plea that he was innocent and ejected him with admirable alacrity from both the hostel and the university. Too ashamed to return home, Caesar worked briefly as a bouncer in a Mumbai nightclub but was sacked when the management had its arm twisted by the local labour union to hire some homegrown goons instead.

A friend introduced him to Salim Pasha, an Afghan carpet-cum-cocaine dealer, who needed a reliable pusher capable of delivering dope and collecting cash from clients across Mumbai. Caesar soon found himself on the speed dial list of a vast number of Mumbai's glitterati. College kids, models, actors, designers, bankers, lawyers, surgeons and politicians—it seemed just about everyone wanted to get high in this hyper city.

Salim Pasha had instructed Caesar that since Gautam was an exceptionally wealthy client, he should make every effort to cater to the dope-head's narcotic needs. Caesar had recently acquired an iPhone from a strung-out, cash strapped teenager who had happily traded his sister's precious mobile for a few grams of coke. Communicating via Skype, Gautam and he had arranged to meet at the secluded Scandal Point, located barely five hundred metres from Behramjee Manor.

Sharing the filthy lock-up with a distraught Ricky Kumar at Breach Candy police station, Caesar Adebayo was not perturbed. He knew his well-networked boss would get him out of jail. All he had to do was keep his mouth shut about Gautam and play along with the police.

'SCANDAL POINT!!!' shrieked the headline emblazoned across every newspaper and television screen in the country. The members of the honourable fourth estate couldn't believe their luck. It had been a slow news week and then Ricky Kumar, upcoming star son, had single-handedly provided them with a luscious, juicy scandal that simmered with the ingredients of a Hindi masala potboiler: take a young, handsome hero, mix in some drugs, pepper with a pusher, garnish with a glamorous girlfriend and fan the flame for weeks.

Intrepid reporters, making up what they lacked in experience with an abundance of enthusiasm, scrambled into action and tracked down the sundry celebrities present at the nightclub where Ricky Kumar had partied before he was busted. Most of the A-listers who had so effusively air-kissed Ricky that evening developed amnesia about spending time with him, fearing the association would also implicate them. A fashion designer whose show Ricky had politely declined, swore, on condition of anonymity, of course, that he had seen the actor snorting coke in the loo with a rolled-up five-hundred-rupee note and subsequently tipping the lavatory attendant with it. The confused attendant, who had amassed a small fortune that night in rolled-up bills, couldn't recall what sort of note Ricky Kumar had so generously tipped him, so the story, though bogus, acquired tremendous credence.

All the waiters testified that Ricky had refused alcohol that evening. This led a television panel of experts to infer that Ricky was undoubtedly on drugs. 'How can anyone in their right mind attend a party in Mumbai and not get high?' thundered an advertising-guru-cum-social-commentator. 'If he wasn't drinking, it's obvious he was snorting. Let's face it, Ricky Kumar was coked out of his head!'

The video footage of Ricky gyrating with Rhea on the dance floor was looped and played endlessly on television as conclusive evidence of his intoxication. The enthralled nation watched in shock, awe and vicarious thrill as the media spun a tantalizing tale of an irresponsible, spoilt rich kid and his night of drug-fuelled debauchery.

Unsurprisingly, one of the biggest beneficiaries of Ricky's arrest was Senior Inspector Madhukar Bobde, who gloated in every interview, 'These Hindi film peoples are always showing us policewallahs to be villains or comedians in their pictures. But I have proved who is the asli hero and who is the complete zero. The long arm of the law is equal for all!'

In fact, Bobde had been elated when, instead of Gautam Goyal, Ricky Kumar showed up at Scandal Point. The pudgy cop had promised the reporters a scoop involving the celebrity son of a billionaire but fortuitously delivered them a Bollywood star instead. Bobde knew there was no evidence to suggest that Ricky had any prior contact with the peddler or that he had gone to Scandal Point specifically to procure drugs. The lab tests had also turned out negative, revealing no trace of narcotics in Ricky's system. But these were piffling technicalities that nobody seemed too concerned with in the midst of the media mayhem.

Fortunately, Ricky's lawyer convinced the magistrate that the evidence against the young actor was entirely circumstantial and he should be released on bail. But, of course, even before Ricky appeared in court, he had been subjected to a sensationalist media trial and pronounced unequivocally guilty.

Gautam Goyal lay face down on his bed and winced as the contemptuous matron dressed his buttock wound. The ferocious Doberman had managed to sink its teeth deep into his derriere and Gautam was concerned about contracting rabies.

'Don't worry, Mr Goyal,' said Dr Behramjee wryly. 'We Parsis may be inbred but our dogs are absolute thoroughbreds. I'm sorry you had to suffer a nibble from Bruno, but you do understand that sometimes I have to be cruel in order to be kind.'

Gautam grunted in response.

'Now, I must go inform your father of this incident. I do hope you will not indulge in any more attempts to exit via the compound walls. If you want to leave, my gates are open during the day—but remember, there is no coming back.'

Gautam weighed his options. He wanted to get the hell out of here and sue the pants off this demented doctor. But he was also concerned that his father would be furious when he learnt that Gautam had dishonoured his promise within days of arriving in Mumbai. Sir Dharmesh had recently issued a stern ultimatum to his second-born to either clean up or clear out. Gautam knew his father was too much of a doting Indian parent to ever disown his only son, but he did fear his wrath. Gautam made his decision. 'I'm truly sorry, doc. This was a stupid mistake. You have my word it will never happen again.'

'I genuinely want to believe you, son. I have seen too many young men and women die miserably from this evil. It's not too late. You have your whole life ahead of you. I'm not saying it's going to be easy. You must promise to meet me halfway, otherwise we'll both be squandering our time.'

Thanks to the canine's chomp, it was not possible for Gautam to sit up and look the doctor in the eye, but he hoped he sounded sufficiently contrite.

'I understand, doc. Just one more chance, please, that's all I ask.'

The doctor's tone softened. 'Very well, Mr Goyal. I'm prepared to give you a final opportunity to redeem yourself. Please don't prove a disappointment.'

As the doctor turned to leave, Gautam called out, 'Doc, could you please not tell my dad about this? He's suffered enough from my recklessness. This will break his heart.'

'Hmm … your friend, Miss Kansal, has already made this request on your behalf. You should follow her example. She has been an exemplary patient, totally committed to turning over a new leaf. For the moment, I am prepared to keep this matter between us.'

Gautam was relieved. As the matron finished her ministrations and departed huffily, taking his iPad with her, he thought to himself, 'It was bloody decent of Sheena to plead my case. She's a useful ally to have around. And now, I must come up with a better plan since the previous one ended up biting me in the arse!'

Rhea Zaveri wept through the nine-hour flight to Antwerp. The past few days had been harrowing and she was in shock at the manner in which events had unfolded. One minute she was pleasuring the man she intended to marry and the next she had found herself bundled into a police van, under the blinding glare of media scrutiny.

The police eventually allowed Rhea to go home after Kapil's lawyer had a chat with the senior inspector and slipped him a bulging envelope with a promise of more to come. In any case, Madhukar Bobde was far more interested in his prize catch and didn't want to be seen hassling a sobbing young woman in front of the press that swarmed the police station.

When Rhea realized that Ricky had been arrested for attempting to buy cocaine and not for public indecency, she was relieved. If they had been caught in flagrante delicto, it would have resulted in an altogether different type of scandal. The veteran lawyer Hotchand Fatwani had coaxed Bobde into not pressing any formal charges against Rhea and advised her to leave the country forthwith. Kantilal Zaveri flew down from Antwerp and bundled her into the return flight before the corpulent inspector realized he had allowed a golden goose to fly the coop.

The last time Rhea saw Ricky was when she was about to leave the police station. She had run to the cell where he was being held alongside a menagerie of leering drunks, pimps and pickpockets. Managing to somehow suppress the reflex to throw up as a fetid cocktail of stale urine, body odours and country liquor assaulted her nostrils, Rhea reassured Ricky that everything was going to be all right. As they clenched hands through the flaking, rusty bars of the police lock-up, Ricky whispered to Rhea that he loved her and would be home soon. Neither of the naïve young lovers realized it would be a very long time before they saw each other again.

'Saala melya kutrya! It is the poor dog who will be needing injections after biting that haraami drug addict.' Waman Dixit cursed Gautam and the fact that despite his best efforts, the insolent offspring of his employer had escaped arrest. The loyal manager had envisaged earning a fat commission from the bribe money Sir Dharmesh would have paid to secure the release of his son. Dixit called the Goyal patriarch in London to apprise him of the developments of that fateful night, prudently omitting to mention his own small part in alerting the police to Gautam's shenanigans. Sir Dharmesh was disappointed to hear that his son had so blatantly betrayed his trust, but also relieved that Gautam was not behind bars.

Dharmesh Goyal was descended from a long line of tradesmen who prided themselves on their financial savvy and sharp mercantile acumen. His mercurial rise from small-time shopkeeper to world-renowned restaurateur had been meticulously calculated. His generous contributions to the Conservative Party in the UK were not made on account of ideological affinity but to buy him a peerage and with it a grudging validation from the white man.

'Family is family—flesh and blood—but business is bloody business and nobody, not even my son, can be allowed to destroy the empire I have spent a lifetime building!' Sir Dharmesh brooded before instructing his manager to visit Gautam at Behramjee Manor and convey, clearly, that if he did not successfully complete his term in rehab, he should consider himself cut off from not only the family but also its considerable fortune.

Waman Dixit drew solace from the fact that he would be the bearer of bad news.

'Ricky Kumar!! Hai Hai!!'

'Ricky Kumar!! Murdabad Murdabad!!'

'Say No No to Drugs!! Say Go Go to Ricky Kumar!!'

A floundering political party that had absolutely no agenda for the upcoming municipal elections had decided that picketing and denouncing Ricky Kumar would be an ideal way to garner cost-effective publicity for their cause. The frenzied chanting and sloganeering by loyal party workers, rounded up from local slums and brought in truckloads to the posh gates of Casa Kumar on Pali Hill, made headlines across the nation.

The leader of the agitation, Pramod Potnis, a toupee-sporting municipal corporator, bellowed into a megaphone, denouncing drugs and urban decadence. He pilloried Ricky Kumar as the embodiment of all that was wrong with the nation's youth and declared it the duty of every patriot to boycott Ricky's forthcoming films and ensure he never worked in Mumbai again. An effigy of Ricky was paraded before the gathered media and garlanded with slippers to demonstrate just how much the party despised the drug-addled actor. For good measure, the footwear-festooned rag doll was set on fire outside Ricky's bungalow to symbolize the purging of evil from civil society.

'Sandal Point!' read the cheeky headline of the *Indian Post* as it reported how the upcoming star was now persona non grata in the city of his birth.

Immensely buoyed by the headlines he was grabbing, the fascist politico announced that he was going on a hunger strike until Ricky Kumar publicly swore to renounce a lifetime of narcotic abuse. A pandal was hastily erected on the street outside Casa Kumar where the rabble-rouser commenced his farcical fast and created even more traffic chaos than usual.

It had been two days since Ricky's release from custody and the young man was reeling from shock, not only at the unexpected departure of his beloved Rhea but also at how he had suddenly metamorphosed from the nation's heart-throb to public enemy number one. Ironically, in all his twenty-five years, Ricky had never dabbled in drugs, not even taken a pull at a marijuana joint.

Hotchand Fatwani, Kapil's lawyer and long-time confidante, sat with the Kumars in their opulent living room, confabulating the next course of action.

'Fucking fat, bald pig! I campaigned for his rival during the last assembly elections. He is taking revenge on me by targeting Ricky!' thundered an agitated Kapil.

Hotchand tried to calm him. 'Look, everyone knows Potnis is an opportunist who's milking the moment, Kapil. Nobody takes him seriously. But it may be a good idea if Ricky leaves town for a bit till things cool down.'

'Why the hell should Ricky boy leave? Let that takloo starve to death outside on the street, ya? Arrey, he won't last even four hours before gobbling up six-seven samosas. Saala bhukkad fraud!'

'Papa, I think Uncle Hotchand is right. Public sentiment is against me, regardless of whether I am guilty or not. Since everybody is convinced I'm a drug addict, perhaps the best way out is to admit it and show I am truly contrite for my actions?'

'Nonsense! Why should you admit to being a charsi when all your medical reports clearly show you are squeaky clean?'

Manju, who had been silent so far, finally spoke. 'Ricky has made a very good point, Kapil. On Oprah's show, I have seen these Hollywood celebrities asking for forgiveness and a second chance from the American public after doing god knows what all hera-pheri in their private life. Maybe Ricky can also benefit from public sympathy if he apologizes for his actions?'

Hotchand Fatwani was impressed at how perceptive the otherwise naive Manju was. 'Exactly! That's exactly how we can turn this whole situation to our advantage. We first issue a public statement that Ricky is willing to seek help and go into drug rehab at some place outside Mumbai for a month or so. When things calm down, he can return, triumphant, as the tragic hero who has redeemed himself. Then, a few months later, you can release Ricky's film and he will have a fantastic debut vehicle with a massive amount of free publicity. You, better than anyone else, know that Indians love a good underdog story, Kapil.'

Kapil Kumar shut his eyes and went into deep thought. After a minute of intense rumination, during which no one dared speak, he erupted, 'Arrey, superb! This is a dhamaakedaar marketing strategy, Hotchand! I will write Ricky's launch film where his character will be a hero turned villain turned hero again! Reel life will be ditto to real life. Ricky boy, pack your bags—you are going into rehab!'

TWO

Sheena Kansal sat astride Gautam's bare back and massaged his sinewy shoulders. She was adept at Shiatsu after having taken a course in Tokyo one summer and her long, strong fingers kneaded deep to expertly release the tension in his torso. With no access to narcotics, Gautam had been experiencing the full onslaught of withdrawal symptoms and Sheena, constantly at his side, tried to help the young addict cope with the torment of rigours, cold sweats and convulsions.

There was a sharp rap on the door and when Gautam did not reply, the matron called out, 'Mr Goyal, visitor for you.'

Gautam, who was even more irritable than usual, snarled, 'I don't want to see anyone. Tell them to go away.'

'Open the door, Mr Goyal. Now!'

Sheena swung off Gautam's back and handed him his pyjamas, whispering, 'You'd better go see. This could be important, Gautam.'

Cursing as he went, Gautam opened the door and was livid to find the ingratiating Waman Dixit standing beside the matron.

'Hello, Gautam baba. How are you keeping? I hope you are fully comfortable here.' Dixit beamed as he peered into the room and caught sight of Sheena sitting on the bed. He smirked knowingly at Gautam, infuriating him even further. 'So very sorry to disturb but daddyji sent me with important message. Fully private and personal matter. Can I come inside, Gautam baba?'

Gautam glowered for a few seconds longer, debating his next move. Finally he nodded, but just as Dixit stepped forward to enter, he slammed the door hard on his face. Outside, Dixit crumpled onto the terracotta floor, clutching his nose and screaming in agony as a flustered matron called out for help. Sheena was aghast when Gautam calmly bolted the door, peeled off his pyjamas and lay down again.

'You shouldn't have done that, Gautam. Now he's going to go tell your dad!'

'I know, but I just can't help myself. That wanker really fucking annoys me!'

Sheena was besotted by this capricious, brooding young man; she was convinced she alone understood his angst and could help him through his ordeal. She hopped on top of him and whispered soothingly as she resumed massaging his back, 'Relax, Gautam. Calm your mind. Concentrate only on healing yourself. Om … Shanti … Shanti … '

Waman Dixit moaned as he caught sight of his bandaged face in the mirror. 'Bhadwa behenchod has fully fractured my nose even before I could talk to him! Imagine what that yeda would have done to me if I had actually given him his daddy's message?'

Even as the poor manager shuddered, an idea slowly began taking shape in his mind. One that would not only feed his revenge but also ensure that he retired a rather wealthy man.

Detective Virendra Dhadda had expended considerable effort trying to get an audience with Kapil Kumar in the past week. It was difficult for a mere mortal to access a Bollywood star, even one whose aura had diminished considerably. Security around Casa Kumar at Pali Hill had been trebled after the incident at Scandal Point and a posse of private guards kept undesirables at bay. The mobile number that VD had managed to source by bribing a film journalist turned out to belong to some other Kapil Kumar, who roundly abused VD when he realized the private eye was yet another imbecile looking for his illustrious namesake and not the tropical fish he specialized in supplying.

Finally, at his wit's end, VD walked up to the security supervisor at the Kumar residence and handed him a manila envelope with a plea that it be urgently delivered to the actor.

Kapil Kumar was ensconced in his maroon velvet upholstered den, chatting on the phone with Ricky, when the maid brought in his tray of afternoon tea along with the envelope. Mistaking it for an important legal document, the actor tore it open and almost choked on his chilli cheese toast when he saw it contained photographs of Rhea fellating his son in vivid close-up. At the back was a telephone number which Kapil realized belonged to the man who intended to blackmail him. The trembling thespian hung up on Ricky and hastily dialled Hotchand Fatwani, requesting him to come over immediately.

It had been a week since Ricky was dispatched from Mumbai to the Suryanamaskar Spa in Goa for his bogus stint in rehab. The opportunistic Potnis had abandoned his fast unto death outside Casa Kumar and instead focussed his energies on beating up migrant bhelpuri vendors in the city after one unfortunate Bihari was caught urinating into his mixing bowl in the absence of a public toilet.

The beleaguered screen legend was beginning to feel that things were finally settling down when Virendra Dhadda suddenly reared his turquoise-turbaned head.

'Oye, Kapilji, I am your very biggest fan. I have seen your every picture, first day first show, papaji. I was bunking class in Bhatinda whenever your fillum was coming and bajaoing ceetees from the front row. By god, you are my hero number one!'

Kapil Kumar could have throttled the smarmy detective who sat before him, but knew he should exercise restraint in dealing with a man who could destroy his son.

'That's why, sirji, I decided, why to go to media with these photos? Khamakha there will be badnaami of Ricky puttar and madamji also. First there was drugs scandal, and now there will be sex scandal. Much better to bring to you only. We can settle directly like gentlemens, kyon ji?'

'Ya, ya—you did the right thing in coming straight to me, Dhadda. Now tell me, what do you want?'

'Your autograph, sirji.'

Kapil was dumbfounded. 'My autograph?'

'Aaho, sirji. I told you I am your very biggest fan. Tussi great ho, papaji!'

The veteran star's heart leapt in hope. He grabbed a pen and scribbled on the notepad that lay on his desk.

The detective interrupted him with a hearty guffaw. 'No, no, sirji, I am definitely wanting your autograph—but on a cheque, please—if you don't mind!'

Kapil was incensed at being manipulated in this manner but managed to keep his cool. 'Good joke, Dhadda, good joke. Now, what amount should I write on the cheque?'

'Only rupees one lakh, one thousand and one, sirji. In the name of Bhatinda School for the Blind.'

'I see. How very noble of you, Dhadda. Is that it or do you want anything else?'

'Only this much by cheque, sirji. Rest nine crores, ninety-nine lakhs you can give in cash.'

Sitting by Kapil's side, Hotchand Fatwani marvelled at the audacity of the man who was toying with his client with such aplomb. In his forty years in the legal profession, Fatwani had come across his fair share of blackmailers, but this sleazebag was in a league of his own. The lawyer decided it was time to intervene.

'I see you are less a philanthropist and much more an extortionist, Mr Dhadda. Ten crores is a lot of money for a set of photos. I think you will have to be more reasonable than that.'

The detective nodded patiently. 'Oye, sirji, maana ke ten crores is a lot of money for a small man like me, but it is petty cash for a Hindi film hero. After Ricky puttar gives one hit film, his proud papaji will be demanding this much money from every producer wanting to sign him, hai na? Think of it only as a small investment for the future.'

Fatwani had to concur; the argument was quite faultless. Successful Bollywood stars earned staggering sums not only by acting in films but also from endorsement deals, international stage shows and by dancing at weddings and film award functions. Ricky could potentially generate ten times this amount, but it was imperative he maintain a relatively wholesome public persona. Fatwani was confident that, in time, the masses would forgive Ricky his alleged drug indiscretion. But two successive scandals might prove detrimental to his fledgling career and no amount of damage control could then salvage the young actor's reputation.

'Why don't you please give me a few moments to discuss this with my client, Mr Dhadda?'

'Oye, no problem, papaji, take your time. I have kept all of today free for this matter only.'

After Dhadda jauntily exited the den, Kapil Kumar became apoplectic. 'Bastard thinks he's going to extort ten fucking crores from me. Let me call bhai in Dubai and fix him once and for all! One bullet in his bheja, that's what he'll get!'

'Calm down, Kapil. Ricky is in enough trouble already, and you think that by calling up some defanged don, this matter will get settled? Those days are long gone when the underworld controlled Bollywood, my friend. I think it's much wiser to negotiate with this fellow directly and simply bury the matter.'

'Arrey, I will bury that bugger first before I give him one naya paisa, ya! I will drink the blood of that dog! I will piss on his grave! I will … I will …'

Kapil Kumar suddenly realized his bluster was beginning to sound as ineffectual as his filmi dialogue. The greying screen hero turned to his long-time friend and trusted counsel. 'What the hell do I do, Hotchand? I'm so bloody scared. What will happen if these photos ever leak out? Ricky, Rhea, Manju, Kaamiya, Kanti, me—we will never be able to survive the shame!'

'Don't worry. Leave it to me. I will try to bargain this fellow down. Whatever it is, it's a small price to pay for your family's well-being.'

Kapil Kumar felt somewhat reassured. 'Thanks ya, and please do the best you can. But you wait and see, I'm going to recover my ten crores from bloody Kantilal. After all, it was his daughter who was blowing my poor beta.'

Kaamiya Zaveri had abundant reason to ensure her daughter fled Mumbai in the aftermath of the now infamous incident at Scandal Point. A battle-scarred veteran of the slings and arrows of middle-class morality, Kaamiya was determined her daughter would not suffer the public censure she herself had endured for the better part of her career as an actress.

Rhea had been provided the finest education that Kantilal's money could buy and was an exceptionally bright girl. But Kaamiya feared her little princess wasn't street-smart and tough enough to survive public shame and scandal. The erstwhile glamour puss had forbidden Rhea from contacting Ricky in any manner and her lovelorn daughter was understandably distraught.

'Why, mum? What wrong has Ricky done? Look around you—everyone does drugs, but Ricky doesn't even touch alcohol. And you want me to break off all contact with a boy I've known since he was born because of some bogus police charge? That is utter crap. Even you can't be that stupid.'

Kaamiya gave Rhea a resounding slap not only for her insolence but also for presenting her points so logically. The mother knew the only way she could win an argument with the debating champion was by beating some sense into her. 'Shut up and do as you're told, Rhea! I don't want to see you hurt, that's all.'

'Wow! Do you even hear yourself? You just hit me saying you don't want to hurt me! You're totally insane—and I'm not going to listen to your bullshit any more!' Rhea stormed out, leaving Kaamiya to lament loudly in Punjabi about how her only child had turned into an abusive ingrate.

As is the unenviable lot of all doting fathers, Kantilal Zaveri was implored by his daughter to go talk to his wife. 'Darling, what is the harm if Rhea speaks to Ricky? The police have obviously framed that poor fellow. Surely you don't believe he is some sort of drug addict? They had only gone to Scandal

Point for the same reason that all young couples go. They were just unlucky to be caught in the wrong place at the wrong time. We must be supportive of Ricky, or what will Manju and Kapil think—that we have abandoned them when they need us most?'

'You think I am an idiot, huh? Just because I didn't pass SSC and go to some fancy school for finishing girls doesn't mean I am a duffer! I have seen more of the world than even you, Kanti—you are a diamond vyapaari, but you don't understand duniya daari! Rhea will be turning twenty-seven soon. Do you know how hard it will be to find her a boy from a good family? Once a girl's reputation is gone, her market value comes tumbling down. Then only gold diggers will come to marry her—for your diamonds!'

Kantilal couldn't help but inwardly smile at the irony of this statement, given he had gladly married Kaamiya despite her own less than sparkling reputation. 'Come on, darling. Times have changed. Youngsters don't think like that any more. Rhea will have plenty of suitors and frankly, why bother looking further than apna Ricky? The kids obviously have strong feelings for each other, otherwise they would not have landed up in this mess, haan? Once this silly matter subsides, we should get them engaged and formalize the relationship.'

Hearing this, Kaamiya flew into a horrid rage. 'My daughter will die a spinster, but she will never ever marry an actor! Do you hear me, Kanti? I forbid you or Rhea from taking that boy's name again. Otherwise, I swear I will take rat poison and kill myself. Do I make myself clear?'

'Yes, but … what's the harm if … ?'

'Not one more word, Kanti … or else I will drink a full bottle of Tik-Twenty and leave a suicide note blaming Rhea and you for my death!'

After more than a quarter century of connubial bliss, Kantilal was all too familiar with his wife's propensity for melodrama, but even he was taken aback by the ferocity of her response. Wisely electing to withdraw before the situation escalated, the hapless billionaire decided it would be easier to talk some sense into his heartbroken daughter than his unhinged and volatile wife.

Waman Dixit accosted Munna Qureshi, one of the ward boys who worked at Behramjee Manor, just as he left the premises after an exhausting twelve-hour shift. Dixit, whose nose was encased in plaster, spoke in a low tone that made him sound somewhat like a ruptured tabla. 'Ay, Munna—you want to make ten thousand rupees for ten minutes of work?'

Munna was intrigued.

'I want you to take this powder packet and offer it to Gautam saab—you know, that angrez ki aulad in room number twelve. Tell him that you want five thousand rupees for it and you can supply him this much daily at the same price.'

'Arrey, but patients are not allowed to keep any cash with them—how will he pay me?'

'Don't worry about the money—you just tell Gautam saab that you trust him and that he can pay you later. I will supply you one packet every day and also pay you five hundred rupees daily for doing this job, okay? All you have to do is pass the packet on to Gautam, gupchup. Whatever money he pays you later is fully an extra bonus for you to keep.'

As Munna pondered this, Dixit pulled out a wad of ten thousand and thrust it at the ward boy. 'Arrey, why are you thinking so much, Munna bhai? With this much money, you will be celebrating Eid every day, haan! It will be raining biryani non-stop in your house from now on.'

Munna nodded as he accepted the money and the little packet of white powder.

Dixit was delighted. 'Shaabaash, Munna! Now be sure you tell nobody about me and don't let anyone catch you giving this to Gautam, kai? I will meet you tomorrow—same time, same place, okay? Ta-ta.'

As the scheming manager gingerly adjusted his safety helmet over his bandaged face and took off on his scooter, Munna grinned and stashed his ill-gotten gains into his knockoff Ed Hardy jeans.

Ricky Kumar waited impatiently in the foyer of the Suryanamaskar Wellness Spa for the car that would take him to the airport. Ever thoughtful, Ricky had spent the last two days hugging and generously tipping the entire staff, obliging them by posing for endless photographs with extended family members who came, in their Sunday best, to gawp at this hunky actor in exile.

Ricky had finally been given the green signal to return home and he was both apprehensive and excited at the prospect of returning to Mumbai, the city he had been so unceremoniously ousted from a month ago.

Ricky's nemesis, the politician Pramod Potnis, had suffered an enormous setback in the interim when his daughter eloped with a migrant Bihari auto-rickshaw driver. To compound his misery, his new son-in-law was a Muslim, and Potnis realized he faced the ignominious prospect of being expelled by the hardliners of his own party who would not tolerate this double-whammy betrayal. Shrewdly deciding to defect to a more liberal, secular political outfit, Pramod called a press conference and proclaimed that he would henceforth champion the cause of all migrants in Mumbai. He reminded everyone that Bombay was a city built primarily by enterprising outsiders of diverse faiths. Hindus, Muslims, Parsis, Christians, Jews had flocked from different parts of India to this cluster of seven islands and contributed towards making it urbs prima in Indus.

Potnis threatened to thrash anyone who dared intimidate migrants, thereby sending a clear message to his former party's top brass. Even though he was a freshly minted liberal, he wasn't averse to getting into a good, old-fashioned street fight.

As Ricky drove through the glistening emerald paddy fields of the Goan countryside, he lowered the car window and savoured the cool, crisp breeze on his face. His month-long stint at the spa had rejuvenated him and he looked forward to a fresh beginning in Mumbai, where he could finally get down to becoming a full-fledged movie star. He was also determined to get in touch with Rhea, who had inexplicably been incommunicado all this while.

Waman Dixit sat across the table from his old friend, Senior Inspector Madhukar Bobde. The decrepit dive they had been drinking in these past four hours had once been a glittering dance bar, one of the finest in the city, where buxom waitresses served whisky by the quarter bottle to leering customers who showered reams of cash on sexy nautch girls. Some of the finest femme fatales in Mumbai had shaken their ample booties in this stellar establishment before the moral police played spoilsport and forced the reluctant constabulary to shut it down.

The two friends cursed the astronomical rents that had resulted in the closure of some of the best-located whore joints in Mumbai and spoke despairingly of how the flesh trade had begun to move out of the city limits, indeed, all the way to Dubai. It was getting progressively harder for respectable middle-class men such as themselves to have a decent night out on the town.

'Behenchod, what do these politicians think? We should go to bloody Mira Road to bajao some Tina or Mina? Arrey, full Kamathipura should be declared a heritage zone and protected by these conservation wallahs! Mumbai's red light district is our national treasure!'

The policeman slurred in full agreement. 'Correct, bhau! Two hundred per cent correct. That's why I started my brothel in Colaba. All are old rent control buildings. Otherwise how can a businessman survive today in Mumbai?'

'Arrey, forget about the bhadwa businessman!' bellowed Dixit. 'What about the common man? How can he survive in Mumbai if he has to commute two hours to work and three hours to fuck? What is the quality of life in this city, haan? It's a major tragedy!'

'Very major tragedy,' concurred the corrupt cop. 'Achha, bhau—let's not get too emotional—tell me, what is the news of that Gautam fellow? Has he done any more tamasha at Behramjee's so I can arrest him?'

'Nai rey, unfortunately, not yet—but I have pataoed a ward boy at the clinic and given him the drug packets you seized from that kaaliya dealer. I told him to supply one to that gandoo Gautam every day. I am sure any day now that yeda's bheja will get fully fried and he will attack someone—just like he attacked me! And then you can throw that charsi into jail.'

'Arrey bhau, why to take so much trouble? Let me simply

arrest him for breaking your nose. We can comfortably squeeze his daddy's balls for a tagda amount to release him, kai?'

'No, no. I don't want his father to think I have personally complained about his haraami son. I have worked there many years, and so I want a much more bigger retirement package for my loyal service.'

The drunken inspector was disappointed. He had made a tidy sum from the Kumars, thanks to the incident at Scandal Point, and was salivating at the prospect of extorting more easy money from the super wealthy Goyals. He consoled himself by recalling what his grandmother used to say: the fruit of patience is most delicious.

Bobde smiled and raised his glass. 'Okay, bhau—but any time you hear he has done something crazy, just dial me, kai? You know I am always at your service. Cheers!'

Dixit rose, lurched across the table and thanked his old friend with a whisky-drenched kiss. 'Cheers, Madhu! I know I can count on you. You are my asli brother from somebody else's mother.'

Ricky Kumar was instantly recognized at Goa airport by legions of domestic tourists who swamped him for an autograph and a photo-op. His recent notoriety had added a new edge to his hitherto squeaky-clean image and Ricky had become more popular than ever, thanks to this bad boy persona. Before he even landed in Mumbai, the news had been tweeted and blogged across the nation that Ricky Kumar was returning home.

Hundreds of fans thronged Pali Hill to catch a glimpse of the new enfant terrible of Indian cinema and cheered enthusiastically as his BMW approached the gates of Casa

Kumar. Ricky could not have asked for a better homecoming and his confidence grew immeasurably as he smiled and waved at the screaming fans and television news crews that surrounded his car. The media ecstatically reported the return of the Prince of Pali Hill and celebrated the fact that the reformed, rehabilitated Ricky was looking better than ever.

'Welcome home, jaanoo! This is all Babaji's blessings!' wept Manju, as she embraced her son after performing a welcome aarti and streaking an enormous tilak on his forehead.

'Hey, Ricky boy! How are you, my bachcha? Did you enjoy your time in Goa? Banged any sexy gori chicks, ya?'

Ricky shook his head and blushed through his tears as his incorrigible father enveloped him in a bone-crushing bear hug. Hotchand Fatwani beamed in satisfaction. His well-calculated gamble had yielded fantastic results. Ricky's homecoming was being projected in the media as the return of the nation's prodigal. It seemed every Indian family felt it was their own son returning to the fold after redeeming himself.

A popular Hindi proverb reminds us that if a man loses his way in the morning but eventually returns home at night, he cannot be thought to have been truly lost. The warm reception Ricky Kumar received upon his return to Mumbai was a testament to how forgiving Indians can be of their idols and the unconditional love they appear to have for someone they genuinely consider their own.

Halfway across town, the man inadvertently responsible for Ricky Kumar's fluctuating fortunes was experiencing his own upheavals. Gautam Goyal had managed to endure the worst of the withdrawal symptoms and was well on his way to recovery.

Though he was no longer physically dependent on drugs, his mind remained a matter of concern for Dr Behramjee. The good doctor feared that Gautam had found no real impetus that would compel him to keep his nose clean.

Dr Behramjee had spent weeks counselling Gautam and even enlisted Sheena's help in motivating the obstinate young man to realize he could have a far more rewarding existence once liberated from the deadly vice. But the strong, self-destructive streak that imbued Gautam's soul was not easy to exorcise and the experienced Dr Behramjee felt it was only a matter of time before his patient reverted to his hedonistic ways.

Munna Qureshi had already earned a substantial amount of money from Waman Dixit and the latter was getting rather irate as he had not heard of any untoward incident involving Gautam.

'Arrey, that chodu charsi broke my nose—just like that—no reason only—and you are saying he has not made any hungama after that? No smashing furniture, slapping the doctor, doing susu in the garden, nothing at all?'

'No, sir,' replied the ward boy. 'He must be very khush with the powder you are supplying, so he is not giving any problem.'

'Oh ho—my plan is fully backfiring.' Dixit panicked. 'I was expecting gandoo Gautam to get bheja fried and attack that Bawa doctor or the matron or saala anybody else so Bobde can arrest him. But this behenchod is now fully behaving himself! His daddy sent me ten lakhs compensation for his damaging of my nose, but I must somehow earn at least fifty lakhs from this bhosdika.'

Waman turned to the ward boy. 'Okay, Munna—no more powder from now on. Our deal is khatam. You tell Gautam that you can't supply any more drugs. Let's see if that works better in making him violent, kai? Here—keep this five hundred—and remember—don't say anything to anybody, okay?'

As the exasperated manager furiously kick-started his scooter and drove off to his mid-city chawl, Munna Qureshi waved him a fond farewell. It was daunting working with recovering drug addicts on a daily basis, but Munna had known it was his destiny to care for those who wanted to escape the clutches of this haraam after his own father had overdosed on brown sugar twelve years ago. Dr Behramjee had taken the orphan Munna under his wing and given him a job at the clinic, an act for which he was eternally grateful. The god-fearing ward boy had no intention of passing on the evil powder to Gautam but saw no reason why he shouldn't make a fast buck off this comical little man with the bandaged face and querulous voice.

The phenomenal public response to Ricky's return spurred Kapil Kumar to begin work on the film that would propel his son to superstardom. With his years of experience as a Bollywood star, Kapil Kumar felt he was ideally suited to write, direct, produce and present Ricky's debut and promptly called up his coterie of cronies who would collaborate on this magnum opus.

First on Kapil's wishlist was the veteran screenwriter, Irshad Habib, now in his late seventies but spritely as a dog in heat. Irshad saab was an incurable romantic and his three divorces stood sterling testimony to the fiery passion that raged within his heart—and his loins. The aged writer had scripted some of the most successful films of the previous century but had been unkindly sidelined by the upstarts who entered Bollywood at the turn of the millennium. Kapil was convinced that Irshad saab's earthy expertise in sensing the pulse of the average cinemagoer made him an ideal candidate to partner with on the story, screenplay and dialogue of his film.

Another key, to-be-enlisted collaborator was the music composer. Kapil had once famously proclaimed that all Bollywood films require at least seven tingling songs to ensure jingling at the box-office. His unequivocal choice was the legendary Debendranath Chattopadhyay, known across the film industry, inexplicably but affectionately, as Jhontu da.

Jhontu da was an inspired musician whose love for world music had led to his lifting several melodies from across the globe. Be it African beats, Middle Eastern Rai, Polish folk songs or Abba classics, Jhontu da adapted and unabashedly integrated them into his thumping compositions. With the advent of the accursed Internet, it was becoming difficult for the music maestro to mask the source of his material and he was fast falling out of favour with film-makers who placed an unnecessary premium on originality. Jhontu da was currently on the fringes of mainstream Bollywood and busy using his talents in Bhojpuri films. The prolific composer had industriously programmed a vast bank of stock music into his trusty Yamaha organ, which he regularly regurgitated. Kapil was convinced that he was just the man for the job because, unlike other music composers, Jhontu da expressed willingness to come to Casa Kumar every day, organ in tow, and warble new ditties for the director in the comfort of his den.

Next was the cameraman. These days some hotshot Bollywood technicians called themselves cinematographers and directors of photography. The word 'cinematographer' was too difficult for Kapil to pronounce and he was damned if he was going to hire anyone who termed himself something so pretentious. 'And I'll tell you what a bloody D.O.P. is—he's a fucking dope, ya? I am not going to work with some pseudo, ponytailed popat with newfangled ideas about lighting, composition, and other such rubbish. Just give me a simple, no-nonsense cameraman who will put the bloody tripod wherever I tell him to!'

W.C. Shah was one such unassuming, unpretentious lensman who had ensured longevity in his profession not due to any cinematic proficiency but through an innate ability to acquiesce to everything the director demanded. Lesser technicians were known to throw tantrums and walk off film sets if they were not given the complement of lights and equipment they had requisitioned. But W.C. was a producer's delight as he managed to make do with the limited paraphernalia provided by penny-pinching production controllers.

Kapil Kumar, in a rare bout of humility, realized that since he was trying his hand at direction for the first time, he probably required some solid assistance with the technical aspects of film-making. He therefore hired what is euphemistically referred to in Bollywood as an 'Associate'. The job of the Associate was primarily to cover up the lapses of a clueless first-time director. An experienced but out-of-work pro or else a promising young assistant is usually offered this job and Kapil, unsurprisingly, opted for the former.

Guneet Mahajan was the director of over a dozen dhamaakedaar blockbusters in the roaring eighties but had fallen on hard times after successive films bombed in the following decade. After working with the A-listers of his generation, Guneet suddenly found his calls to producers unanswered. The stars he approached to act in his films respectfully declined, citing 'date issues', another Bollywood euphemism that allows actors to diplomatically claim they have the sincere inclination but no time to work with a flop film-maker. Guneet had been encountering 'date issues' for the past fifteen years. The call from Kapil Kumar, after an eternity, was most fortuitous. The impoverished director, though disappointed at being asked to play second fiddle, tearfully thanked him and swore to become both his left and right hand.

In a similar fashion, Kapil Kumar recruited a slew of familiar faces he had worked with over three decades in the film industry. 'I have assembled an army of veterans,' exulted the screen legend. 'They are all seasoned warriors who will go into battle with me. My film will have youth on screen and experience off it. Now comes the fun bit. I must find a sexy new heroine to star opposite Ricky boy!'

Dr Behramjee smilingly certified Sheena Kansal as drug free and fit to leave his clinic, completely rehabilitated and ready to begin life afresh. He was not as willing to give Gautam a clean chit but knew there was nothing more he could do to help the stubborn fellow.

Gautam, drained from four weeks at Behramjee Manor, wanted to leave the chamber of horrors at the earliest. However, he did not feel up to returning to freezing London and facing his father and thus gratefully accepted Sheena's offer to go spend some time in Delhi.

Sheena had stayed two extra weeks at the clinic to ensure Gautam had some company and moral support while he dried out thoroughly. She was ecstatic to have him as her houseguest and looked forward to showing him off to Delhi society as her new boyfriend.

Dr Behramjee escorted them to the gates of his sprawling manor. 'Good luck, you two. Stay clean and stay strong. Don't give in to temptation and remember, if you ever need a friend to talk to, I am only a phone call away.' The diminutive doctor hugged Sheena tenderly and then extended his hand towards Gautam. The six-footer looked down at his tiny tormentor and did something entirely unexpected. He grabbed hold of Dr Behramjee, enveloped him in a tight embrace and broke down, weeping uncontrollably.

Munna Qureshi, who was carrying Gautam's luggage, also shed a smiling tear, knowing he had contributed in his own small, twisted way towards saving the soul of his fellow man.

THREE

'What the Indian public is looking for in a Hindi film heroine is a slutty Savitri. A virgin-whore, ya? We need to find a girl who is a sangam of these two qualities, Ricky boy! She must have the face of an angel and the body of an apsara—massive boobs with a slender waist and a big, juicy ass. Like those Khajuraho-type sculptures. Get it?'

Ricky blushed but said nothing. He was amazed his chauvinistic father could objectify women in this manner without an iota of shame. But Kapil 'King Cock' Kumar was not being lascivious. He was merely expounding his theory of what Indian audiences wanted to see on screen.

'Today's girls are all carrom boards, ya? No dudhdoos, no buttocks, nothing! And what the bloody hell is this size zero nonsense, haan? The average Indian male fantasizes about taking a heroine to bed—he needs something fleshy he can hold on to and squeeze. Tell me, how can you dabaao a woman who is ...'

'Papa, please—stop it! I get what you're saying.' Ricky was a puddle of embarrassment.

'Arrey, let him continue, beta—your father is speaking a lot of sense.' The septuagenarian writer, Irshad saab, was hugely aroused by Kapil's vivid description of the anatomical requirements of their film's leading lady.

Sprawled in his den at Casa Kumar, surrounded by his chamchas, Kapil was in his element after downing the fourth large peg of Johnnie Black. 'Haan, so where was I? Yes, so that's why today's films are flopping left, right and bloody centre. First and foremost, we must find a new face. Actually, a new body!'

'But why not cast one of the top heroines, papa? So many have been sending feelers through their secretaries that they are keen to star opposite me.'

'Nonsense! We don't want a known face to piggyback on your debut and steal your thunder. This is your launch pad, Ricky boy; the focus has to be on you. Besides, audiences today are hungry for a fresh pair on screen.'

'Yes. Hungry for a fresh pair of breasts on screen!' cackled Irshad saab and collapsed in mirth.

Kapil Kumar held up his hand to silence the randy old man. 'Irshad saab! I do hope you will give better dialogues than this one. Otherwise, we will have a super-duper flop on our hands!'

The aged writer looked crestfallen and began to apologize profusely. 'Maaf kijiye, Kapilji—it was just a spur of the moment joke and I was ...'

Kapil Kumar could not keep a straight face any longer. 'Arrey, if on the spur of the moment you can come up with such gems, imagine what seeti-maar dialogues you will write for Ricky, ya?' Kapil exploded with laughter and raised his hand to high-five the immensely relieved comic genius.

As they rolled about the red velvet sofa in paroxysms of drunken hilarity, Kapil's other assembled cronies realized this was their cue and began to laugh boisterously. The hooting and backslapping continued for another fifteen minutes before Kapil Kumar staggered to his feet and declaimed, 'Gentlemen, let's call a press conference and announce a nation-wide hunt for a new heroine. The publicity we generate will be huge! After all, it is every girl's wet dream to star opposite the handsomest hero in Bollywood, my boy, Ricky Kumar. Cheers!'

The sycophants raised their glasses and looked around the room to toast their crown prince, but Ricky had long slipped out of his father's den and gone to get a good night's sleep.

'I totally adore Delhi in winter. It's so beautiful waking up to the misty mornings and cuddling round bonfires at night. For me, it's all about long walks in Lodhi Gardens and hot chocolate at Delhi Club. Man, it's sometimes easy to forget you're in India. You could be in New York or Berlin or Paris. Okay, maybe not Paris—'coz that's just like my absolute favourite city in the universe—but hey, you know, Delhi is Delhi. It's home, man!'

As Sheena prattled on, Gautam smiled. He was relieved to have escaped the miserable confines of Behramjee Manor and Mumbai, that infernal city he would forever associate with the trauma of cold turkey. Gautam gazed outside at the majestic gulmohar trees that lined the broad avenue they were driving down and felt at peace. He turned to Sheena and kissed her tenderly on the lips.

She blushed and withdrew, whispering, 'Hey, not here. Mustn't let the driver see. He'll spread it all over the servants' quarters!'

Gautam was annoyed. He didn't like people contradicting or correcting him. He recoiled and looked huffily out the window.

Sheena tried to pacify the prickly young man. 'Hey, I'm sorry. I didn't mean to hurt your feelings, Gautam. It's just that we don't behave like this in front of the staff. It's simply not done. It has nothing to do with you. It's just the way I am, okay?'

'Well, fuck you. I can't stand hypocrites who pretend to be goody two-shoes and then do all sorts of shit behind closed doors.'

Sheena was mortified. She saw the chauffeur watching her tear up in the rear-view mirror, alerted by Gautam's raised voice. 'Please, Gautam. Not here, I beg you. I'm so sorry. I didn't mean to upset you, man. I'm really sorry.'

Just as quickly as he had erupted, Gautam calmed down and took the trembling Sheena in his arms. 'No, I'm sorry, love. It's not your fault. You know what a messed-up bloke I am. I lose all control sometimes. It's a problem I need to address. Promise you won't give up on me?'

Sheena snuggled in the warmth of his embrace, reassured. This petulant bad boy was her new project and she had no intention of giving up on him. Rather, she was determined to reform Gautam Goyal and get him to marry her some day.

In the last decades of the twentieth century, a number of film stars, politicians, stockbrokers and sundry nouveau riche folk who had made their fortunes in Mumbai, aspired to embellish their homes in the latest fashion. At the time, the ultimate arbiters of taste in the city were a pair of upper-crust ladies who reigned supreme as Mumbai's most sought-after interior decorators. Both women, one Parsi, the other Punjabi, came from solid middle-class stock but had married old money and assiduously went about positioning themselves as style mavens. While one was a light-eyed beauty and a natural charmer, the other was dumpy and abrasive but knew a thing or two about design. Thanks to their husbands' formidable influence and their own relentless ambition, this double act soon transformed the aesthetics of several upscale homes across the city. Manju and Kapil Kumar, then a newly married couple, anxious to be accepted by Mumbai's elite, had felt obliged to engage the duo's services to adorn the large bungalow they had so proudly purchased in suburban Pali Hill, Bollywood's answer to Beverly Hills.

It took the design virtuosos two years to titivate the interiors in their signature eclectic style, replete with Italian marble-clad walls, calligraphy-inscribed Mughal columns, latticed Rajasthani windows, perspex dining furniture and massive murals that paid homage to the genius of Botticelli, Rembrandt, Michelangelo and other European masters. Since having a home decorated by these ladies was considered the definitive status symbol amongst the Bombay beau monde, it was imperative that every project they executed closely resembled the other, so guests would have no trouble identifying their handiwork and marvelling at their bravura.

When the revamp of the Pali Hill bungalow was complete, the doyennes of décor presented the excited Kumars with the keys to their new residence. At the entrance, an ornate plaque fashioned from railway sleeper wood and etched acrylic dubbed the abode 'Casa Kumar'. Initially, the ostentatious edifice which looked like an unholy amalgam of the Sistine Chapel and Salim Chishti's tomb overwhelmed the mild-mannered Manju and even the highly flamboyant Kapil. But they were so in awe of its venerated decorators they dared not say, let alone change, a thing. The Kumars meekly moved in and gradually began to regard Casa Kumar as their home and it was here that their only child was lovingly raised.

Now that Ricky was about to embark on his film career, Manju summoned the city's leading astrologer for a consultation and insisted Kapil be present for this vital meeting. Ricky was excused from attending, as Manju feared the fortune-teller might say something that could potentially upset her sensitive son.

Pandit Kripashankar Trivedi sat cross-legged on the white shag carpet in the opulent living room of Casa Kumar and chanted 'Om' as he waited for his seventeen-inch laptop to boot. Manju gazed reverently as the celebrated seer proceeded to cross-reference Ricky's birth date with the time he was born. He then computed the most auspicious moment for the mahurat of her son's soon-to-be-launched film.

'According to the alignment of the planets, the mahurat must be done on the third of March at four thirty in the morning,' pronounced the pandit.

'What rubbish!' snorted Kapil Kumar. 'We don't even have a script, let alone a heroine. How can we launch Ricky's film so soon? And who the hell is going to attend a mahurat at four thirty in the bloody morning, huh? Arrey, find some sensible date and time in April or May when we can go on the floors.'

'Sorry, Kapilji, but all dates are inauspicious for eight months after this one. They are simply not favouring Rickyji's chart. It is best to hold the mahurat as per my advice and shoot the rest of the film as and when you are able.'

'Bloody bullshit! How can I shoot for one day and wait for another two months before taking my next shot? What sort of ponga pandit are you?'

Manju quickly interjected before her brusque husband could offend the aged astrologer further. 'Panditji, is it not possible to do some pooja or havan to change the mahurat dates?'

The pandit patiently explained, 'Of course I can do so madamji, but please trust me, this is the very best date and time to launch the film. This will result in a silver-jubilee hit.

Otherwise, I can guarantee only recovery of production cost at the box-office excluding marketing, print and publicity.'

Pandit Trivedi was something of a Bollywood specialist, widely in demand with the superstitious film fraternity. A staggering seventy per cent of the movies churned out by the world's most prolific film industry were flops that did not even recover their cost of production, let alone turn in a profit. It was not surprising then, that the denizens of tinsel town actively sought divine assistance in all their ventures.

'So, you are personally guaranteeing me a silver-jubilee hit if I launch the film on the third of March at four thirty in the morning?' asked Kapil Kumar, amazed at the pandit's pluck.

'Correct, Kapilji. Once I give you the proper spelling of the name of your film, you will be assured of box-office success. Have you thought of a title yet?'

'Arrey, I told you, I don't even have a script, so how can I have a bloody title, ya? Are you listening to anything at all or only babbling your own bloody bullshit?' fumed Kapil, ignoring Manju's fretting.

'Kapilji, the title is more important than the story these days. It is best that your film begins with the letter "G".'

'Jee, panditji,' said Kapil Kumar with mock reverence.

'Also, one more thing. As the director and producer of the film, it would be much better to change the spelling of your first name and add one more "K", to make it Kkapil.'

Kapil Kumar rose with folded hands and bowed before the astrologer. 'Panditji, I have been a household name across the world, wherever Hindi films are watched, for the past thirty years. And you are telling me that I should change the spelling of the very name that two generations of film-goers have grown up adoring?'

The pandit nodded sagely. 'Only if you want a guaranteed silver-jubilee hit.'

'I will hit you for a fucking silver-jubilee before I change even one hair on my testicles!' thundered Kapil Kumar. 'Get the fuck out of my house before I personally kick you and your bloody computer out of here. Today a producer is lucky if his film runs for even four weeks in a multiplex and you are guaranteeing me a silver-jubilee run of twenty-five weeks? What sort of gullible ghanchakkar do you think I am?'

Pandit Trivedi hastily snapped his laptop shut and scurried out of Casa Kumar. This former junior electrical engineer had toiled for years at a low-paying government job until he hit upon the idea of quitting his profession and pursuing his hobby full time to become an astrologer to the stars. The date of every successful film's launch and release, its title, the astrological charts of the principal cast and crew were assiduously studied by Kripashankar Trivedi, who soon adopted the prefix Pandit as his popularity began to grow. He had diversified into Vaastu, Feng-Shui and numerology and made a small fortune by changing the way half the highly insecure film community spelt their names.

Pandit Trivedi knew that no one could predict the box-office fate of a film. But this former minion of the Municipal Corporation loved how the movers and shakers of Bollywood obeyed his every diktat in their desperate quest for success. The astrologer, who had succeeded primarily in changing his own fortunes, enjoyed fraternizing with the stars but today he discovered that occasionally, when you come too close to one, you're liable to get burnt.

'Fucking fraud! Why the hell do you insist on bringing these jokers into our house, Manju? Don't you trust me? I have been in this industry for over three decades! Who better than me to know exactly what sells and what doesn't? We don't need to rely on mumbo-jumbo nonsense!'

Manju nodded. She was appalled but she knew better than to reproach her temperamental husband when he was throwing one of his infamous fits.

'I'm so sorry, Kapil. I was simply trying to help our Ricky after all the bad luck he's been having. I trust you completely, and I know you will make a big blockbuster for my jaanoo. He is lucky to have such a talented father. And I am so very blessed to have such a sensible husband.'

Having mollycoddled Kapil for ten more minutes and successfully assuaged his bruised ego, Manju retreated to her bedroom and made plans to visit Babaji's ashram in the Himalayas. She was convinced her son had fallen prey to the evil eye and only this great ascetic possessed the power to rid him of his curse. The young actor had suffered immensely the past couple of months and his mother wanted to ensure that he got all the help he needed to achieve the greatness he was destined for.

The two-storeyed Kansal Villa in the upmarket enclave of Delhi's Golf Links was divided equally between Nina and Jagjit Kansal. The once lovely Nina had claimed the top floor of this eight-bedroom Art Deco bungalow as part of her divorce settlement ten years ago. It was there that she resided, in the heart of Lutyens's Delhi, with her two daughters, Sheena and Mini.

Her ex-husband Jagjit Kansal occupied the floor below and lived the charmed life of a successful, single politician. Delhi proffered an array of delectable divorcees of every age who were happy to jump into bed with this suave maverick. It was not that Jagjit was a particularly good-looking man, but the clout he wielded in the corridors of power made him an attractive proposition for lonely ladies and they regularly trooped in and out of his well-appointed home.

With great power comes great depravity and Jagjit was no stranger to accusations of great corruption. However, the former lawyer was adept at staying two steps ahead of his detractors. He managed to remain in power and out of jail while better men than him found themselves either incarcerated in Tihar or worse, exiled to political wilderness.

Jagjit learned from his major domo Murugan that his elder daughter had returned from Mumbai with a young man who was currently lodged in one of the guest rooms upstairs. He instructed Murugan to find out through the domestic grapevine what the name of this chap was and where precisely he hailed from. Jagjit Kansal may not have been a hands-on father, but he monitored every move his children made, primarily to ensure they never compromised him politically or left him open to blackmail. He had supported Sheena both emotionally and financially when she announced her decision to check into Dr Behramjee's clinic and was pleased his attention-deficit elder daughter had managed to stick it out in Mumbai for six weeks.

Nina Kansal, on the other hand, couldn't be less bothered what her two kids were up to. They were young women now and therefore competition for the male attention she personally craved. Three decades ago, Nina Pujji, determined to transcend her small-town existence, had entered the Miss India pageant with a view to conquering the world. Unfortunately, her strong equine features, though striking, were not quite what the judges were looking for and she was sorely disappointed to emerge the second runner-up that year.

Downhearted but not defeated, the tenacious Nina decided to accept the marriage proposal made by Jagjit Kansal, an ambitious student leader at Law College, who was besotted with the fiery Punjabi kudi. With her looks and his wit and their combined ambition, Nina and Jagjit made a formidable team. They scaled the political and social ladder to emerge as a pre-eminent power couple in Delhi. Once successful, Jagjit, with his affable charm and incredible influence, became prone to obliging helpless young women who sought his assistance. Provided they reciprocated his largesse with sexual favours, of course. Nina meanwhile made two unsuccessful attempts at producing a son and blamed her sagging breasts and straying husband on the birth of her daughters. Overweight and insecure, Nina hit a mid-life crisis. She had spent years transforming from Ludhiana lass into society swan and resolved once again to re-invent herself and reclaim her status as a top Delhi diva. Gymming and botoxing herself senseless, she sexed up her wardrobe and went on a rampage seducing as many men as she possibly could. Hardly discerning, she bedded a considerable number of married men in the National Capital Region and was understandably not very popular with wives.

Now Nina was enamoured of the brooding, handsome chap Sheena had brought back from rehab and made efforts to ensure their new houseguest felt welcome.

'Gautam, you must make yourself at home, dahling. Mini is away so there are plenty of rooms to choose from, in case you don't like sleeping in the guest bedroom.'

Nina's husky voice was as cultivated as her socialite persona and Gautam was instantly annoyed by her Anglo-Ludhianvi accent. 'If there is anything you need, puhleese don't hesitate to ring for Rosie. Otherwise, feel free to call me. Any time.'

Gautam smiled broadly. 'I'll be sure to ring for Rosie. Thank you, aunty.'

That dreaded word had the desired effect, sending a shiver down Nina's Versace–sheathed spine. 'Gautam, puhleese! No aunty-shanti. I am Nina, just Nina. You know I had Sheena when I was only sixteen? People insist I cannot be her mother, that I must be her sister. Some even say younger sister! Can you imagine!'

'Randy, backstabbing bitch,' thought Gautam.

He had shagged his fair share of older women, but Nina, with her painted face, bulging boobs and predatory manner, repulsed him. He turned to Sheena, who was squirming with embarrassment as her mother made a blatant play for her boyfriend.

'Sheena, I have to agree. I don't think anyone would believe Nina is really your mother.' Nina preened as Gautam continued, 'Actually, Nina, you remind me so much of Lady Tremaine.'

Nina was flummoxed but did not want to betray her ignorance of English aristocracy. 'Well, thanks, dahling! I will take that as a massive compliment, coming from someone as debonayaar as you.' She leaned over and kissed Gautam close to the lips. 'Now, please go to bed and have only sweet dreams. Goodnight, dahlings!'

As Nina flounced off, her daughter rolled her eyes. 'I warned you, didn't I? My mother's a complete character!'

Gautam grinned and grabbed Sheena, kissing her passionately in the doorway between their rooms. They staggered around in a flurry of passion, bursting through Sheena's bedroom door and finally fell onto her bed, locked in a frantic embrace. When they finally disengaged, Sheena licked her lips. 'Mmmm . . . Yummy!'

Then a jealous thought stabbed her. 'Hey, who the heck is Lady Tremaine?'

'Oh, you know, she's the wicked stepmother from Cinderella.'

Sheena squealed in delight and flipped around on the bouncy mattress to land gently atop Gautam. She started to slowly unbutton his shirt and leaned in close to whisper, 'So then, Prince Charming, shall I wear my golden slippers to bed tonight?'

'Nyaah. I much prefer red stilettos, babe. Always have. Always will.'

Ricky Kumar didn't mind in the least when people called him a mamma's boy. He loved his mother dearly and could speak with her freely on matters that most kids preferred keeping from their parents. Ricky had confessed to Manju that he was in love with Rhea and wanted to marry her as soon as he had established himself as a Bollywood hero. The twenty-five-year-old was adamant he should be able to support his wife financially and grant her every luxury she desired. Kantilal Zaveri would undoubtedly leave his vast fortune to his only daughter, but Ricky proudly declared he would never accept any money from his in-laws, nor indeed his parents, once he was up on his own feet.

'Ah, the idealism of youth,' sighed Manju. 'My son is such a good boy but so very naïve in the ways of the world. Thank god, we are here to launch him and ensure he doesn't really have to struggle in life.'

Ricky drew inspiration from the story his father loved to recount of his struggle to make it big in Bollywood. How he had arrived in Mumbai all those years ago, from his small village in Punjab, travelling ticketless and third class on the

Firozpur Janta. How his poor but proud parents, ashamed their only son wanted to become a bhaand, a lowly actor, had disowned him. How he had slept on railway platforms and eaten only one meal a day as he walked from studio to studio, hoping to meet a producer or director who would be willing to cast him. How he had been humiliated by the biggest names in the business and swore that one day they would line up at his door, just as he had waited for weeks outside theirs.

It was a stirring saga of courage, tenacity and the triumph of the human spirit, but it was also bogus. Kapil was actually the son of a wealthy Amritsar-based surgeon, who had dispatched the good-looking but dim-witted stud to study medicine in Mumbai. Instead, Kapil became obsessed with the anatomy of the girls in the college drama department. Rather than attend tedious lectures on histology, he preferred to dabble in histrionics and participated in several amateur productions. He landed his break when spotted and cast by a well-known film director who was judging an inter-college drama competition. Karambir Singh Minhas promptly dropped out of medical college and re-christened himself Kapil Kumar. He then embarked on a lustrous career in Bollywood, with the blessings of his father, who was eternally grateful he would not have to support his duffer son for the rest of his years.

The mythology that Kapil had built around his ascent was cobbled together from the true stories of the struggles of several other actors. Somewhere deep down, the filmi icon felt guilty and even ashamed he had made such a name and earned so much money for essentially doing nothing more than sporting garish costumes, mouthing inane dialogue and prancing around trees. Kapil had tremendous respect for his surgeon father, who saved lives every day, and knew he could never be half the man his brilliant papa was. The perks of his own job were, however, fantastic, and Kapil Kumar proudly and loudly and often claimed to have banged every actress he worked with.

Young Ricky would have been disillusioned to learn that, in actuality, his dad was a lucky sod who had hit the big time without really having to pay his dues. But middle-class Manju was keen to perpetuate the myth to teach her son the value of hard work and humility. And the ever-obedient Ricky had learned this life lesson well.

'I just can't understand why Rhea isn't responding to my calls, Mamma?' said Ricky. 'Can you please try Aunty Kaamiya in Antwerp and find out if she's okay? I'm really worried about her.'

'Of course I will, jaanoo. Now you don't worry any more about anything. Soon we will go meet Babaji in Rishikesh. He will sort out all your problems.'

Gautam had declined to fly out from London to Delhi for the grand opening of Masala Magic four years ago. His elder sister Rani had accompanied their father on the trip eastward while he whooped it up at home in the West End. Now, walking into the expansive restaurant for the first time, with Sheena by his side, Gautam felt chuffed that his family owned such a stunning property.

Sheena was a familiar face on the capital's social circuit and no stranger to the gossip pages either. She had suddenly dropped out of sight six weeks ago and there had been some whispers about her having left town to enter rehab. Some speculated she had checked into Betty Ford and others swore she had been sighted getting a much-needed nose job in

Zurich. The buzz quickly went round the glitzy restaurant-cum-lounge-bar that Sheena Kansal was back in town with a dishy Brit-Asian hunk on her arm.

Hip-hop Hooda, the exuberant in-house Jat DJ, grabbed the mike to announce that Delhi's favourite party animal, Sheena baby, was back in da house. Gautam was soon identified as the NRI munda who owned dis joint and everyone gave a big shout out to dis uber cool couple that was here to rock da night. Oh yeah!

A fair few of the well-heeled crowd gathered that Saturday night knew Gautam from their annual pilgrimages to London or were at least familiar with his hell-raiser reputation. They were disappointed, therefore, when both Gautam and Sheena remained sober that evening and indulged in no untoward antics. The paparazzi that hovered outside the restaurant were annoyed they would have nothing more salacious than pictures of the hugging happy couple to feature in the next day's edition of the gossip glossies. Sheena, mindful of Dr Behramjee's warning that they were vulnerable to toxic shock after weeks in purgatory, ensured Gautam stayed away from the bar. Sober in the midst of bonhomie after a long time, Sheena hugged her friends and smilingly introduced her new boyfriend to them.

'They are all bloody stick insects!' roared Kapil Kumar as he flung a set of photographs in the air. 'Arrey, I want to see some flesh. Khaate-peete ghar ki ladki honi chahiye—girls who enjoy eating, drinking, fucking, ya?'

The scandalized casting director got down on his knees and hastily gathered up the portfolio pictures of the dozen aspiring actresses he had short-listed to show the volatile film-maker.

'Now get out. And don't come back to waste my valuable time until you have some proper pathaka to show.'

As the casting director fled, Ricky politely chided his father. 'Papa, please. No one will work with us if you shout and scream like this.'

'Arrey, nonsense! They know this is my andaaz, my style of functioning. I need to whip these lazy lumps into producing results, otherwise they will simply sit all day on their fat fucking arses!'

Before Ricky could reply, there was a knock on the door and the aged Irshad saab entered, carrying with him a polythene bag. 'Salaam, Irshad saab,' said Kapil, waving him in. 'Have you come from sabzi shopping in Pali Market?'

The geriatric writer winked as he plonked on the couch beside Kapil. 'Well, you could say I have been shopping. Not for vegetables but for ideas, janaab.' He bumptiously pulled out a stack of eight DVDs and spread them before the veteran actor. 'Kapil sahab, these are the top grossing Hollywood films of last year. My grandson ordered them from Amazon. Romance, comedy, action, drama, science fiction, thriller, murder mystery and horror. Just choose one and we can start writing our script.'

Ricky was aghast. Though there was a long and inglorious tradition of plagiarizing Hollywood films in India, he certainly didn't want his debut to be an international rip off. Nevertheless, he kept quiet, not wanting to offend a senior writer.

'Irshad saab, do you think I am a bloody DVD director?' thundered Kapil, using the pejorative term for local auteurs who shamelessly copied entire scenes after watching the originals on video. 'You think I am some fucking faltu who will make a frame-to-frame remake of a foreign film?'

Irshad saab quavered. 'Ama, this is only for inspiration. We have such little time for scripting before you go on the floors, so I thought we could ...'

'Never! Never! Never! My subject has to be completely original,' said Kapil loftily and stood up to declaim. 'This is why the goras laugh and call our film industry Bollywood. Because we have forgotten our own film culture and have blindly started copying everything from Hollywood. But the times have changed, Irshad saab, and we must also change with the times.'

Ricky was proud his father had decided to take a stand on intellectual property rights and was championing the cause of originality in Hindi cinema. 'Precisely, Papa! We have to set an example for the nation's youth.'

'Arrey, nation's youth ki maa ki chut!' bellowed his father. 'We have to worry about being dragged to court by those bastard Hollywood buggers!'

Some of the biggest names in the Hindi film industry had been guilty of filching entire plots, characters and dialogue from foreign films. For years, the country's archaic copyright laws had ensured that local producers could blatantly remake a blockbuster and get away without paying a paisa in royalty. But recently a few major American studios had decided to take action and sought injunctions against illegal remakes. As a result, there were several Hindi films awaiting judicial clearance before they could be exhibited in cinemas. The producers, all friends of Kapil, rued the day they had invested in international knockoffs.

'Irshad saab, you want me to twiddle my fucking thumbs and pay interest through my arse to those bloodsucking financiers while my film rots in the cans, ya?'

'Tauba, tauba ... not at all, janaab,' mumbled the screenwriter. 'Please forgive me. I promise I will come back to you in a few days with a minty fresh story.'

Polythene bag in hand, Irshad saab exited Casa Kumar, silently cursing its owner. 'Doesn't this pompous fool realize that nearly a dozen of his hit films have been lifted directly from video? I should know, I wrote them!'

'Thanks, Papa. I was worried for a moment you might go along with Irshad saab's plan.'

'Don't you worry, Ricky boy, we are going to make a dhansoo picture together. I've already got an original idea ghoomoing in my head. It's a remake of one of my old films.'

'Papa, I thought we were going with an original idea?'

'Of course we are, Ricky boy. The original film was originally original. Not some copy, ya? Nowadays, making a remake is the latest trend in Bollywood. You remember my blockbuster, *Pardesi Pardesi?*'

Ricky had seen his father's golden-jubilee film several times. An action adventure romantic social about a poor village bumpkin who immigrates to England to work as a cook at an Indian restaurant but eventually becomes the head of an international smuggling syndicate. He then realizes he has made millions but lost the respect of the village belle he was in love with. He finally decides to give up everything and returns to India after having won the gratitude and respect of the entire nation through this sacrifice, but most importantly, he wins the heart of his ladylove.

Ricky pondered this for a bit. There was something audacious and retro about remaking the eighties kitsch classic for a modern audience. The curious public would flock to cinemas to see the star son play the role once immortalized by his father. Also, the parable of redemption and forgiveness fit perfectly with Ricky's personal journey of hero turned villain turned public hero. The more he thought about it, the more he liked it.

'Papa, it's an absolutely fucking brilliant idea! Let's do it. Let's remake *Pardesi Pardesi*.'

Kapil Kumar was ecstatic. Not only had he cracked the plot for a super-duper hit film but also his son had finally grown the gonads to use the 'F' word in his presence. Kapil Kumar welled up with joy and proudly hugged Ricky. 'Fuck, fuck, fuckity fuck! My wimpy boy has finally become a man!'

The Delhi society pages splashed pictures of Sheena and Gautam on their night out at Masala Magic and anointed the duo the new IT couple in town. The hooking up of the good-looking, loaded restaurateur with the politically connected party girl became the topic du jour.

Gautam thoroughly enjoyed the attention being showered on him. His family owned the hippest hangout in town, his girlfriend knew just about everybody worth knowing, and the Delhi edition of the *Indian Post* hailed him as one of the handsomest men in India. Gautam realized he had the city at his feet within a week of having arrived there. The memory of the harrowing time spent in Mumbai began to fade and Gautam Goyal immersed himself in the blessed existence that was his life once again.

A well-known Delhi wag, Mukesh Menda, then broke a salacious story in his widely read gossip column in the *Delhi Dispatch*:

> Hello, my luscious *laddoos*! *Garma garam* gossip in the middle of freezing winter! We all know *apni Dilli ki billi*, Sheena Kansal, is having a torrid affair with that stud muffin *launda* from London, Gautam Goyal. These two latest lovebirds were last spotted doing kootchie kookoo at

Masala Magic, which is owned by Gautam's *crorepati pita*, Sir Dharmesh Goyal.

But did you know that party-hearty Sheena, daughter of our upright *neta* Shri Jagjit Kansal actually met her loaded loverboy in rehab at the famous Behramjee Clinic in Mumbai?

Yes, it's absolutely true, my jolly *jalebis*! A little tweety birdy informs me that these two fans of Uncle Charlie were forced into drug detox by their parents. And that's when they first laid (eyes on) one another! It seems *sayani* Sheena would sneak into Gautam's room every night to keep warm and only return to her own empty *kamraa* in the morning. Must be shivering from Cold Turkey, *hain na*, honeybunches? Wink, wink!

Not only that but *suna hai ki* the *natkhat* NRI playboy was bitten on his bottom by Dr Behramjee's *wafaadaar kutta* Bruno, when he tried to escape the clinic by climbing over the wall one night. *Bechaara* Bruno, hope he recovers soon!

Anyway, we wish this ex-junkie *jodi* all the very best. Let's hope their newfound love (and lust) will help them keep each other's noses clean. Otherwise, they can always apply for a couple's discount rate in rehab the next time. Wot say?

Toodle-oo, my gorgeous *golgappas*. Stay tuned and stay snug till next week's hot, hot goss!

This tawdry piece of tattle spread like wildfire. The electronic media picked it up and ran the story as a lead, given it had the three ingredients vital for any juicy scandal: celebrity, sex and drugs. Stock images of Gautam and Sheena were flashed across the country, proclaiming the veracity of the aspersions cast on the lovers. While some newspapers and television reports lauded the efforts of the young couple to get clean, most dwelled on the seamier side of their liaison as also their individual colourful pasts. Gautam's infamous escapades as a London wild child were raked up and gleefully reported to the Indian public and Sheena's misadventures as a Delhi party girl were also enumerated for the nation's benefit. Their parents were unwittingly dragged into the melee and it became a veritable family circus as personal details about Sir Dharmesh and the messily divorced Nina and Jagjit Kansal were made public. People who had never even heard of Sheena Kansal and Gautam Goyal were suddenly privy to their intimate secrets, thanks to a healthy interest in the scurrilous lives of the rich and famous.

Mukesh Menda was soon fatigued from shuttling between the offices of news channels in Delhi and Mumbai. But being a dedicated media darling, he delicately dabbed his brow and soldiered on, giving interview after interview where he pontificated on how vital it was for the young lovers to stay clean and wished them the very best for a rosy future together. The catty social commentator refused to accept that he had violated the privacy of two individuals and maintained that public figures were fair game, open to media scrutiny. He skilfully evaded prickly questions about whether his story had diminished Sheena and Gautam's chances of remaining sober in light of the public humiliation.

'My job is only to hold a mirror to the foibles of society. I am not liable for the consequences of their irresponsible actions. If you can't stand the heat, don't play with fire,' hissed the eloquent Mukesh. 'Frankly, I blame the parents—they need to supervise their kids. I don't know much about Dharmesh Goyal, but I can tell you, if Nina and Jagjit Kansal had been better parents, their daughter would never have become a drug addict.'

Mukesh pursed his plump lips and steadfastly refused to divulge the source of his sensational information, citing journalistic confidentiality.

Soon after the story broke, the sniggering started amongst the glitterati.

'Breaking news! Sheena and Gautam are getting married. They will now live as a "Joint" family!' An SMS, widely forwarded across town.

'What do Sheena and Gautam offer their guests at home? Pepsi or Coke?' The pithy tweet posted by a socialite who had effusively hugged Sheena only the week before.

'Sheena and Gautam—elite members of Delhi's HIGH society?' A Facebook post that was 'liked' by over nine hundred friends.

Gautam was a jaded veteran of jibes, thanks to the British tabloids, and inured from embarrassment. But Sheena was inconsolable, wholly devastated by the negative publicity. Her shenanigans had been kept out of the press by her politician father so far. She was reeling from how vicious and personal the attacks were, now that the gloves had come off.

'I realize that everything they said about us is true. We did meet in rehab and I did sneak into your room every night, but it sounds so sleazy. I feel so dirty and violated. Oh god, I just want to crawl under a rock and die!' sobbed Sheena.

'Don't worry, babe. This will become yesterday's news tomorrow. You have to remain focussed and not allow these wankers to mess with your mind.'

Gautam lay down next to Sheena and stroked her face gently just as she had done through his worst phase of rehab. Through a kaleidoscope of tears, Sheena smiled weakly at the beautiful boy by her side.

That which does not kill you only makes you stronger, the Nietzsche-spouting Dr Behramjee had taught them. Sheena resolved to dig deep and find the inner strength to overcome this new adversity. She swore she would never fall back into the abyss she had only recently crawled out of.

Jagjit Kansal also made a solemn promise that day. The powerful politician swore that Mukesh Menda would pay a heavy price for the havoc he had unleashed on the Kansal family.

Babaji, venerated by thousands of devotees across the globe, looked nothing like the other fashionable godmen of his generation. He eschewed a flowing beard and dressed in a simple cotton kurta-pyjama rather than the silk robes in vogue among his peers. He lived and worked out of an austere ashram he had established twenty years ago near Rishikesh, nestled in the foothills of the craggy Himalayas. Babaji devoted his energies to running charitable institutions. He was especially involved with improving the deplorable condition of the girl child and preached against female infanticide, which was widely, albeit covertly, practised throughout India.

Manju had insisted Ricky visit Babaji for a darshan so he could be blessed and purged of the 'buri nazar' of jealous rivals. The aspiring actor was a rationalist at heart and only agreed to make the trip to indulge his mother, who he knew revered the holy man. He looked around the serene ashram, situated in an apple orchard surrounded by snow-clad peaks, and wondered what Babaji would say about his future.

A young attendant led them down a red-brick path to the simple log hut where Babaji received visitors. Upon first meeting Babaji, Ricky instinctively bent to touch his feet, but the charismatic guru stopped him and enveloped the young actor in a warm embrace instead.

'Bow before no one but God. Or those that are truly worthy of your respect, son. At the moment, you are undoubtedly here at your mother's behest. I cannot allow you to touch my feet until I have genuinely touched your heart.'

Ricky smiled at the understanding of the prescient man. He was instantly impressed by Babaji's humility as also his command of the language. His accent suggested he had received a formal education at an English-medium school. Possibly abroad? Ricky wondered.

Manju apprised Babaji of the turmoil in Ricky's young life and exhorted the guru to help her son.

'Manju, everyone must first learn to fall before they can truly rise. Ricky has a strong destiny written for him. Once he charts his own course, it will be smooth sailing for your son.'

'But, Babaji, he needs to be protected from the evil eye. I was hoping you could rid him of the curse that a jealous rival has definitely put on him.'

Babaji shook his head and smiled indulgently. To Manju's disappointment, he refused to perform an exorcism ritual or even give Ricky a talisman.

Instead, he turned to Ricky and said, 'You have a bright future ahead of you, son. Remember, you can only expect to win the hearts of others when your own is truly clean.'

So, Babaji was not a miracle-performing poseur but a true spiritualist, Ricky thought, relieved.

'Babaji, I want to ask you about my friend—a special friend, Rhea. We had recently become very close but she has suddenly disappeared from my life. I don't know what to do.'

Babaji's face broke into a smile and he dismissed Ricky's concern with a wave of his hand. 'Do nothing, son. Do not pursue her. When the time is right, she will appear just as suddenly as she disappeared. Concentrate only on the task at hand. Focus and you will reap the benefits.'

A young attendant politely intervened to indicate the audience with the holy man was over. Babaji rose and held out his arms to embrace Ricky, but the new disciple chose instead to bend and touch the master's feet.

Irshad saab trundled into Casa Kumar with a thick box file tucked under his arm. He had spent six sleepless nights toiling over a screenplay that would serve not only as Ricky's debut film, but more importantly, mark his triumphant comeback as a top-notch Bollywood scriptwriter. The geriatric was exhausted but elated, having produced an original piece of work after several decades.

Kapil Kumar was engrossed in a music sitting with Jhontu da, so Irshad saab dutifully sat in a corner, awaiting his turn to confer with the mercurial first-time director. A 'sitting' is Bollywood parlance for an extended meeting where the writer or music composer sits with the director in his lair, quaffing alcohol and brainstorming.

Jhontu da was in fine fettle and belted out one thumping song after another on his trusty organ. 'Wah wah, shoobie doobie boom boom. Waka waka, chika dika ho ho. Yabba dabba yabba dabba bang bang, Maka naka maka naka toot toot!' In the absence of lyrics, the music maestro improvised gibberish to accompany his tuneful compositions.

'Arrey, superb, Jhontu da! Khoob bhaalo gaan! Let us shortlist this song for Ricky's introduction. Now what about the item number? We need to insert a zabardast cabaret song before the interval to excite the audience and ensure they come back after the toilet break.'

'Don't waarry, dada! I bhil gib my bhest ephort. You bhil hab public going crazy. Thees ees amaar promise.' Jhontu da's thick Bengali accent was difficult to comprehend at the best of times but mercifully he let his music do most of the talking.

'Fantastic! Now we need to compose four original songs and we will remix three old songs from the original film, ya?'

Irshad saab pricked up his ears. His libido and his hearing were both in good shape, but he needed to reconfirm what he had just heard. 'Excuse me, janaab, but did you say you were remixing three songs from some other film?'

'Of course. What's the point of making a remake if we don't remix the film's superhit songs?'

'But which songs? And from what film?' asked the perplexed geriatric.

'Arrey, *Pardesi Pardesi* had three super-duper hit songs. Don't you remember, Irshad saab? Jhontu da—one two three four!' Jhontu da needed no further prompting. 'Oh baby, come to the disco dandiya. Oh baby, let's do the disco dandiya!' he crooned.

Film songs of the eighties were not renowned for the nuance of their lyrics and also left a lot to be desired in terms of musicality. 'Oh baby, baby! Dandiya! Dandiya!' trilled Jhontu da.

'Stop. Please stop. I beg you!' cried Irshad saab.

Jhontu da did not appreciate being interrupted mid-flow, but he could see the elderly gent was distraught.

'Janaab, are you saying you are remaking *Pardesi Pardesi*?'

'Of course we are, Irshad saab. Did nobody tell you that?'

'No! And why would you? I am only the poor scriptwriter. And naturally, nobody values the writer in Bollywood. After forty years in this business, my words are even more worthless than my Remington typewriter today.'

'I am so sorry, Irshad saab, but I swear I told Guneet to inform you. Kyon, Guneet, you forgot to call him or what?'

Guneet Mahajan, the associate director, looked askance as Kapil pointed at him, but realizing he was expected to cover up the lapse on Kapil's part, sportingly apologized. 'Forgive me, Irshad saab. We were waiting to receive permission from the film's original producer for the remake rights. We got the green signal only today. We wanted to share the good news with you in person. Here, let me pour you a Scotch to celebrate.'

'Huzoor, I have not slept for six days because I was writing an original story for you. At least hear me out once before you decide to remake another film.'

Kapil Kumar put his arm around the wrinkled writer. 'Irshad saab, we will definitely hear your story, minty fresh, when we make our next film. Right now, we are launching Ricky boy in and as *Pardesi Pardesi*! Have a drink, janaab—it will help you sleep tonight. Cheers!'

'I'm an Islay man myself, Gautam. There's nothing quite like an Ardbeg to transport you straight to bonnie Scotland, wouldn't you agree?' Like many educated Indians, Jagjit Kansal was prone to lapsing into a faux clipped accent when speaking with those whose native tongue was English.

The politician poured two stiff measures and handed one of the Riedel malt glasses to the young man who sat in his mahogany-panelled study. Jagjit had grown up in a provincial town in north India, but had cultivated a veneer of western sophistication over the years. He now drank only single malts, had developed a penchant for Havanas, played golf every weekend and had the interiors of his home replicated in the style of a Surrey mansion he had once seen in *Horse & Hound*.

'Slangevar, sir!' Gautam clinked glasses with his host and took a slow sip of the amber whisky. It was gratifying to savour the iodine and peat distilled within the potent dram. He realized it had been nearly six weeks since his last tipple and marvelled at his own ability to abstain for as long as he had.

'I thought it was high time we met, son. Particularly in light of this whole media fiasco.' Jagjit sat back in his weathered Chesterfield armchair and smiled. 'You seem to have had quite a remarkable life, if what we've heard and read this past week is even half-true.'

'Well, to be honest, the reports of my excesses aren't that highly exaggerated. I've been a bit of a lad. But I assure you that's all in the past.'

'That's good to know. I'm glad you've decided to sober up. It was certainly high time for Sheena and I'm proud that she made this decision all by herself. As a father, I haven't always been there for her, but I realize it's time to participate a little more actively in my daughter's life.'

'Sheena's a great girl. She really helped me get through rehab.'

'Did she now? How wonderful for you. Speaking of rehab, any thoughts on who might have leaked the details of your stay at the clinic?'

'Not a clue, sir. But if I ever find out, I swear I'll kill the wank ... er ... bloke!'

'There's no need to do that, son. Just let me know and I will take care of it.'

Seeing Gautam's face suddenly change colour, Jagjit

laughed. 'I obviously mean I'll ensure he never causes Sheena and you any trouble again.'

Gautam smiled uneasily. He had heard stories from Sheena about Kansal's army of goons—loyal 'party workers' who vandalized newspaper offices, roughed up rivals and generally intimidated anybody who dared protest against their beloved leader. Kansal was not a person to be messed with and Mukesh Menda had taken a huge risk in not only writing so brazenly about the politician's daughter but also condemning him personally on national television.

'So, tell me. What news of your father? How is he?'

'He's very well. A bit upset over the brouhaha, as you can imagine, but otherwise in the pink. I didn't know that you know him.'

'Well, I certainly know *of* him. As I'm sure he knows of me. Do give him my regards when you speak with him next. Perhaps we could discuss doing some business together?'

'Yes, sir. I'll definitely convey your message. I'm sure he will be very pleased to hear it. Well, I think I'd better pop back upstairs and check on Sheena. Thanks for the drink and I look forward to another one with you soon. Goodnight, sir.'

There was a long history of matrimonial alliances in the Kansal clan, which had prospered over the centuries by marrying wisely. Jagjit mulled over the possibility of entering into a similar accord with Dharmesh Goyal. 'My druggie daughter is besotted with Sir Dharmesh's dopehead son. It seems like a match made in heaven.'

The sexy VJ, Kimi K, introduced Ricky Kumar on her television show *India's Hottest Hunks* in such orgasmic terms that the young actor turned crimson before he even walked onto the shimmering set. A gaggle of girls, who comprised the live studio audience, went berserk when Ricky, dressed in an impeccably fitted Armani suit, entered and blew a kiss in their direction. It took a long time to calm the hysterical audience before Kimi could finally put her first question to her handsome guest.

'Ricky, you're so amazingly good looking that it's totally unfair there's just one of you for all of us! Am I right, girls?'

The girls vociferously agreed with the skimpily clad anchor and began to chant Ricky's name.

'Ricky, you were recently in the news for all the wrong reasons. Is there anything you want to say to all your fans who stood by your side?' continued Kimi in her Lokhandwala twang.

'Yes, absolutely. I want to thank each and every one of them. I'm so very sorry I disappointed my fans, my family and most of all, myself. I made a huge error of judgment and I do hope the people of India have found it in their hearts to genuinely forgive me.'

Sexy Kimi turned to the audience. 'What do you say, girls, have we forgiven Ricky Kumar his one mistake?'

Expectedly, the girls let out a roar of approval.

Kimi looked at Ricky appreciatively and gave him two thumbs up. 'So, tell me. Does an ordinary girl even stand a chance with Ricky Kumar? Would you possibly consider dating someone from our studio audience or from among your millions of female fans watching this show at home?'

'Absolutely!' said Ricky earnestly. 'I'm just a regular guy who's hoping to find the girl of his dreams. In fact, I'm currently looking for a girl who might be willing to star opposite me in my debut film.'

Ricky turned and looked directly into the camera he knew had him in close-up. 'So, if any of you girls out there think you have what it takes to be my desi heroine in *Pardesi Pardesi*, log on to our website below and submit all your details . . .'

Ricky suddenly trailed off mid-sentence and looked up towards the control room. 'Shivani, do I really need to say this bit looking straight into camera? Doesn't it also seem really contrived if I announce the website details?'

'Cut, cut, cut!' A stern female voice boomed from above. Shivani Mehta was the top celebrity publicist in Mumbai and didn't appreciate her clients questioning her expertise. The dynamic spin doctor had come on board to manage Ricky's career after Hotchand Fatwani strongly recommended her to Kapil Kumar.

It was Shivani who had planted all those stories in the press, claiming the Indian public had forgiven Ricky, the stories which eventually paved the way for his return from exile. The gushing tweets, blogs and Facebook campaigns were all orchestrated by her. The image consultant had also entirely stage-managed the media frenzy upon Ricky's arrival in Mumbai. The masses of fans gathered outside the gates of Casa Kumar were junior artistes, professionals paid by Shivani to carry placards and scream out Ricky's name, as were all the girls who comprised the hysterical studio audience today.

The marketing maven believed Ricky could be a superstar. However, he was raw and required careful steering. In addition, he now needed to shut the fuck up and follow her instructions. Shivani leaned into the studio mike and snapped, 'Let's stick to our script, Ricky. Trust me, it sounds far more sincere to viewers back home when a star speaks directly to camera. Come on; let's retake that last bit. No more wasting time. Make-up, dada, clear the sets, roll camera and action!'

The pony-tailed director of *India's Hottest Hunks* bristled at being sidelined by the tough bitch who was calling the shots on his show, but he didn't dare say a word as he sat in the control room and watched Ricky Kumar meekly follow instructions. Ricky knew Shivani was being paid bigger bucks than Irshad saab to script the story of his success. He was also beginning to understand that his enormous public popularity was actually the result of careful media manipulation.

Sir Dharmesh received an urgent call from Nazareth. The manager of Masala Magic's Delhi branch informed him that the Municipal Corporation had revoked their restaurant licence with immediate effect. Apparently some urban conservationist seeking to protect the environs of the Qutub Minar had filed a public interest litigation with the courts. Since the restaurant fell within five hundred metres of a historic site, the authorities had decided to shut it down.

Sir Dharmesh made a quick mental list of his contacts in Delhi to determine which fixer he could call to sort out the problem. He spoke to a few of the usual suspects, but no one seemed to know precisely how to tackle the matter. He was assured, however, that the matter would soon be resolved; it was merely a function of paying off a mid-level flunkey. Sir Dharmesh was a master of damage control and knew how to firefight the multitude of problems that inevitably arose in the course of running a restaurant business. Zoning laws, municipal permissions, liquor licenses, kitchen safety permits, fire department NOCs—these were only a few of the hurdles that needed to be jumped. Each city in each country threw up a unique set of challenges that required the equanimity of an experienced administrator. Sir Dharmesh possessed this in abundance and it was the reason behind his sustained success in a notoriously fickle trade, where fancy eateries opened with great fanfare only to close down in months. The shrewd entrepreneur wasn't perturbed, therefore, that his flagship Indian eatery had been forced to down its shutters for a couple of days. He took this setback too in his stride.

The phone rang again. This time it was Gautam on the line.

'Hi, Papa, any news?'

'Not yet, betaji. But you know how it is in Delhi. This culture of "ho jayega". Everyone promises. But when and how, nobody knows.'

'Do you want me to speak to Jagjit Kansal about this, Papa?'

'Let's give it a little more time, betaji. No point being obligated to him if it can be sorted out at a lower level, hai na?'

Sir Dharmesh knew the further down the pecking order the matter was settled, the cheaper it would be for him.

'Right, Papa, but I did tell you that he said to convey his regards and also mentioned he wanted to discuss the possibility of doing some business together.'

'Yes, Gautam. But it's much better to keep such people at an arm and a legs' distance, you know?'

'Okay, Papa, but if you need me to speak to Kansal, just say the word. Take care and give my love to Rani.'

Having disconnected, Sir Dharmesh thought to himself, 'There has been no shortage of female company in Gautam's life. This is obviously one more bang-bang situation for my badmaash betaji. Finally he will have to settle down with a girl of my choice only. Meanwhile, let him have his fun with Kansal's daughter. What goes of mine?'

The hunt for Ricky Kumar's heroine had gathered momentum. Thousands of hopefuls sent in their applications to the website he had publicized on TV. The traffic on the site was so heavy after Ricky's appearance on *India's Hottest Hunks* that the server crashed twice the very evening the episode aired.

Thousands more sent in their photographs by post and a flood of mail from different parts of the world inundated Casa Kumar. The hapless casting director was given the unenviable task of wading through this massive pile to shortlist only those photos that were worthy of Kapil Kumar's attention.

Ricky joined the search, scouring each application received on the website, hoping to find one face that would leap off the computer screen. That girl would become his new heroine and together they would embark on a dazzling career as shining stars of the silver screen. Unfortunately, none of the girls seemed to fit the bill.

Ricky walked into the den where Shivani Mehta was in conversation with Kapil Kumar.

'Come, come, Ricky boy. Shivani and I were just discussing the fantastic response to your heroine hunt!'

'Yes, isn't it amazing, Papa? But it occurs to me that all these girls are going to feel very hurt when they realize they have been rejected,' said Ricky. 'Why don't we send each of them a letter from me, with an autographed picture, to soften the blow?'

'Nonsense! Have you any idea how much that will cost? I want to see my hard-earned money spent on-screen, not donated to some bloody courier company, ya?' Kapil paused for a moment. 'Unless, of course, someone wants to come in as a promotion partner? What do you think, Shivani baby? Can you speak to some courier wallahs?'

The seasoned image consultant shook her head. 'I hardly

think any company will want to be positioned in the hearts of people as the bearer of bad news. But Ricky has come up with a good idea. This will not only consolidate the fan database but also embellish his lover-boy image. We can begin by responding to the online applications. And don't worry, Kapilji, sending out emails doesn't cost that much,' said Shivani wryly.

She turned to the young actor. 'Ricky, why don't you go draft that rejection letter and show it to me? I'll have my office action this and also send out a press release stating what a sensitive and caring young man you are.'

Ricky was pleased his idea had gone down well but a little offended by her patronizing tone. Shivani had an air of condescension about her and often spoke to Ricky as if he were a schoolboy. He said nothing, however, and went off to his room to compose the letter for the heartbroken hopefuls.

Once Ricky was out of earshot, Shivani spoke. 'Kapilji, does Ricky genuinely believe you are going to find your new heroine by sifting through these silly applications? Surely he knows this is a marketing ploy to generate publicity for the film.'

Kapil smiled indulgently. 'Arrey, Shivani baby, I am keeping Ricky boy informed of our strategies strictly on a need-to-know basis. He is a very bhola-bhaala fellow. Why trouble him with unnecessary details? Let him concentrate only on becoming a superstar, ya? Rest, we are there to handle.'

Two weeks had gone by, and the doors of Masala Magic remained resolutely sealed. In the interim, Pink Paisley, another swanky restaurant, announced its opening in central Delhi. Its young owner, Happy Walia, scion of a dodgy, arms-dealing family, was married to an ex-Bollywood hottie, Tina Sharma.

A few years ago, Tina had realized that after a decade in the Mumbai film industry, she remained a struggling starlet and needed to establish herself as a trophy wife before her market appeal was lost. Harpreet 'Happy' Walia was ready, willing and loaded, so Tina bid goodbye to Bollywood and settled down to a life of leisure in Jor Bagh.

The launch party of Pink Paisley promised to be a mega event. The invitees included not only the movers and shakers of Delhi but also a sizeable contingent of Tina's film friends from Mumbai. The glamorous Bolly brigade was flying in on a special charter to grace the opening night with their luminescence. Some were charging a fee to make a professional appearance, but most were coming to show solidarity with an old colleague. Among them was Ricky Kumar, who had known Tina socially in Mumbai and was rather fond of the bubbly actress who had sadly never quite managed to make it.

Ricky was encouraged to attend the Delhi event by Shivani Mehta, who insisted the actor needed to raise his popularity in the capital by making a couple of high-profile public appearances. Delhi was Bollywood-obsessed, she explained. Moreover, there would be massive media coverage accorded to the red-hot Ricky, whose film was scheduled to go on the floors very soon. The fact that Shivani's company was being paid a substantial amount to corral as many celebrities as possible for the party was only incidental.

Sheena Kansal had known Happy Walia since the days when he had repeatedly flashed his peepee at her in Tiny Tots Nursery. They had grown up together and were paid-up members of the Delhi rich-kid clique. Happy had been smitten with Sheena, but she could never reciprocate the affections of this lovable doofus and, much to his dismay, decreed him her rakhi brother. But that was all in the past. Happy was now deliriously living up to his name, having married the lovely Tina, who had expeditiously produced a son to keep her in-laws equally elated.

Sheena had kept a low profile since Mukesh Menda's exposé. Happy, however, threatened never to speak to her if she ducked out of attending his big night. The emotional blackmail worked on Sheena, who was also being prodded by Gautam to get out of the house and on with her life.

The rich and almost famous in India don't really require an excuse to party, but it helps to have a theme around which a celebration can be built and marketed. The event managers entrusted with the task of organizing the launch of Pink Paisley came up with the ingenious idea of hosting the festivities on the eve of Republic Day so guests could not only make it their patriotic duty to party till they puked, but also comfortably nurse their hangovers in bed the next day, a national holiday.

Twenty-fifth January thus became a red-letter day in Delhi's social calendar and the neighbourhood of Pink Paisley was bathed in a fuchsia glow as tinted halogen lights illuminated the night sky. The media presence was understandably large. The ubiquity of film stars guaranteed national press coverage of what was otherwise merely a local restaurant opening.

Ricky, who placed enormous premium on being punctual, was one of the first of the filmi guests to arrive. Alighting from his limousine at the striking pink-painted gates, he walked down the plush red carpet amidst a flurry of flashbulbs, overwhelmed by the deafening screams of fans. As tutored by Shivani, he gave suitable sound bytes to various news crews, waxing eloquent about the restaurant and explaining he was here to support his dear friend, Tina. He pretended not to hear the impudent question about whether he remained hooked on drugs and informed the nation that the hunt for his new heroine was very much on and they should keep sending in fresh applications. He agreed it was entirely possible he might find a new co-star here this evening and proclaimed that he unreservedly loved the kudis of Delhi. He then blew a loving kiss to all his fans watching back home, urged them not to drink and drive and conserve energy by switching off the lights and fans when leaving a room.

When he finally managed to extricate himself from the media swarm, Ricky entered the cavernous restaurant, done up in a highly original Punjabi Baroque style with massive pink chandeliers and life-size paisley motifs stencilled across wall-to-wall mirrors. The young heart-throb had barely caught his breath when he was accosted by a zealous mob of star-struck local invitees. They each insisted on a photo and enthusiastically hugged Ricky as though he were a long-lost brother. This was followed by a demand for autographs, personally made out to names like Goga, Gudda, Babloo, Ponty and Tutu.

Being a celebrity is an exhausting business, thought Ricky, as he fled to the restaurant's magenta-tiled toilet. Happy Walia, with his keen eye for detail, had ensured there were slabs of dry ice in each of the vagina-shaped urinals so that a steady stream of smoke emerged whenever someone used the facilities. It was amusing the thick fog Ricky generated as he relieved himself in this uniquely designed loo.

As he ringed his hands, four large, egg-shaped pink pods lined up against the opposite wall piqued Ricky's curiosity. He went over for a closer look and slid open the door of one.

Ricky Kumar was startled to find Gautam Goyal sitting inside on a commode.

Greatly disturbed, Ricky stumbled out of the lurid lavatory and bumped into Tina Walia, the gracious hostess of the evening's festivities. 'Ricky, darling! How are you? Thanks so much for making it down. This means a lot to Happy and me!'

As Tina hugged her old friend, she realized he was trembling and his face was clammy. 'Hey, you okay?'

'I'm fine! Sorry, I was a little thrown back there. So, umm ... congratulations.'

'Are you sure you're all right? What happened?'

'Honestly, I'm okay. I ... I ...'

Just then, Gautam Goyal exited the loo and caught sight of Tina and Ricky in conversation. Gautam stopped momentarily to glower at Ricky and strode away, disappearing into the throng. Tina noticed the young actor averted his eyes under Gautam's gaze.

'Are you upset seeing that Goyal fellow? He's here with Sheena Kansal. What happened in there? Did he say or do anything to offend you?'

'No, no.'

'Please tell me, Ricky? If he's making you uncomfortable, I can ask him to leave the party.'

'No, Tina, please, there's really no need for that.'

'Ricky, you're still shaking! Tell me what's wrong, darling? I'm totally beginning to worry about you!'

'Relax, Tina. It's nothing. I ... accidentally walked in on Gautam in the loo.'

'Right. And that's what has upset you so deeply? Come on, Ricky, I wasn't born yesterday. Tell me what happened in there.'

'Well ... I, er ... I ... saw Gautam snorting coke in one of the pods.'

'What? Oh my God!'

'Yeah. And it shook me up pretty badly. I ... I really can't afford to get involved in a drug scandal again, Tina. You ... you understand?'

'Of course! I completely understand, Ricky. Believe me, we have a zero-tolerance policy here for any sort of substance abuse! Wow—and to think those two only just came out of rehab! I'd better go tell Happy. I'll catch up with you later, darling. Enjoy yourself, and thanks for telling me.'

As Tina left, Ricky shut his eyes and tried a breathing exercise he had learnt at the Suryanamaskar Spa to help calm his pounding heart. Tina's persistence had left him with little choice but to lie about what had engendered his panic attack. No one could ever find out the real reason why Gautam Goyal had such a disquieting effect on Ricky Kumar.

Mukesh Menda, bon vivant and gossipmonger extraordinaire, was in conversation with Happy Walia when Tina finally located her husband. Mukesh had a tacit quid pro quo understanding with the restaurateurs he wrote positive reviews for. He could wine and dine at their eateries and never be bothered with the tedium of paying a bill. The five-star hotel that once made the mistake of asking Mukesh to cough up the money for the extravagant birthday bash he had hosted on their premises was still, three years later, reeling from his savage diatribes.

The freelance free-loader was waxing eloquent about the unique décor of Pink Paisley to its excited owner. 'Happy, honeybunch, just leave it to me. I'll write you a glowing piece in my Sunday column. It's time Delhi had a spanking new hot spot. Masala Magic was well on its way to passédom, so your timing is impeccable!'

'Thanks, Mukeshji, we very much appreciate your support. Please come by any time as our valued guest. Jai Mata di!'

'Oh, I'll certainly be back, sweetie. Now excuse me, I must visit the little boys' room. I hear there are some delightfully naughty touches in there?'

As Mukesh Menda traipsed off, Tina, who couldn't possibly have informed her husband about Gautam's narcotic transgression with Mukesh around, quickly apprised him of the situation. The couple decided their best recourse was to inform Sheena and let her tackle Gautam, since he had come as her guest.

Gautam Goyal had not been having a particularly good day. His stomach had begun gurgling a couple of hours ago, probably a result of all the spicy aaloo chaat that Nina Kansal had plied him with at tea. He then had quite a time convincing Sheena to agree to step out in the evening and finally some wanker had walked in on him mid-crap, in that absurd egg-shaped loo that didn't even lock properly. Now his tummy had started rumbling again, and he needed to head back to that hideous, bloody bog.

As Gautam entered, he saw Mukesh Menda carefully combing his blonde-highlighted hair in the mirror. The sight of this despicable gnome who had unleashed such a scandal with his scurrilous writing infuriated Gautam and he strode up behind the preening columnist.

'Oy! You're Mukesh Menda, aren't you?'

Mukesh froze at the sight of Gautam's reflection. Afraid the looming six-footer might be in the mood for revenge, Mukesh tried to bluff his way out.

'No, no, I'm not. Actually, I'm the owner of this restaurant, Happy Walia. Pleased to meet you. And you are …?'

'Don't lie to me, you sodding bum sucker! I recognize you from the telly. You have some nerve messing with other people's lives!'

Mukesh was petrified. He had heard of Gautam's mercurial temper and feared the volatile drug fiend might attack him. He decided his best bet was to make a run for it and he bolted towards the exit.

Gautam instinctively lunged at the fleeing hack and brought him down on the pink cement floor with a rugby tackle. Mukesh started yelping and screeching as the two of them rolled about on the ground. Managing to somehow extricate himself from Gautam's clutches, the squealing scribe scurried on all fours towards the safety of one of the lavatory pods and rapidly latched the door behind him.

Gautam banged furiously on the door. 'Come out, you coward! Let's talk man to man! I want to know why you wrote all that bollocks about Sheena and me.'

Mukesh cowered inside the egg-shaped shell, knowing it wouldn't take Gautam long to break down the flimsy door. 'I'm so very sorry. I never meant to harm you in any way, Gautam!' he bawled.

'Really, now? So you write filth about people because you want to help them, is that it?'

'No, no. It's not like that. I was only reporting information I had been given. Please don't hurt me, Gautam!'

'All right, then—tell me who told you all that rubbish about Sheena and me and I promise I won't touch you!'

Mukesh had few options at this point. It was better to placate Gautam than to aggravate his temper by holding out.

'You swear on your mother you won't hit me if I tell you?' Mukesh simpered.

'Yeah, I swear!'

'It was your sister, Rani.'

Gautam was dumbfounded. His sister and he had never quite gotten along, but Gautam couldn't imagine why she would set him up in this manner and how she could possibly have had access to all that information.

'You're lying, you sodding twat! And now I'm going to bash your brains in when I get my hands on you!'

'I swear it was Rani!' wailed the trembling journo. 'She emailed me all those details about Sheena and you.'

'Oh yeah? And how do you even know her, you sick fuck?'

'I … I … met her four years ago in Delhi when she came down for the opening of Masala Magic. We became friends, and I even introduced her to some local lesbians. We've kept in touch ever since.'

Gautam's head began to spin. The fact that Mukesh did know Rani had been firmly established as only a close circle was aware of her sexual proclivities. 'So, why did Rani ask you to write all that shit about me?' shouted Gautam.

'I honestly don't know! She mailed me some material a few weeks ago saying this was an exclusive scoop I could print. I had no idea it would snowball into such a big story. You have to believe me, please!'

Gautam slumped to the floor, clutching his head, trying to make sense of the information he had been given. Why had his elder sister backstabbed him in such a vicious manner? How had she gathered all those details about his stint in rehab? What could she possibly hope to achieve by publicly humiliating him? As these questions swirled in Gautam's mind, he realized he needed to head home to London and confront Rani.

A few minutes later Mukesh Menda timidly called out. 'Hello? Gautam? Are you there?'

'Yes I am, Mukesh. It's okay. You can come out now.'

'Umm … I'd prefer to stay in here if it's all the same with you.'

'Come out, Mukesh. I swore on my mother I wouldn't hit you. Do you think I would renege on that promise?'

Mukesh cautiously opened the door of the perspex pod and stepped out. He smiled sheepishly at Gautam, who squatted defeated and forlorn on the cold floor.

'I'm truly sorry for the harm I've caused you, Gautam. May I please go now?'

'Yeah. Naff off.'

Relieved, Mukesh headed towards the exit when Gautam called. 'Oy, Mukesh! One moment.'

Mukesh stopped in his tracks and slowly turned around.

'I want you to take off all your clothes.'

For once, the social commentator was at a complete loss. He stared bug-eyed at Gautam who suddenly snarled at him. 'Didn't you hear me? Take off all your bloody clothes or I'll fucking rip them off you.'

Already shivering, Mukesh disrobed in the freezing winter evening and handed Gautam his blue velvet suit as instructed. Gautam sauntered out with the pile of designer duds and a picture on his mobile phone of a stark-naked Mukesh Menda. It was unlikely the fearless columnist would have anything nasty to write about Sheena Kansal and Gautam Goyal in the near future. He had been duly warned that photos of his inch-long penis would otherwise be put on full public display.

Ricky Kumar clutched his pounding head and moaned as he sat in a quiet corner of the Delhi airport lounge, waiting to board the flight home. The six tequila shots he had downed the night before, in a desperate attempt to calm his nerves, had played havoc with his system. Ricky had spent most of the night and the better part of the morning throwing his innards up all over the pristine Carrara marble bathroom of his hotel suite. He had decided against taking the afternoon charter flight back to Mumbai, the prospect of two hours with a planeload of raucous filmi colleagues too daunting. Feeble attempts to eat something met with little success as his stomach refused to keep anything down.

Hungover, hungry and feeling sorry for himself, he woozily boarded the late evening flight and buckled himself in. He had requested the hotel travel desk to purchase and block the adjacent seat so he could travel undisturbed. He intended to switch on his noise-cancellation headphones, cocoon himself from the world and, hopefully, snooze all the way back.

The flight attendant asked for his meal preference but upon seeing Ricky recoil at the very mention of Chicken Chettinad, realized her VIP passenger wasn't keen on savouring the airline's fabled in-flight cuisine. She smiled understandingly and returned a few moments later with a glass of cold water and a blister pack of Disprin. She allowed two tablets to effervesce gently in the clear plastic cup before handing it to Ricky. Unsure whether he would be able to keep down the fluid, Ricky took a few tentative sips of the fizzing libation before eventually draining the contents of the cup.

When the flight attendant returned to clear the tray, Ricky smiled weakly at her and it was then that he noticed his ministering angel was an exceptionally good-looking young woman. Her ample bosom and well-rounded buttocks filled out her cherry red uniform. She had exquisite, expressive almond eyes and luscious lips that seemed to rest in a permanent pout, suggesting the promise of wicked pleasures. Her nose was aquiline, in the manner of many north Indian beauties, and her flawless complexion completed the mesmerizing look that was best described in the words of Kapil Kumar: a true 'Slutty Savitri'. Preeti, her name tag read. She was the perfect embodiment of Kapil's virgin-whore—that prized creature that Indian men aspire to take not only to bed but also straight home to their beloved mummy.

'Hopefully you'll start feeling better in a bit, sir. Once we are airborne, you can decide if you want to eat something. May I get you anything else?'

'No, thanks. I'm all right. Well, actually, I'm anything but all right but I appreciate your concern.'

'It's my pleasure, sir. I saw you on the news last night. It seemed quite a rocking party. That's why I thought you might prefer a Disprin instead of our Dum Aaloo.'

Ricky caught the sliver of an impish smile playing on Preeti's lips and laughed aloud at her little jibe. His head throbbed when he spoke, but somehow the effort was well worth it. 'Oh, absolutely! Last night I had my first drink in a year, and I have a feeling I won't be having another one anytime soon!'

'Good for you, sir. Now if you'll please excuse me, I have to go demonstrate the safety procedures.'

Ricky found himself unable to stop gaping at this vision of delight as she stood on tiptoe and arched her magnificent body to remove the demo seat belt and oxygen mask from an overhead bin. Her pert derriere strained against her tight-fitting skirt and Ricky felt a stirring in his own nether regions even as he gazed admiringly at hers.

There were only two other passengers sitting up front on the flight to Mumbai that evening. One was the recently suspended minister for housing, the other a prominent builder under the CBI scanner. Both had flown to Delhi to attend the Republic Day parade, both had sought an audience with the party high command but had been tersely turned away. Bonding over their woes, the duo huddled together and bemoaned the fate of the nation, leaving Preeti free to devote her energies to the handsome, hungover actor.

Preeti lost little time in informing Ricky that she was a film buff and aspired to be an actress. The responsibility of being the family's sole breadwinner had compelled her to take up this stable airline job. She had, however, managed to model for some local brands back home in Panchkula and she declared earnestly that she would give anything for an opportunity to screen-test for the part of the village belle opposite Ricky in *Pardesi Pardesi*. Ricky, who was already enamoured of Preeti, gave her his mobile number and she promised to come across the next day to meet the legendary Kapil Kumar.

The history of Indian civil aviation is replete with tales of how some of the wealthiest men in the country ended up marrying stewardesses they had met on the national carrier. From airhostess to society hostess, from the trolley to the lolly, as it were, there was a formidable list of female cabin crew that had landed high fliers in the friendly skies.

Twenty-two-year-old Preeti Bhasin was determined to hitch her own ride to fame and fortune and fervently hoped Ricky Kumar would help realize her dreams. Fortunately for Preeti, Ricky had a soft spot for flight attendants as his own mother had first met his filmstar father while serving him on board an Air India flight to London twenty-five years ago.

Would history repeat itself, wondered Ricky. Would this chance encounter with a beautiful stewardess remain merely that or would it grow and develop into something more meaningful? And what of his relationship with Rhea? Would she be forgotten as just a memorable dalliance or would she once again enter his life as Babaji had assured him she would? All these questions wafted through Ricky's mind even as waves of sleep gradually started washing over him. Mercifully, his hangover and the meeting with Preeti had succeeded in distracting Ricky from that brief but unsettling encounter with Gautam Goyal.

'Fuck you, Sheena! I haven't touched any sort of shit since we left rehab. So, if some git has been going around town claiming he saw me tooting in a loo, he's obviously lying!'

'Why would Ricky Kumar, of all people, lie about something like this, Gautam? What could he possibly have against you to make such a wild accusation?'

'I have no sodding idea who this Kumar twat is, but I swear I'm going to kill him for talking shit about me!'

'He's the son of a famous Bollywood star and an old friend of Tina Walia. Happy told me that Ricky swears he saw you doing coke last night in one of those pods. How could you do this to me, Gautam? I'm not like you. I can't hop from one scandal to the next. Can you imagine what will happen if word gets out? Mukesh Menda will have a field day with the story!'

'Oh, I wouldn't worry about Mukesh. I've neutralized that bum bandit, good and proper!'

'Oh my god! What have you done to him, Gautam? Please tell me you haven't beaten him up? We don't need a police case on our hands right now!'

'Don't worry about the police. You just tell me where I can get my hands on Ricky Kumar so I can teach him a lesson about fabricating fairy tales!'

'Don't you dare go anywhere near him, Gautam! In any case, he's probably flown back to Mumbai today. I want you to know I'm furious you've started snorting again and I don't want you around me any more!'

'Fine! I'm fed up with you and your whole fragile rich bitch bollocks as well, you know? So don't worry about me hanging around any longer. I'm taking the first available flight home.'

'Really, now? So, you're going to run away without owning

responsibility for your actions? That's incredibly mature, Gautam!'

'I'm not running away. I'm leaving because I'm done with this sodding country and I'm certainly done with you!'

'What? Listen, I'm upset because I think you're lying to me. But can we please just calm down? You know I want you here with me, Gautam. I . . . I need you!'

'Look, Sheena. This was fun and I'll always be grateful for everything you did for me, but I do need to get back to London now. So let's end this right here, okay?'

'Gautam, please. Don't do this. I am so sorry I doubted you. I love you so much! I was hurt and angry because I thought you'd started snorting behind my back!'

'It fucking disgusts me that you would so easily believe the lies of some random Bollywood brat, Sheena. It doesn't say very much about your faith in me or about the strength of this relationship, does it? So, I'd rather naff off. The sooner the better.'

'Gautam, please! We've been through so much together. You are not seriously ending this, are you?'

'Look, I told you—I genuinely need to get home and I'm not into any of this long-distance shit. So let's make a clean break, all right? It will be better for both of us.'

'That is the most selfish, callous thing I have heard in my whole life! I fucking stood by you through four bloody weeks in rehab! And now you're dumping me over one lousy misunderstanding? You know what? You're right—let's end this because it could never have worked in the long run. You're not only a hopeless cokehead but also an emotionally retarded dickhead. So, yeah, fuck off, Gautam! And leave me the fuck alone!'

FOUR

'Ricky boy, you were absolutely right! This girl is an Apsara—a total fucking pathaka! What luscious boobs and what a fantastically juicy arse! And let's not forget that face. Arrey, she is ekdum perfect gaon ki gori material. Well spotted, son. You truly are a chip off the old cock!'

Ricky turned crimson, both in embarrassment and delight that his father had so glowingly approved of Preeti as the new heroine of *Pardesi Pardesi*.

Earlier that day, the cameraman W.C. Shah had erected a makeshift studio within Casa Kumar. Preeti arrived at four and was sent to get her hair and make-up done. The wardrobe mistress rustled up a suitably low-cut ghagra-choli, a size too small, to emphasize Preeti's ample curves. A few lines of dialogue were loudly recited by Irshad saab whilst the aspiring actress sat getting her hair styled. She was meant to parrot them on camera for the benefit of the director.

Going by the prominent bulge in Kapil Kumar's trousers, it was obvious that Preeti had passed the screen test. The screen veteran enveloped his ecstatic protégé in a bear hug and presented her with a wad of cash, informing Preeti she should consider this her signing amount as the heroine of his magnum opus. Kapil also commanded Preeti to quit her flying job forthwith, as he intended to take her under his wing and groom her into a screen goddess.

Ricky proudly embraced his grateful new co-star and told her how delighted he was that she had nailed the part. This film, he graciously promised, would be as much a launch pad for her iridescent career in Bollywood as it would be his.

After being subjected to a barrage of blessings and effusive hugs from Kapil's assembled cronies, particularly Irshad saab, Preeti extricated herself and went to the washroom to change out of her costume. She gazed in awe at the wall-to-wall reproduction of Botticelli's *Venus Rising*, the ornate Swarovski chandelier, the swan-shaped gilded faucets, the lapis-lazuli inlaid jacuzzi and fuchsia-silk-upholstered chaise longue. This bathroom in Casa Kumar was bigger than the apartment she shared with her family in Panchkula.

Preeti was aware that less than twenty-four hours ago she had been just another flight attendant. And now her life had been irrevocably altered. Preeti Bhasin stared at herself in a massive Art Nouveau gilded mirror and began to cry. The trickle of tears turned into a torrent as she sat on the chaise longue and sobbed, thanking the universe for its munificence.

Rani Goyal decided to launch a counter-offensive when her enraged brother confronted her in London.

'So you really want to know why I leaked your sordid little secrets to Mukesh Menda? I'll tell you, Gautam. It's because I wanted to teach you a lesson. And to let the world know just what a good-for-nothing wastrel you are! You have done nothing but snort and shag your way through life. And at the age of thirty, your crowning achievement is that you managed to spend a month in rehab. And you almost screwed even that up, didn't you?'

Gautam looked askance as his sister spewed venom. 'Yes, but that's all old news, Rani! What I don't understand is why, now, when I'm trying so fucking hard to get my shit together, you are adamant on creating all this trouble for me. What is your bloody problem?'

'You're the problem, Gautam! I am the first-born of this family. I've slogged fifteen years to help build this company while you gallivanted—drinking, puking and fucking all over the countryside. But it seems, now that you're back from rehab, Papa wants to make you the majority shareholder of Masala Magic.'

'What? I … I had no idea!'

'It's so unfair! And the only reason he's doing it is because you have a penis and I don't. He's such a chauvinist—wanting to leave his empire to his beloved son even though it's his bloody daughter who's been doing all the work!'

Gautam was thrilled to learn of this unexpected development. If his father was keen to induct him into the family business and give him a sizeable chunk of the company, the newly rehabilitated junkie was quite prepared to rise to the challenge. But Gautam knew it was vital to placate his insecure and vindictive sister who was, after all, second in command at Masala Magic.

'You've got to believe me, Rani—I knew nothing about this. I promise I'll speak to Papa. There's no way he's going to cut you out of your fair share.'

'Oh, thanks, Gautam! That's all I need—for you to plead my case with that Neanderthal. He will be proud his precious son is being so considerate towards his poor lesbo sister. Look, I have no doubt Papa will throw a few crumbs my way, but I deserve at least half, if not the lion's share of this company. And I'm fully prepared to fight for my rights!'

'Listen to me, Rani. I don't want a confrontation with you. I know you've worked hard. You deserve to inherit half of Papa's wealth. So, I give you my word—I will never deprive you of what's rightfully yours. I love you, Rani—you know that. Now come here and give your little brother a hug.'

Gautam felt a twinge of pity as he embraced his unremarkable-looking sister who had been blessed with a sharp intellect but precious little beauty. He knew she'd struggled with her sexual orientation and was secretly jealous of her handsome brother who effortlessly attracted all the women she would have liked to his bed.

Comforted by Gautam, Rani felt contrite for her reckless actions. 'Look, I'm sorry I created all this trouble for you, Gautam. I honestly had no idea that the info I passed on to Mukesh would erupt into such a scandal. I guess, thanks to me, you're a household name in India now?'

Rani gave a rueful smile as Gautam laughed. 'Well, I can't say I didn't enjoy some of the attention. But how did you get to know of all the goings-on in Behramjee's clinic? Did you have someone follow me?'

'I didn't—but Papa certainly did. He was getting daily reports on your every move from our local office manager. I simply read those e-mails and passed them on to Mukesh Menda.'

'That worm Dixit was Papa's spy, eh? I should have guessed. I'm glad I broke the bastard's nose. Serves the snoop right!'

'It apparently cost Papa ten lakh rupees to keep Dixit from filing a police complaint against you. Papa was tempted to have you thrown into jail for a bit to teach you a lesson. But the thought of his little brat being buggered in an Indian lock-up was too much for him to bear.'

'You know, I'm so glad Papa chose to keep me on at Behramjee's. It was a living hell, but completely worth it in the end. I promise you, Rani—I'm on the straight and narrow now. So, please let's put this bad blood behind us and make a fresh start, shall we?' Gautam looked his sister in the eye as he spoke and she scrutinized his face for any sign of insincerity.

'Hmm … I wonder if this is the new, improved Gautam or if you're pulling another one of your con jobs on me? I guess only time will tell.'

Kapil Kumar made plans to send Preeti for a four-week crash course to the Bollywood acting guru, Professor Godbole. Much like his illustrious namesake from Forster's *A Passage to India*, Professor Godbole aspired to be both wise and enigmatic. He derided the Method school of acting and lived by the maxim that all performances in Hindi cinema should be spontaneous and unrehearsed.

'There is no Method in my madness. But there is much madness in my methods,' cackled Godbole, who had squandered several years in the sixties trying to establish himself as a film hero before finally settling on becoming an acting teacher.

Thirty-five years ago, Kapil Kumar himself had been dispatched to Godbole's Academy of Acting to learn a few tricks of the trade. The syllabus had then comprised the staples of becoming a successful Hindi film hero, requirements like horse riding, stunt fighting, playback syncing, dialogue dubbing and disco dancing. Not much had changed over the past four decades at Godbole's Academy, but his roster of illustrious alumni ensured he remained the most sought-after acting coach in town.

Ricky had spent three months under the professor's tutelage and hated every moment of his time at the academy where half his batch-mates sucked up to him, hoping he would serve as their meal ticket in Bollywood, while the other half openly mocked him as the spoilt son of one of the leading hams of Hindi cinema.

Ricky preferred a subtler, less theatrical approach to acting, but Kapil Kumar advocated the importance of playing to the gallery. He urged Ricky to cultivate a unique set of mannerisms that the audience could associate with the aspiring hero. 'Nobody in India wants to spend their hard-earned money to watch some pseudo, arty-farty acting on the silver screen, ya? The public comes to the cinema hall to see a star. They want to watch their hero thrash the villain so they can daydream about bashing up their own bloody bosses at work. They come to see the sexy heroine being seduced by the hero so they can fantasize about her when they are banging their plain-Jane wives at night. They want to see a star doing action, emotion, comedy, tragedy, dance and romance. They want total paisa-vasool so for three hours they can pretend they are super studs and forget how fucked-up their lives actually are. Always remember that, Ricky boy. Your job as a Hindi film hero is only to give the paying public what they want. So never, ever, try to be a Brando in Bollywood!'

Gautam's coterie of friends, all progeny of remarkably wealthy parents, had organized an extravagant bash to welcome their former coke buddy home. This elite circle of Londoners had partied together since their teenage years and even though they were now in their thirties, many of them married and parents, they socialized and snorted with the same fervour as before. All that had changed in the past fifteen years were the names of the establishments they frequented when out on the town. A few nightclubs had fallen out of favour with the Hooray Henrys and others had been forced to shut shop, unable to withstand the competition from newer, hipper hotspots. Ordinary Londoners couldn't afford to go out that often as jobs began to dry up and the economy floundered. But the party never ended for this bunch of moneyed hedonists, who had reserved the private lounge at their perennial favourite, Tramps, to celebrate the return of the bad boy of Belgravia.

A gaggle of giggling Sloane Rangers engulfed Gautam, playfully smothering him in Bollinger-soaked kisses even as the Mayfair mob raucously toasted his return to the fold. The DJ spun a series of Bollywood and bhangra tracks in deference to Gautam, the evening's guest of honour. The crowd gyrated vigorously to these thumping beats, clumsily parodying the moves they saw in Hindi films.

In the midst of this pulsating orgy, Gautam caught sight of a stunningly attractive Indian girl, swaying sensuously by herself in front of the mirrored wall, unmindful of the male attention focussed on her. Gautam slowly made his way across the room to her. The girl was moving in perfect sync with the music, her eyes shut, and she looked even more stunning up close. She was statuesque, flaunting long, well-toned limbs and a full figure. Her tightly fitted purple Herve Leger dress stopped short after barely covering and accentuating her curvaceous derriere and the audacious V of her neckline showcased a pair of immaculate breasts that moved seductively to the rhythm of her dance.

Gautam had seen his share of provocatively dressed knockouts at various clubs around the world but this girl was in a league of her own. Besides, she looked desi, and he found the combination of overt oomph and Indian good looks irresistible. As one song ended and segued into the next, the girl opened her eyes and saw Gautam staring directly at her. She glared at him and he hastily averted his gaze, embarrassed at being caught gawking. Then, deciding it was better to seize the opportunity than retreat, he walked up to her, held out his hand and introduced himself suavely.

'I know who you are,' she said matter-of-factly. 'You're back from rehab in India and everyone is curious to see whether you're going to behave yourself tonight. Nobody believes Gautam Goyal can stay sober for long.'

'Wow. Are you always this subtle with people you've just met?'

'Yup. Pretty much. I find it's easier to speak my mind. If people don't like what I have to say, that's too bad. A girl like me has no trouble finding friends.'

Gautam laughed, taken with the spunky sexpot. He leaned close, ostensibly to be heard over the music.

'So, who are you here with tonight? And how come we've never met?'

'Oh, I'm from out of town—just visiting a friend for a couple of days.'

'And ... is this a male friend that you're visiting?'

'No, she's not, last time I checked.'

'That's a relief. So, uh ... I would love to take you out some time and show you the sights.'

'I'm sure you would,' she replied evenly.

'So, what do you say? May I take you to lunch tomorrow?'

'Well, that depends ...'

'On what?'

'On whether I want to hang around with you after breakfast.'

Gautam couldn't believe his ears. This voluptuous woman had brazenly propositioned him, even as he was planning to woo her with his standard seduction routine: lunch at Nobu followed by a helicopter ride over London.

'All right, then—let's go! Do you need to say bye to your friend?'

'Not really.' The girl gestured at an attractive blonde snogging a young Asian man in the corner. 'I think my friend's got plans of her own.'

Gautam grinned and took her by the hand to lead her out of the heaving nightclub, smugly aware he had just scored with the hottest girl in the house.

The Goyals lived in an imposing three-storeyed mansion in Belgravia, at the heart of central London. The ground floor comprised opulent living and dining areas, and on the second floor Sir Dharmesh resided in and conducted his business. The third level was shared between Rani and Gautam and housed a plush home theatre lounge with two additional bedrooms for guests.

Sir Dharmesh believed it was vital to reside at the correct address and be chauffeured around town in the right automobile in order to be truly accepted by the Brits. As a young man, he had aspired to drive a Rolls-Royce, but when he could finally afford one, he was advised that the Bentley was the vehicle of choice among aristocrats. Three Bentleys were acquired, in different colours, so Sir Dharmesh could arrive at the House of Lords in a vehicle that matched the shade of his Savile Row suit. He famously hired a distant cousin of the Queen to design the interiors of his mansion and forked out a king's ransom for the privilege of boasting he had a minor royal on his payroll. Of course, the upper echelons of British society continued to deride Sir Dharmesh as a nouveau riche social climber and tittered at his mangling of the English language, even as they attended his lavish parties and solicited generous contributions to assorted charities. The erstwhile shopkeeper from Rajasthan was, however, impervious to their snotty remarks and insisted on attending the races at Ascot each year in top hat and tails, even though he had no interest in horses, or indeed, any form of gambling.

Gautam pulled into the basement garage in his Maserati, still disbelieving of his immense good luck. Exiting his gleaming red sports car, he strode across to the other side and swung open the door for his companion. Even though she alighted expertly, swivelling her hips to keep both knees together, it was apparent she wasn't wearing any underwear. This got Gautam even more aroused and his mind raced with possibilities, all the things he intended to do once he got her upstairs.

Pressing the lift button for the third floor, Gautam suddenly exclaimed, 'Hey, you know what? You haven't told me your name.'

'Why do you want to know? Isn't anonymous sex a lot more fun?' she teased.

'Well, it's hardly anonymous, is it? You seem to know everything about me.'

The girl laughed. 'That's very true. Okay—hi Gautam, I'm Meneka.'

'Meneka. Now that's an unusual name. What does it mean?'

'It's actually derived from a Sanskrit word which loosely translates to "sexy seductress who's going to bang your brains out".'

Meneka certainly lived up to her name. Uninhibited in bed, she exulted in pleasuring Gautam and willingly acceded to his every kinky request. Nor was she shy about demanding he go down on her, repeatedly, through the night, even when he was spent and looking for a little time to recoup. Utterly insatiable, she managed to arouse and entice him into one last round of frenetic fucking by offering to let him penetrate her taut behind. Finally, when she was convinced her new lover was incapable of any more exertion, she allowed him to fall asleep. Snuggled under the quilt, her head resting on Gautam's muscular chest and sated after several orgasms, Meneka smiled to herself as she drifted off to sleep.

Preeti Bhasin only moved to Panchkula, the middle-class township on the outskirts of Chandigarh, when she was sixteen. She spent her formative years in Lucknow, where her father Sukhwant Bhasin was a mid-level bureaucrat with the U.P. State cadre. Preeti attended the Sacred Heart Convent where Sister Thomas, a missionary nun, introduced her to the works of Shakespeare and the poetry of Wordsworth. A bright student, she excelled in dramatics and languages, speaking fluent English, Hindi and Punjabi, her mother tongue.

Sukhwant Bhasin's career had not advanced as rapidly as those of his IAS batch-mates because he resolutely refused to accept bribes or ignore illegal activities in his area of jurisdiction. The state machinery had little use for such an honest, upright officer and regularly shunted him to insignificant postings in remote areas where he could do minimal damage.

Sukhwant was on one such punishment posting in the hinterland of Uttar Pradesh when he uncovered a major diesel smuggling operation, carried out in connivance with the local police, politicians and mafia. Realizing his efforts to shut down the racket were coming to naught, Sukhwant decided to bring the matter to the attention of the national media. He was confident that by exposing the modus operandi of the corrupt officials through the press, he would be able to help cleanse the rot in the system. Unfortunately, the local journalist whose help he enlisted turned out to be on the payroll of the local MLA. They conspired not only to teach the obstinate bureaucrat a lesson but also to send a chilling message to other uncooperative officers who might be posted here in the future.

In broad daylight, a gang of ten men barged into Sukhwant's office and dragged him out onto the street. There, as a crowd gathered, they beat him mercilessly with their lathis and doused him with the very diesel whose smuggling he had been trying to shut down. They then set him alight in front of dozens of eyewitnesses and watched in smug satisfaction as he burnt to death.

The subsequent investigation and police report, conveniently conducted and filed by the same people who had perpetrated the crime, stated that Sukhwant Bhasin had committed suicide by immolating himself in front of his office after having been caught red-handed extorting a huge bribe from a local businessman.

The treacherous journalist wrote a damning article about the corrupt IAS officer and branded him a coward for choosing to end his life rather than face criminal prosecution. The cold-blooded public execution of an honest bureaucrat was deftly perverted into a macabre morality tale. The national media picked up the hideously distorted version of the truth and reproduced it as gospel.

Sukhwant's distraught wife Harleen tried in vain to clear her husband's name but no matter where she turned she was met with deafening silence. Every single eyewitness, even Sukhwant's colleagues who were present on the spot, refused to testify against the criminals, fearing they too would meet a fiery end.

Eventually, the family had little option but to leave Lucknow in disgrace. They moved in with Preeti's maternal grandparents, who lived in a one-room tenement in Panchkula, desperately hoping the shameful tale of the corrupt, cowardly Sukhwant Bhasin would not follow them there. As if murdering Sukhwant and hounding his family out of the state were not enough, the government also posthumously suspended his pension, since he had been found guilty of abusing public office.

Harleen Kaur had once nurtured high hopes for Preeti but this heinous twist of fate meant all her dreams were shattered overnight. A barely educated, conservative Punjabi woman, she found it hard to accept that her once over-protected daughter had to take up an airline job just so the family could survive.

When Preeti called and excitedly informed her mother that she had been selected as the new heroine opposite Ricky Kumar, Harleen took a bus to Amritsar and went to bow her head in gratitude at the Golden Temple. After having paid her respects to the various gurus, she sat at sunset by the molten lake waters that reflected the Sri Harmandir Sahib and indulged in a luxury she had denied herself all these years. Harleen Kaur finally allowed herself to weep.

The next morning, Gautam woke to one of the most erogenous experiences of his life. He lifted the fluffy goose down quilt to find the woman of his dreams gently fellating his penis even as she tenderly massaged his balls. Gautam loved that Meneka relished nibbling and sucking on him, teasing him towards a climax and adeptly stopping short, just before he could come. She delighted in playing with him for a tantalizing twenty-five minutes until he could bear the blissful torture no longer and begged her to release him, finally, in a bout of utter ecstasy. As he lay panting in bed, Meneka crawled up and kissed him passionately, giving him a taste of himself.

'Mmm ... Good morning. So tell me, was that good for you?' she asked mischievously.

'Oh God, yeah—that was amazing. Actually, everything about you is fucking amazing!'

'I know. Aren't I fantastic?' She giggled as she kissed him again. 'Now it's your turn to return the favour, big boy.'

Gautam grinned. His tongue was still a little sore from the vigorous workout the night before. He slid one hand beneath Meneka's firm buttocks and lifted her off the bed a few inches. Grabbing a pillow with the other, he slid it under her and slowly started to work his way down from her bountiful breasts, past her belly button, till he reached her already moist labia. As he skilfully set to work, darting and flicking his tongue over her neatly manicured mound, Gautam knew he had met his equal in the exquisite and audacious Meneka. With his head buried between her legs, he wondered how much longer she intended to stay in town but knew he could only have his answer after he had given her an exceptional orgasm. Employing the little tricks he had picked up over the years, he continued pleasuring the writhing Meneka with his tongue and gradually introduced a finger up her anus. She moaned, initially in pain and then in frenzied delight and almost rolled off the bed as Gautam dexterously brought her to a climax that was both agonizing and euphoric.

'Oh man ... that was so good!'

'I endeavour to provide complete satisfaction.' Gautam smirked, relieved he had managed to measure up to her sexual prowess.

'So, my sister was right—you totally are a fantastic fuck!'

'Well, thank you kindly, I ... hey ... wait a minute ... who ... who's your sister?'

'Sheena Kansal,' she replied matter-of-factly.

Gautam jumped off the bed, aghast. 'You're Sheena's sister? Bloody hell! Why didn't you tell me last night?'

'And risk losing out on going to bed with you? No way. I thought it wiser to wait till we were done doing the dirty,' she said, a wicked gleam in her eye.

Gautam clutched his head and paced the room, appalled at having repeatedly rogered the younger sister of the girl he'd dumped in Delhi less than a week ago.

'Oh fuck ... fuck ... this is so wrong. This is just so wrong!'

'Oh come on, Gautam—what are you getting so worked up about? It's not as if you were cheating on Sheena or anything, right? From what I understood, you guys broke up in Delhi. I happened to bump into you at the club last night and figured I'd find out first-hand what the fuss regarding Gautam Goyal was all about.' Meneka stared approvingly at the young stud's sculpted torso and dangling penis and gave him a lascivious wink.

Flustered, he grabbed one of the pillows from the bed and held it in front of him. 'Listen ... I ... I ... really think you should get dressed and leave.'

Meneka began to laugh. 'Oh, so now you're getting all bashful after having fucked me up the arse last night? For Christ's sake, Gautam, I never pegged you for such a prude. We had fun, didn't we? That's all that should matter.'

Gautam stared at the resplendent, amoral creature that sat naked on his bed and rapidly began to rationalize why he shouldn't feel guilty about having slept with the sister of an ex-girlfriend. After all, it was Meneka who had knowingly propositioned him, so the onus lay on her, and not him. And if she didn't have a problem with it, why should he?

Meneka sensed Gautam required further convincing. 'Listen, don't overthink this. I'm only here for another three days. So let's just enjoy each other and then go our separate ways, okay?'

Gautam nodded and slowly lowered his pillow, much to Meneka's satisfaction. 'That's a good boy! Now come back here and bang me one more time before breakfast. I'm famished.'

Ricky Kumar was at his wit's end. Rhea continued to remain incommunicado despite the barrage of phone calls, emails and text messages he had sent her. At his behest, his mother had tried reaching Kaamiya several times in Antwerp, but she refused to come on the line. The maid at the Zaveri mansion was polite but firm. Memsaab was busy and would return the call, she said. After four such calls and assurances that the previous messages had indeed been conveyed, Manju gave up trying to speak with her old friend. She tried explaining to her heartbroken son that it was futile to keep calling, but Ricky refused to accept that Rhea could so cold-heartedly cut him off without any word of explanation. Babaji had assured him that one day she would re-enter his life just as suddenly as she had exited it. But the lovelorn young man was running out of patience.

Ricky had majored in English Literature at Mumbai University and knew from his reading of the classics that he had spent the better part of his life as a passive hero. His parents, particularly his father, had determined his every action and were now charting the course for his future. Ricky was grateful for everything they had done for him, but he yearned to stand on his own feet, to be the master of his destiny.

He promised himself he would not be the eternal procrastinator like Hamlet but a man of action, like Alexander. He would seize the day and conquer new worlds. In his newfound determination, he ran through the milestones he had passed in the pursuit of this persona.

He was proud of how he had tackled the media onslaught after the incident at Scandal Point—with courage and equanimity.

He had displayed grace under pressure as Hemingway had dictated a real man should.

He had emerged triumphant from this trial by fire and re-affirmed his status as the nation's new heart-throb.

He continuously strove to present himself as a sensible, level-headed young man.

He was acutely conscious of and eternally grateful for the privilege of being born to wealthy parents.

He was unfailingly polite and courteous, especially to those less fortunate than him.

He wasn't unduly vain or obsessed with his looks, despite being aware that most people found him maddeningly handsome.

He was a faithful friend and dutiful son.

He was god-fearing but not superstitious.

He was poised to become the next big thing in Bollywood.

Women fantasized about jumping into bed with him.

Given all this, why the fuck was Rhea Zaveri not returning his calls?

Sir Dharmesh was accustomed to bumping into his son's beautiful conquests at breakfast. It was standard practice to ply all of them with a hearty meal before dispatching them in a taxi, usually never to see them again.

The Goyal patriarch derived vicarious pleasure in noting the assortment of stunners Gautam had bedded. These ranged from English debutantes to Eastern European models to daughters of various international diplomats. It wasn't often Gautam brought home a Brit-Asian girl and when he did, she rarely stayed the night. Most needed to get home before their parents awoke or were too embarrassed to face Sir Dharmesh in the morning, aware that he knew their families well.

While Sir Dharmesh encouraged and even exulted in his son's sexual peccadillos, an entirely different set of rules applied to his daughter. Rani had been strictly forbidden to bring home any male, or indeed, female friends after her father discovered those ostensibly innocent girlie sleepovers were actually sinister lesbian assignations. The single parent was aghast that his first-born was attracted to women and had tried in vain to cure her of this horrible perversion. After two Harley Street psychiatrists had claimed nothing was mentally wrong with Rani and foolishly counselled he should accept her for who she was, Sir Dharmesh sought recourse by visiting several godmen across India.

One revered sadhu in Varanasi swore that, within a fortnight of her drinking a potion made from the testicles of a tiger, Rani would be exorcised of the terrible curse. This only resulted in her becoming violently ill, which led Sir Dharmesh to visit a Tantrik baba in Kolkata. The baba insisted Rani be sent to spend the night with him so she could fully experience the joys of sleeping with a man. Keen though he was to rid her of the affliction, Sir Dharmesh could not bear the thought of this hirsute, ash-smeared ascetic penetrating his daughter and promptly discarded the proposal.

Rani had initially resented and even rebelled against her father's bigotry and sexist double standards but had eventually given up arguing with him. She came to accept that if she wanted to continue to live under his roof, she would have to abide by his rules. Her poor father, she knew, felt shamed within the conservative Indian community, repeatedly having to decline marriage proposals and make excuses for his daughter's single status; at the age of thirty-five, she was well past the sell-by date for eligible Indian girls.

Father and daughter finally arrived at an understanding. He promised not to interfere in her personal life if she was discreet about her sexual proclivities. Rani began to spend the night at the home of her partner if she was in a serious relationship or otherwise check into a hotel if she sought a quick dalliance, the tab of which would be picked up by the company and written off as a business expense.

Seated at the dining table this morning, waiting for his children to make an appearance, Sir Dharmesh was taken aback to see Meneka walking in with Gautam. She was wearing one of Gautam's shirts in an attempt to cover her scanty evening dress, but it only made her look sexier. Sir Dharmesh experienced a faint stab of jealousy, knowing that his son had spent the night fornicating with this exquisite beauty.

'Good morning, Papa.'

'Good morning, betaji.'

'Papa, this is Meneka,' said Gautam, flaunting his latest catch.

'Hello, Meneka, pleased to meet you. I'm Dharmesh Goyal.'

Meneka had been warned not to divulge her last name, as Gautam didn't want his father to make the connection with either Sheena or Jagjit Kansal. 'It's such a pleasure to meet you, uncle, I've heard so much about you.'

'Achha? So what all lies has my betaji been telling you about me, hain?' asked Dharmesh jovially, even as he inwardly cringed at being called 'uncle' by this sexy creature.

'Oh please, I didn't need Gautam to tell me anything. Your legendary reputation precedes you. In fact, for the last six months in New York I would only eat at Masala Magic when I craved some authentic ghar ka khaana. It's amazing how you keep the quality so consistent across all your restaurants.'

Sir Dharmesh beamed, flattered by her praise. 'Oh, thank you very much! So, you were in New York, haan? And what were you doing there—holidaying, working ...?'

'Actually, I was studying acting at the Lee Strasberg institute.'

Gautam looked at her, impressed, as Sir Dharmesh said, 'Acting, haan? So, you want to become a heroine? In Bollywood or in Hollywood?'

'Well, I'm happy to try my luck in both places. Wherever I get a break, I suppose?'

'Very sensible. A beautiful girl like you will have no trouble getting leading roles in Hindi movies, kyon Gautam?'

'Oh absolutely—I can picture her drenched in a sari, jiggling her bum and singing a duet with some podgy hero.' Gautam winked.

'Come on! That's the worst stereotype of actresses in Indian cinema. I'm sure there's a bunch of fantastic roles out there for women,' Meneka countered.

'Oh yeah? Well, good luck with finding those,' sneered Gautam. Meneka glared at him.

'You know, betaji, there have been some great heroine-oriented Hindi films like *Pakeezah* and *Mother India*,' proclaimed Sir Dharmesh.

'Oh puhlease ... all melodramatic bollocks,' Gautam snorted.

Meneka was quick to retort, 'Have you even seen *Mother India*, Gautam? What an incredible performance by Nargis.'

Before Gautam could reply, his father interjected.

'You know, I used to meet Nargisji regularly when she visited London in the good old days. Dutt saab and she loved to eat at our little restaurant in Wembley. My wife Sakshi and I would tell her we were her biggest fans and she would joke she was an even bigger fan of our shahi koftas.'

'Oh really? Wow, what a privilege to have known Nargisji personally.'

'Wonderful woman—simply wonderful. We lost her too early due to cancer. Even Meena Kumari and Madhubala passed away before their time.'

'Truly, such a tragedy. Such fine actresses.'

'But that's life, you know—you can never predict when your turn will come. Gautam's mother also left us so suddenly ...'

Overcome with nostalgia, Sir Dharmesh started to hum the melancholic anthem from *Mother India*, '*Duniyaa mein hum aaye hain toh jeena hi padega ...*'

Embarrassed, he suddenly stopped and looked sheepishly at Meneka only to realize she had melodiously picked up from where he had left off. '*Jeevan hai agar zahar toh peenaa hee padega.*'

Sir Dharmesh smiled fondly at Meneka as she encouraged him to sing along. '*Aurat hai woh aurat jise duniyaa ki sharam hai, sansaar mein bas laaj hi naari ka dharam hai.*'

As the irony of these lyrics dawned on Meneka, she grew self-conscious at being so inappropriately dressed. She trailed off with a discomfited smile.

'Very nice, beta—you sing beautifully. God bless,' said Sir Dharmesh with sincere affection. 'I wish you all the very best for a bright future.'

'Thank you, uncle.'

Seeing Meneka blush, Gautam realized he could potentially spend the rest of his life with this girl. She had floored him from the moment he laid eyes on her, and here she was, charming his notoriously judgmental father within minutes. But Gautam knew Meneka would be returning to India in a few days and it would be futile to try to pursue a long-term relationship with her.

Suddenly, Gautam felt like singing a melancholic tune of his own.

FIVE

'Come, come, Ricky boy, I want you to meet Meneka Kansal. She's come to see us through my old friend, Lalit Thukral, all the way from Delhi.'

Ricky looked at the gorgeous girl who sat on the sofa in his father's den and smiled warmly at her. 'Hi Meneka, I'm Ricky.'

'Hello, Ricky. It's such a pleasure to meet you.' Meneka remained seated as she extended a perfectly manicured hand.

The young actor was instantly struck by the girl's innate confidence and poise. Other aspiring actresses, unschooled in social graces, were often anxious to please and would have jumped up to greet him.

'So, you've come to Mumbai to become an actor?' asked Ricky.

'Yes, I've only just graduated from the Strasberg institute. I'm now back in India to try my luck in the movies. Lalit uncle and my dad are business partners, so he's known me since I was a child. He insisted I fly down to meet with Kapilji and you.'

Meneka spoke impeccably, without any trace of an accent, unlike Preeti, who occasionally betrayed her small-town roots by mispronouncing certain words. Ricky also approved of Meneka's understated make-up and chic ensemble—well-fitted jeans with a white silk top, top buttons undone to provide a glimpse of décolletage. The shoes and handbag were unmistakably designer, yet discreet. Even her elegant solitaire studs didn't shout for attention; rather, they whispered wealth. Meneka's pedigree was beyond question and Ricky found himself instantly drawn to this strikingly beautiful woman.

'Wow, Strasberg—that must have been quite an amazing experience?' Ricky was in awe.

'Ricky boy, I'm thinking maybe we could cast her as Sonia, what do you think?'

As Ricky mulled over his father's suggestion, Meneka politely interjected.

'Excuse me, Kapilji, but is Sonia the heroine's name in the film?'

'No, not exactly,' said Kapil Kumar. 'Sonia is actually the second lead. You see, *Pardesi Pardesi* is the story of a love triangle. Ricky plays Bhola, a simple village boy who is in love with Gauri, the sarpanch's daughter, ya? Bhola is framed in a murder by the villain and runs off to London to escape the Indian police. There, he works as a cook in an Indian restaurant. The restaurant owner's daughter is Sonia—a completely westernized girl who has grown up in England. That is the role I am thinking of for you.'

'Oh wow. Thank you, Kapilji—that's really very kind. So, please tell me what happens between Sonia and Bhola?'

'She is the rich girl. He is the poor boy. Sonia falls for Bhola, but Bhola loves Gauri. That's the basic love triangle, get it?'

'Yes, I think I do. So Bhola obviously re-unites with Gauri in the end and they live happily ever after?' The disappointment in Meneka's voice was palpable.

'Ya, ya—but don't worry,' said Kapil reassuringly. 'Sonia dies in the climax after saving Bhola from the villain's bullets. It's a very sympathetic role. The audience will weep baaltis after seeing your amazing self-sacrifice.'

'I see. Please forgive all my questions, Kapilji. I missed seeing the original version of *Pardesi Pardesi*.'

'Arrey, don't worry. But you must see it soon, ya—it's one of my golden jubilee hits. I got my first Filmfare for that role.' Kapil proudly pointed towards a large, illuminated glass cabinet that was stocked with an array of trophies and awards he had picked up over his long tenure in Hindi cinema. A few were prestigious awards from reputed institutions, given in recognition of his talent, but the majority were from dubious organizations like the Trombay Cine Club and Bhagalpur Footballers Association who readily doled out these honours to anyone who bothered to show up to receive them.

Meneka looked suitably impressed. 'So, may I ask who played Sonia's character in the original version? '

'Arrey, that was played by apni Ragini. It was one of her early movies but what an outstanding performance!'

'Ragini. But didn't she play a negative character in most Hindi films?' asked Meneka, suddenly wary of being cast as a vamp in Kapil's remake.

Ricky decided to intervene. 'Um ... Raginiji has been a very versatile actress and she played a variety of roles through her career. Some of these did have shades of grey, but she always ended up winning the audience's heart.'

'Oh, I'm sure it's a terrific role, and I would be so honoured to play the part if I am lucky enough to land it,' said Meneka diplomatically. 'But I wonder if there is any possibility of my reading for the lead role of Gauri?'

'That's impossible!' exclaimed Kapil Kumar. 'We have already cast another girl, Preeti Bhasin, and announced her name in the press. Also, your face is too hi-fi to play a simple gaon ki gori. No, trust me—you are better off in Western roles. Audiences will bajao ceetees seeing a girl like you in a bikini, not in a ghaagra choli.'

Ricky was embarrassed by his father's forthrightness but in tacit agreement that Meneka was better suited to play the role of the sophisticated and anglicized Sonia.

Meneka seemed to take Kapil's earthy critique in the right spirit. 'I understand, Kapilji. Thank you so much for giving me this opportunity. May I have a copy of the script so I can prepare for the reading?'

'Arrey, forget about the script—that is still being written! I will tell Irshad saab to help you with a few lines of dialogue that you can mug up on the spot. We will shoot your screen test tomorrow at noon. You just come wearing something really sexy, okay?'

'Okay, Kapilji. Thank you so very much!' said Meneka sweetly, confident she had landed her first role in a Hindi movie.

Ricky escorted Meneka to the driveway of Casa Kumar and held open the car door for her. As she was about to get in, Meneka turned and planted a kiss on Ricky's cheek. 'Thanks, Ricky—you're such a gentleman. I do hope we get to work together. I would love to get to know you better.'

'Likewise, Meneka, I have a feeling you're going to be perfect for the part. I'll see you tomorrow at noon.'

As Meneka's car drew out of the gate, Ricky felt blessed. He would be working with not one but two exceptionally attractive women.

When Ricky re-entered his father's den, Kapil Kumar boomed, 'What a bloody sex bomb! Ricky boy, mark my words—if that girl can act even ten per cent of how hot she looks, she will rock this role! It's so good to meet young girls with some meat on them. Mazaa aa gaya!'

'Meneka's the full package, Papa—looks, poise, pedigree, and I'm sure some serious acting as well. She's definitely destined to go places.'

'Ya, ya, I'm going to sign her tomorrow only before she gets picked up by some other producer. Now, let me call Jhontu da and tell him to start composing a zabardast cabaret number. I want this girl to totally sizzle on screen.'

Sir Dharmesh summoned Gautam to his preposterously ornate office, situated on the second floor of their mansion in Belgravia. Lady Rosalind, the interior decorator, might have been a distant cousin of the Queen but that didn't automatically imbue her with the characteristic British reserve. Rather, given carte blanche by Sir Dharmesh, this unabashed Francophile had allowed both her imagination and budget to run wild as she strove to re-create her vision of Versailles in the heart of London.

Sir Dharmesh sat like a modern-day Sun King on an oversized throne festooned with an ermine canopy, featuring two ferocious lions and a golden sunburst, which denoted that this was a seat of exalted power and glory. Surrounded by gilded frescoes and floridly upholstered furniture and oblivious to how ridiculous he looked, the undisputed monarch of Masala Magic ruled his culinary empire with an iron fist.

'Betaji, you know I am so proud you have returned after successfully detoxicating yourself. You also know that some day, when I am dead and cremated, all this will be yours. Of course, Rani bitiya will be here to help you run the company, but finally you are the man of the house and, therefore, head of the family, hai na?'

'Yes, Papa.'

'So, as a man, you need to take some responsibilities also, betaji. I have never stopped you from having your fun. I am happy you are enjoying all the things I never had when growing up. But I want you to also start taking your career very seriously now.'

'Just tell me what you'd like me to do, Papa,' said Gautam earnestly.

'I want you to start working at one of our restaurants as an assistant manager, Gautam. That is the very best way to get hands-on experience. You must learn how to man-manage the staff and customers and also tackle day-to-night running problems of the business.'

'Absolutely. I'm happy to do that. Where do you suggest I start?'

'We will start you off here only at our Hyde Park branch, betaji. I will speak to Reddy, the general manager, and fix a meeting for tomorrow, okay?'

'Ace! I look forward to starting. Thanks for believing in me, Papa.'

Sir Dharmesh was pleased that Gautam had so readily acquiesced to beginning work. The patriarch was convinced that if his wastrel son had a full-time job, he would be less likely to fall back into his old pattern of drug abuse. He was also keen to have Gautam at home so he could keep a vigilant eye on him.

Sir Dharmesh believed in employing a carrot-and-stick approach in his dealings. He had talked tough and threatened to disown Gautam when he had gotten out of control. That ploy had worked admirably and now he intended to put his recently rehabilitated son to work by dangling a juicy reward. If Gautam believed he stood to inherit most of Sir Dharmesh's wealth, he was unlikely to do anything to disappoint his father.

Despite his personal issues with his daughter, Sir Dharmesh had no real intention of denying Rani her fair share of the spoils. She was a hard worker and an intelligent girl but lately had started flexing her muscles unduly, taking some independent business decisions that had annoyed her father. The shrewd restaurateur was afraid the ambitious girl was becoming too big for her boots and decided it was time to cut her down to size. Accordingly, he circulated a rumour that he intended to make Gautam the majority shareholder of Masala Magic. The fear of losing everything to her younger brother would effectively clip Rani's wings and ensure she never lost sight of who was boss around here.

Gautam was ecstatic with the developments and anxious to prove himself. But he also possessed within him a deeply vengeful streak. He had been biding his time, waiting for an opportune moment to strike at his sister for her great betrayal. Rani had drawn first blood by leaking information about his private life to the press and Gautam yearned for retribution. The younger Goyal resolved to first establish himself within the company and settle scores when he could inflict maximum damage.

On a chilly, mid-February morning, Jagjit Kansal took his customary constitutional around the sprawling Lodhi Gardens. A cold wave had gripped the nation's capital and shrouded it in a blanket of dense fog, but this did not deter Jagjit from his routine in the historic park, where many of the men who currently ruled Delhi perambulated daily. Besides two gun-toting commandos, accompanying Jagjit that morning was his younger daughter, Mini, who had excitedly retuned from Mumbai the previous day with the news that she had been cast opposite Ricky Kumar in his debut film.

Jagjit wasn't exactly pleased his daughter had elected to make a name for herself in Bollywood, where lascivious film-makers were known to prey on vulnerable young women. Lurid tales of the legendary Mumbai casting couch abounded and many a wealthy Delhiwallah fantasized about turning producer solely in the hope of bedding a buxom starlet or even, perhaps, a bona fide Hindi film heroine. The suave politico had heard several such stories from Lalit Thukral, his business partner who dabbled in film financing, lending large amounts of cash at astronomical rates of interest to Mumbai producers who could not raise loans from banks or legitimate financial institutions.

But Jagjit knew his little Meneka, aka Mini, was a big girl now and could take care of herself. He also knew from bitter experience that telling his headstrong daughter what not to do would only serve to alienate her further. Whilst her older sister had borne the brunt of their parents' acrimonious divorce and sought refuge in drugs and alcohol, Mini was far less self-destructive. She rarely drank and she abstained from narcotics. But Jagjit was aware his younger daughter harboured enormous resentment and anger within her and could be a ruthless, manipulative creature.

Meneka had realized early in life that she possessed a unique ability to charm men into giving her precisely what she wanted. Over the years, she had honed that skill into a fine art, using her beauty and overt sexuality to advantage.

Jagjit had bankrolled Meneka's stint in New York and asked his partner Thukral to use his influence among Bollywood producers to help get his daughter a break. He was proud she had landed a role in a prestigious film within a day of arriving in Mumbai. He would ensure word went around tinsel town that she was Jagjit Kansal's daughter and, therefore, not to be messed with.

'So, when and where do you begin filming?' queried Jagjit.

'In a couple of months in London, Dad. But I have to be in Mumbai next week for costume fittings and stuff.'

'And you're sure this is what you want? A career as a Hindi film actress.'

'Yup. Pretty much.'

'It's a notoriously fickle industry, Mini. You have to be prepared for a lot of ups and downs,' said Jagjit sagely.

'Yeah, yeah—I know all that, Dad. I also know the shelf life of a Bollywood heroine is very short. After a few years, audiences get bored and want to see fresh faces on screen. But I really want to give this a shot.'

'Okay—as long as you're going into it with your eyes open.'

'It's bloody unfair isn't it, that the rules are so different for men? Hindi film heroes never seem to retire. Kapil Kumar was around for over thirty years and some of the actresses who debuted opposite him ended up playing his mother. Can you imagine?' Mini scoffed.

'So what are you saying? That you want to end up playing Ricky Kumar's mother?' Jagjit teased.

'No, Dad. I'm saying I want to end up as Ricky Kumar's wife.' Meneka turned and gave her father a sly smile.

Jagjit chortled and lovingly put an arm around his daughter. 'Well then, I wish you the very best, my darling. And if you require any assistance, you know I'm always there for you.'

'Thanks, Dad, I really appreciate everything you're doing for me.'

'I'm glad I can be of help, Mini. By the way, how is Sheena these days?'

'Well, you know we don't really speak that much, Dad. But, from what I understand, she's pretty upset things didn't work out with that Gautam chap.'

'I just hope she doesn't fall back into her old ways. That would be a real shame,' said Jagjit wistfully.

'I hope so too, Dad. No man is worth crying over. Now, if you'll excuse me, I'm going to go run a couple of rounds. Got to look sensational for my big debut!'

As Jagjit watched Meneka sprint away, he was pleased that at least one of his daughters had imbibed the valuable life lessons he had tried to inculcate in them. Jagjit had always preached the efficacy of jungle law as he firmly believed that urban existence was about the survival of the fittest.

'Eat or be eaten,' he would sermonize. 'There is absolutely no room for human weakness and silly sentimentality when there are so many predators on the prowl.'

Shivani Mehta was chuffed with the way things were shaping up on *Pardesi Pardesi*. The casting of Preeti Bhasin as the film's heroine was a publicist's delight. Here was a beautiful, small-town girl, personally discovered by Ricky Kumar when she served him on board a flight from Delhi to Mumbai. This was precisely the stuff that compelling underdog stories were made of. The Indian public would lap up the rags-to-riches tale of a young woman who had been plucked from the masses after a nationwide hunt. On the other hand, Meneka, daughter of politico Jagjit Kansal, was a sophisticated Delhi rich bitch and would serve as the perfect foil to middle-class Preeti.

Shivani could now have a field day planting stories in the press about how these two beauties were vying for Ricky Kumar's attention. News would be strategically leaked over the next few months of filming, of how Ricky was first involved with one girl and then with the other. Eventually, of course, Preeti would win Ricky's heart and they would go on to become the nation's sweethearts, generating massive audience interest and free publicity in the process. On opening night, the young lovers would attend the movie premiere together, hand in hand, and thereby ensure phenomenal news coverage across print, television and the Internet. The entire marketing and publicity campaign was carefully explained to Kapil Kumar, who was impressed at how masterfully Shivani intended to manipulate public sentiment.

'Shivani baby, you're a bloody genius! What a dhansoo strategy. I owe Hotchand big time for finding you. Mwah!' exulted Kapil as he hoisted himself from his maroon velvet swivel chair and planted an extravagant, wet kiss on the publicist's cheek.

'Thanks, Kapilji. It's all in a day's work,' said Shivani, as she discreetly tried to wipe away his slobber. 'Now, what about the chief guest for the mahurat? Should we approach someone like the chief minister or the governor to give the inaugural clap?'

'Arrey, why do we need these political types? Are we launching a feature film or some family planning clinic?' snorted Kapil.

'Okay then—how about a senior actor from the industry? Someone who can give his blessing to the new generation of actors?'

'Arrey, again you are barking up the wrong tree, Shivani. What will some old retired actor do except try and hog all the publicity? We don't need any outsider chief guest. I will be my own cheap guest!'

'As you wish, Kapilji. These were simply suggestions ...'

'I know, I know—but who better than me, as director, producer and presenter of the film, to give the clap for my own remake?'

Kapil Kumar was clearly keen to have his moment in the spotlight and Shivani knew better than to argue with the pompous egotist on such matters. 'Excellent idea, Kapilji. I will send out a press release on this and also arrange to fly in journalists from all over the country for the mahurat.'

'Ya, ya, we must create a national hungama with the launch of *Pardesi Pardesi*. After all, this is not just the launch of Ricky Kumar but also the momentous return of Kapil Kumar!'

'I beg your pardon? What do you mean the return of Kapil Kumar?' Shivani was baffled.

'Shivani baby! I have decided to cast myself in the film!'

'As Ricky's father?'

'No, no, his father is already dead in the movie. I will be the surprise twist in the film.'

'What surprise twist, Kapilji?'

'I will play Romy Punj, the owner of the restaurant in London where Bhola comes to work!'

'But ... but ... haven't you already signed Pradip Kapoor to play that part?'

'Yes, but I have changed my mind. I will play the role of Romy now. Pradip can keep the signing amount. No problem.'

'So, let me get this straight—you will now be playing Sonia's father in the film? Right?'

'Right! No, no, wait a minute. I think I will look too young to play her father. So let's change the character. I will play Sonia's older brother instead!'

'Kapilji, when were you planning to tell me this? My marketing strategy will need to be reworked if you are also appearing in the film,' said Shivani, exasperated.

'Arrey, I have only just decided to cast myself in the picture a few minutes ago, Shivani baby. Isn't it a genius idea?'

'Well ... you mentioned you wanted to keep your role a surprise for the audience? That's pretty good strategy, Kapilji.' Shivani really didn't want Kapil to distract attention from his son's debut.

'Hmm, actually, maybe it's much better if we publicize my role from now only. That way all my fans can come rushing first day, first show to see the film. What do you think, Shivani? Much better strategy, ya?'

Shivani knew it was futile to reason with the man. 'Either way is okay with me, Kapilji—you decide, you're the boss.'

'See, that's why I love working with you, Shivani baby. You fully understand and appreciate true genius.'

Shivani smiled indulgently at Kapil Kumar. The only reason she continued to tolerate this opinionated fathead's blather was because she genuinely believed that Ricky Kumar was destined to be the next big thing in Bollywood. And Shivani was determined to take full credit for having created a superstar out of a scandal-ridden star son. This would be her greatest triumph and re-affirm her status as the city's pre-eminent spin-doctor. And if that meant having to suffer this babbling fool of a father, so be it. In the end, Shivani Mehta would come out on top.

Within four weeks of starting work, Gautam had found his feet at Masala Magic. Charming the patrons and displaying an innate ability to tackle operational issues with decisive tact, he transformed from belligerent spoilt brat to level-headed team player. In so doing, he managed to earn the respect of his co-workers, who were initially wary of the boss's infamous son. Instead of going clubbing with his friends, the notorious playboy stayed late every night at the restaurant and came home directly to a decent night's rest. It seemed the drug haze had magically lifted to reveal a clear-thinking, intelligent young man who remained focussed and driven by the task at hand.

Sir Dharmesh was elated with the daily reports he received on Gautam's progress and felt both proud and relieved that his son was finally proving his mettle. The only person who was worried by Gautam's new-found discipline was his sister.

Rani Goyal had been secure in the knowledge that her irresponsible younger brother would never amount to anything. He had never posed a serious threat to her, for she knew that even if Sir Dharmesh did make him the titular head of the company, she would continue to remain the brains behind the operation. But with Gautam showing tremendous aptitude at work, Rani became anxious. Her plan to discredit her brother had only succeeded to the extent that she had managed to humiliate him in public. Unfortunately, that coward Mukesh Menda had revealed to Gautam that it was she who had leaked the information about his shenanigans at Behramjee's clinic.

Rani had little doubt Gautam would ruthlessly engineer her ouster once he had gathered enough experience to run Masala Magic on his own. She knew she had to formulate a new, foolproof plan that would ensure her future within the company. Mercifully, these were early days yet, and Gautam had a long way to go before he could begin to assert himself.

Filming on *Pardesi Pardesi* had begun in earnest. The veteran art director, Ramakant Chitnis, had lovingly recreated an entire village in Mumbai's Film City studio. Of course, this sprawling set was his utopian imagining of pastoral India—replete with picture postcard Swiss cottages, American mid-west style barns and even a Dutch windmill turning torpidly in the background for good measure. In the midst of this bucolic idyll was a gaudily painted well, from which the beauteous Gauri would daintily draw water as her beau Bhola warbled romantic ditties to woo her.

From day one, Preeti Bhasin validated the faith Kapil Kumar had reposed in her. She slipped effortlessly into her role as a naïve village belle. All wide-eyed and innocent, the novice exuded both oomph and charm in ample measure. The camera adored Preeti, as did the crew. There was no dearth of high-maintenance divas in Bollywood, who would report late to work and bicker about their hair, make-up and wardrobe. This refreshingly good-natured and talented newcomer was a delight to work with.

Ricky, meanwhile, had been facing a tough couple of days playing the rustic simpleton. His Hindi diction was undeniably weak, a result of having been educated at a terribly expensive English-medium school. His anglicized dialogue delivery sounded inauthentic and Kapil Kumar grew impatient with his son's less than stellar performance. The frustrated first-time director kept bellowing 'Cut' each time Ricky fumbled a word, shattering the inexperienced actor's confidence further. Kapil also insisted Ricky emote larger than life, which the young lad found difficult to do, given that his own instinct was to underplay scenes.

Finally, after a week of filming, an incensed Kapil summoned Ricky to his vanity van and tore into him. 'Ricky boy, I've told you a hundred times not to try and be a bloody Brando in Bollywood, ya! Why can't you understand that? From now on, I'm going to act out each and every scene for you. You just copy whatever I do, okay?' railed Kapil.

'But how can I blindly ape you, Papa? I've got to develop my own style of acting. Otherwise people will say I'm a carbon copy of Kapil Kumar.' It wasn't often Ricky stood up to his father, but he knew it was imperative to voice his concerns.

'Arrey, you just bloody do what I'm telling you to do!' Kapil thundered. 'And don't call me papa on set! Over here I am not your father but your director and also your bloody producer and presenter! From this moment, you will call me "sir". Is that understood?'

'Yes, sir.'

'Good! Guneet has given me a very good suggestion that we can dub all your dialogues in post-production. So, don't worry about your fancy angrezi accent baazi. Just concentrate on acting like a proper hero, okay?'

'Yes, sir,' mumbled Ricky, feeling anything but a hero.

'Excellent! Now let's get back there and ....'

Suddenly, a blood-curdling scream was heard outside, followed by anguished cries for help. Ricky and Kapil rushed out of the van to find Irshad saab, the septuagenarian writer, flailing on the ground with a large, buxom woman sitting on top of him, pummelling his face with all her might.

As several unit members rushed to disentangle her from atop the yelping writer, the woman let loose a torrent of filthy abuses. 'Motherfucking pervert! Have you even seen your face in the mirror? Do you have any idea how old you are? And you have the guts to grope my arse? I'll teach you a lesson you will never forget, you son of a smelly whore!'

'Calm down, calm down,' said Kapil Kumar to the enraged

woman, who was evidently an extra hired to play one of the villagers in the film. Her low-cut blouse and tightly wrapped sari had obviously aroused the randy old writer and he had decided to cop a feel.

'Arrey, what do you think—we are all prostitutes or something?' she roared. 'We may be junior artistes, but we will not tolerate such molestations. I will complain to the police and to our union and have this shooting shut down.'

A number of junior artistes started rallying round their affronted colleague and threatened to quit en masse. Ricky was appalled by Irshad saab's behaviour but realized he had to placate everyone before matters got out of hand. He walked up to the aggrieved woman with folded hands.

'Behenji, I am begging you to please forgive Irshad saab. He is old enough to be your father and is now losing his mind due to dementia. I can personally assure you, we have the highest respect and regard for you all. We are all co-actors working in unison to make this film. This is my debut, and I beseech you to please bless me with your support.'

Mollified by the young actor's assurances and touched by his sincerity, the junior artistes relented and agreed not to press charges. Irshad saab was hastily bundled into a rickshaw and dispatched to a nearby clinic.

'Well done, Ricky boy!' said Kapil once the crowd had dispersed. 'These unions are very powerful and could have caused us a lot of trouble. You did a great job of calming things down.'

'Thanks, Papa … I mean, sir,' said Ricky.

'Arrey, call me papa only!' said Kapil, as he smothered his son in a bear hug. 'You must learn not to take everything I say so seriously, Ricky boy. You know I am just as nervous as you are. In fact—doubly nervous! Not only is this your acting debut but also my directorial debut, ya? I come on set every day, and my legs start to wobble. I'm terrified of making a bloody fool of myself in front of everyone. So, I am venting all my own insecurities on you. I love you, son. Don't worry—you're going to be great in this movie. And I'm going to be even greater! Together we are going to make one motherfucking super-duper platinum-jubilee hit picture. Right, Ricky boy?'

'Right, Papa,' said Ricky, smiling.

Sheena Kansal had spent the last couple of months tending to a broken heart. She berated herself for having naïvely expected Gautam to be considerate of her feelings. Despite everything she had done for him, that self-absorbed, cold-blooded cad had upped and left overnight, leaving her alone and devastated. Sheena's self-esteem was at an all-time low. She was tempted to dull her pain using an old, familiar crutch. But she knew that if she sank back into substance abuse, escaping its soporific, seductive clutches yet again would prove impossible.

Meanwhile, Mini had been cast in a film opposite Ricky Kumar and would soon become a successful heroine. Of the two siblings, Mini was the real beauty and also considerably brighter and far more ambitious. Sheena knew that most people thought of her as the loser older sister. The only time she had scored over Mini was when she landed Gautam Goyal as her boyfriend. But that bastard had dumped her before Mini could even return from New York. Sheena decided it was time to stop floundering in self-pity and find a vocation that would keep her mind engaged and, hopefully, off Gautam.

Sheena belonged to an echelon of glamorous Delhi girls, born to moneyed parents, whose sole objective was seemingly to snare an even wealthier husband. Most of her friends had already married exceedingly well and produced babies who were being expertly raised by nannies. Some of these young society swans were content being ladies who lunched, but others aspired to do something a little more rewarding with their time.

A few had decided to launch themselves as fashion designers. But rather than enrol at a fashion institute and learn the nuances of drape and design, they had shrewdly enlisted the services of a local master tailor who did all the dreary darzi work while they preened on the society pages, flaunting their respective labels.

Other comely lasses declared they were interior designers, again, without having received any formal training. Apparently, being rich automatically imbues one with impeccable taste and aesthetics and these self-assured ladies, therefore, went about desecrating the urban landscape with impunity.

A few ingénues had a gem of an idea and positioned themselves as jewellery designers whilst a bevy of beauties became art dealers and opened galleries in their garages despite being unable to distinguish between Frida Kahlo and Freida Pinto.

It was easy to snigger at these high-society debutantes, and most of Delhi did so with relish. But, ironically, it was this very set of divas that had the last laugh, chortling all the way to the bank, having achieved enviable success within an admirably short period of time. This was because the charmed circle of uber rich women formed a tight coterie—indeed, a cartel—which supported and sustained them in every amateur enterprise. The daughters and wives of industrialists, politicians, hoteliers and other entrepreneurs ensured they bought each other's 'designer' clothes, jewellery and art. They commissioned their friends to decorate their homes and patronized their vanity projects in a tacit quid pro quo. Extensive media coverage was ensured by the presence of their celebrity chums, and it helped that many magazines and television channels were owned by their families.

The great Indian middle-class gaped in wonder and aspired to be like them someday. Everyone wanted to join these perfectly manicured mannequins exultant in their mediocrity.

At the age of twenty-five, Sheena realized she had no real, formal education that could render her gainfully employed. But she had an innate flair for art and had excelled at art class in secondary school. Hitherto known only for her propensity to splash the town red, Sheena decided to try her hand at painting, aware that, if not her talent, then her father's clout would ensure that any exhibition of her work was an instant sell-out.

Manju Kumar had taken an immediate shine to Preeti Bhasin. The affable, down-to-earth girl reminded Ricky's mother of herself and the two spent hours swapping stories and bonding over their experiences as former flight attendants.

Manju was eager her son forget Rhea and get on with his life. She was convinced Preeti possessed all the requisite qualities to be Ricky's girlfriend and perhaps wife someday. The mother decided to play Cupid and sought to engineer a romance between the co-stars. When she sounded out Kapil, he encouraged it whole-heartedly as that was precisely what Shivani's publicity strategy called for.

'Arrey, superb! Reel life and real life will be same-same. Just like you and me, haan, Manju? You remember how you first brought me a Patiala peg of Chivas on that flight, twenty-five years ago. And I kept polishing it off and asking for more because I wanted to talk to you again and again.'

'Yes, how can I forget? You got completely drunk and passed out. We had a real tough time waking you up at Heathrow,' Manju affectionately chided her husband.

'Arrey, I only got drunk on love, Manju meri jaan—totally bloody punch-drunk on love! Now, it's our son's turn, ya?'

Ricky was not at all receptive to the idea of kindling a romance with Preeti. 'Mamma, please. First of all, she's a colleague. Also, you know I'm having a tough time playing this Bhola character. I need to focus on acting at this point. I can't afford any distractions and frankly, nor can Preeti. I appreciate what you are trying to do, but trust me—it's not a good idea.'

Reluctantly, Manju had to agree with her son. Ricky was certainly not performing as well as expected, and an on-set romance was probably the last thing he needed.

'Okay jaanoo, I'm sorry I brought it up. I promise, no more interference while you're shooting. But once you're done, I want you to start thinking seriously about Preeti. She's such a lovely girl, and you're far too handsome to remain single for very long.'

Ricky grinned at his mother's praise but was glad he had managed to convince her to back off. He didn't want to tell her that he still nurtured ardent hopes of reuniting with Rhea. And if at all he were to consider getting involved with another girl, it would be to the far more urbane and sophisticated Meneka Kansal.

Much to Rani's dismay, Sir Dharmesh decided it was time to transfer his rehabilitated son to the strategy and planning division, the nerve centre of their business empire. This was Rani's area of expertise and she guarded her precious fiefdom with ferocity. When her father instructed her to take Gautam under her wing and teach him the ropes, she was livid but could not refuse.

'Those saala goras managed to colonize India by following a policy of divide and rule. They encouraged the local rajas to fight among themselves and meanwhile established their own might within our country. Clever bastards,' thought Sir Dharmesh, who sought to employ this very strategy while dealing with his offspring. 'Let my children squabble. As long as their loyalty is to me, I am happy. In fact, a little sibling rivalry will encourage them to perform better.'

A few weeks into work at the head office, Gautam came up with a suggestion at their Monday morning brainstorming session. 'Papa, I've noticed that given the proximity and favourable currency rate, thousands of Indian tourists visit Thailand every year but find it difficult to find pure veggie nosh there. Almost all Thai dishes are prepared using fish sauce or shrimp paste—even the so-called veg ones. So, why don't we consider opening a chain of low-cost restaurants across Thailand that specialize in serving pure Indian vegetarian fare?'

'Hmm ... very interesting idea, betaji.' Sir Dharmesh's sharp mercantile mind began to whir. 'We know that most Indians prefer to eat only desi bhojan when they travel abroad. That's why we get so much business from package tour operators who bring their customers to eat at our restaurants. These tourwallahs are forced to bring along special cooks from India so pure veg tourists can be guaranteed shudh shakahaari meals, without a teeny-weeny trace of meat, otherwise they will all become dharambhrasht. Yes, this could certainly be a big opportunity for us. What do you feel, Rani bitiya?'

'On the face of it, it doesn't sound like a bad idea, Papa. Obviously we will need to study the ground realities first.'

'Yes, of course. Gautam, why don't you go visit some popular tourist hot-spots like Bangkok, Phuket and Pattaya and see if your idea is viable? Prepare a feasibility report and bring it to me. If I approve it, this can be your first solo independent project.'

'Cheers, Papa. I'm positive this will be a huge money-spinner for us,' replied Gautam, elated.

'Let's hope so, betaji. I'm happy to see you're thinking out of some box. Keep up the good work!'

Rani was a little envious that her brother had come up with such a clever idea. But she was also glad, for Gautam would be going away for at least a couple of weeks. And if the Thailand project did get green-lit he could be out of her hair for several months, even a year or two, perhaps. Rani suddenly became rather enamoured with the idea of the Goyal empire setting up a chain of restaurants in Thailand. In fact, the more the merrier, she thought. As long as it got Gautam out of their father's sight.

SIX

After six weeks of filming in Mumbai, the unit of *Pardesi Pardesi* moved to London, where the remainder of the movie was to be picturized. The British capital had long been a favoured destination for Bollywood, as it not only provided scenic locales and easy filming infrastructure but also had a sizeable Asian population. Increasingly, Hindi movies featured among the top grossers at the UK box-office and many desi producers banked heavily on returns from this profitable overseas territory.

Kapil Kumar had once had a substantial fan base in London and looked forward to returning to the city he considered a second home, having filmed and fucked there regularly over the past three decades.

Ricky loved the vibrant metropolis too and had fond memories of vacationing there every summer with his mother. He would accompany her dutifully on shopping expeditions to High Street Kensington and Oxford Street, where Manju would buy him clothes from Selfridges and then lingerie for herself from Marks and Sparks. As a reward for his good behaviour, she would take him to Hamleys on Regent Street and get him a toy of his choosing. Though she promised herself never to spoil him, Manju invariably succumbed to that adorable smile and those wide brown eyes that beseeched just one more Lego set or Matchbox dinky car.

Mother and son would sometimes spend the afternoon in Hyde Park, feeding the swans and pedal boating on the Serpentine. Having worked up an appetite, they would hail a black cab and head to the Ritz for a decadent afternoon tea comprising Ricky's sinful favourite: freshly baked apple and raisin scones with strawberry preserve and clotted Devonshire cream. Sometimes they would catch a musical in the West End or a movie at the Leicester Square Odeon and stroll down to Chinatown to dine on crispy Peking duck.

Returning to their plush Mayfair service flat, which they rented every April, Manju and Ricky would curl up in front of the telly and tuck into a box of Macintosh Quality Street chocolates. In pre-liberalized India, families could only indulge their appetite for Western goodies when they travelled abroad, or else source them through visiting relatives, or sometimes locally, at a substantial premium, from the neighbourhood smuggler. Manju would buy a suitcaseful of Ricky's favourite chocolates and carefully ration them to him in Mumbai through the year.

When Manju thought Ricky had fallen asleep, she would quietly light up a 555 State Express cigarette and savour the rapture of fine roasted tobacco as it swirled round her palate, down her throat and into her lungs and exhale the seductive smoke leisurely, through her nostrils. Smoking was the only vice Kapil Kumar discouraged and for one month, every year, Manju covertly indulged in this forbidden pleasure. Young Ricky never let on that he knew his mother's little secret and maintained this discretion even as an adult. Everyone—even mothers were entitled to some privacy.

Manju Kumar had elected not to accompany her husband and son on this visit to London but chose, instead, to spend the month at Babaji's ashram. Ricky looked forward to this section of the filming, as his character would transform from village bumpkin to suave international smuggler, corrupted by the evil West. The young actor realized he hadn't quite done justice to his role in India and hoped to do a better job playing the more debonair avatar of Bhola.

Preeti Bhasin had enacted her part as Gauri to perfection, and it was time for Sonia to enter the picture. Meneka Kansal flew in from Delhi to join her co-star in London. Over the past couple of months, she had adhered to a punishing dietary and workout regimen prescribed by her personal trainer and looked sensational. Her on-screen persona was that of an arrogant, spoilt brat, disparaging of everything Indian, until she falls in love with Bhola and realizes the folly of her ways. Though the role had negative shades, Meneka was convinced she could bring depth and nuance to her performance and establish herself in Bollywood as an actress of substance. Besides, she wanted the highly desirable Ricky Kumar to fall madly in love with her and had little doubt she would soon have him wrapped around her perfectly manicured pinkie.

The local production manager Gogi Padda had arranged permission for filming at a mid-sized Indian restaurant in Southall, where a substantial number of London's Asian community resided.

On the first day of filming, word quickly spread through the bustling neighbourhood that Ricky Kumar, the Indian heart-throb, was shooting at Tandoori Palace along with his father, yesteryear filmstar Kapil Kumar. Within an hour, an excited crowd had gathered outside the restaurant to catch a glimpse of the two Bollywood heroes. Kapil and Ricky were thrilled by the overwhelming turnout and came out of the restaurant to wave and blow kisses. When they went back inside, the crowd grew unruly and started chanting Ricky's name. The noise was deafening and it became impossible to continue work.

Ricky decided to step outside to calm the crowd. He grabbed a megaphone from one of the assistants, climbed atop a stack of crates and beseeched the throng to quieten down. But the boisterous crowd roared louder each time Ricky spoke, in no mood to listen to his imprecations. By now, several young punks had joined the gathering of fans and they began to heckle Ricky and jostle the private security guards employed to protect the film unit.

As a scuffle broke out between the guards and these hooligans, the crowd turned hostile and started assailing the restaurant with an array of projectiles. A beer bottle hurtled towards Ricky, catching him on the shoulder and narrowly missing his face. Seeing Ricky hurt, Kapil dashed out and dragged his son back into the restaurant even as police sirens began to blare in the distance.

Eventually, it took two units of London's riot police an hour to disperse the mob. All this while, the unit members cowered inside the restaurant. An anxious Meneka clung to Ricky, who was himself pretty shaken up by the manner in which the crowd had suddenly turned on him. One minute they were a group of adoring fans and the next, a vengeful mob. It had happened to him before, when overnight he had gone from being media darling to irresponsible dopehead. Fame, Ricky had come to realize, is a truly fickle monster.

Kapil Kumar was furious with his production manager. 'What the fuck have you done, Gogi? You couldn't find a more sensible location for us to shoot in? Ricky is lucky to have got away without a serious injury! That mob could have killed us! What the hell are we supposed to do now?'

Gogi Padda had organized dozens of Bollywood shoots

in London and was aware that the locality was less than ideal for filming. He had decided to risk it because Tandoori Palace belonged to his wife's cousin. The enterprising production manager had struck a deal to receive a hefty kickback from the restaurant owner in lieu of inflated location-hire charges. But his lucrative plan had backfired. Not only was the restaurant damaged, he also had an apoplectic producer on his hands.

'I'm very sorry, Kapilji, but don't worry. I will find you another location within the next couple of days.'

'Arrey, what don't worry? Every day that is wasted thanks to your stupidity will cost me thousands of pounds. Do you know what the bloody rupee exchange rate is? It costs a bomb to shoot here in London. It would have been much cheaper for me to erect a set in India only!'

Overhearing this heated exchange, Meneka had an idea. She went up to Ricky who was trying to calm his sputtering father. 'Listen, Ricky. I know Gautam Goyal reasonably well. His family owns the Masala Magic chain of restaurants. Would you like me to call and ask him if there is any possibility of filming at one of their properties?'

Hearing Gautam's name, Ricky blanched. He did not intend to see that bastard again and certainly didn't want to be beholden to him in any way. 'No thanks, Meneka. It's very sweet of you to offer but I'm sure Gogi can arrange another location soon.'

The harried production manager butted in, 'Menekaji, that's wonderful. If you know the Goyals personally, nothing like it! They have so many restaurants all over London, they could definitely help us out.'

Ricky whipped around and snarled, 'Why don't you concentrate on doing your fucking job, Gogi, instead of asking other people to do it for you!'

'Sss ... sorry Rickyji ... it's just that since Menekaji herself offered to use her contacts ... we can get the location much cheaper this way and ...'

'Menekaji is one of the stars of this film—not some production flunky,' Ricky barked. 'If you can't find a new location on your own, it's better we sack you and find someone who can!'

Meneka and Kapil were as taken aback as Gogi by Ricky's response.

Kapil decided to intervene. 'Ricky boy, if Meneka knows the owners personally, there's really no harm if she speaks to them.'

'Yes, there is, Papa. We can't expect her to take favours from her friends. Let Gogi go find another restaurant.'

'Arrey, all Meneka will do is provide an introduction. They will obviously charge us for using the place, so where is the question of taking any favours? You don't mind, do you, Meneka?'

'Not at all, Kapilji. I'm happy to help in any way I can. Ricky, honestly, it's not an issue.'

'Well, I still don't think it's a good idea. But do what you want. I don't care!' Ricky stormed off, leaving the unit wondering.

Meneka was in a quandary whether she should call Gautam at all. Then Kapil came up to her and whispered, 'Arrey, don't worry about Ricky boy. I think he's just shaken up after today's tamasha and simply needs to cool down. You please call your friend and help get us out of this bloody mess.'

Meneka was astute enough to figure out that Ricky was hiding something. She was determined to find out what it was.

Gautam was nursing an Armagnac at Bangkok's trendy Sky Bar when his phone rang. The view from the popular nightspot, situated atop the sixty-three-storeyed Lebua Towers, was spectacular. The city sprawl twinkled below, a carpet of fairylights. Pagodas, palaces, temples, tenements, condos, massage parlours, hotels and brothels all packed cheek by jowl, in chaotic yet congruent coexistence.

For a single man, there were many delights to be found in this legendary sin city, but rather than pick up some frisky tourist or dial an escort service to provide companionship for the evening, Gautam was content to sit by himself and soak in the ambience. His recce around Thailand had gone exceedingly well, and the idea of opening a chain of Indian vegetarian restaurants seemed more viable than originally envisioned.

Seeing Meneka's name suddenly flash on his mobile made his heart skip a beat. The four days and nights they had spent together in London had been exhilarating. Marathon sex sessions, interspersed with visits to some of the finest restaurants and nightclubs in town—it was a joyous 'fuck feast' as Meneka had naughtily dubbed it. And then, all too quickly, she was gone, leaving him to wonder what might have developed between them had she stayed.

'Well, hello! How are you?'

'Gautam, hi! I'm great, thanks. Just got into London a few days ago.'

'Brilliant! I'm in Bangkok at the moment, but back tomorrow. How long are you staying?'

'Oh, I'm in London for at least a month—shooting my first film here! Isn't that cool?'

'Ace—well done, you! So, is this some sort of Bollywood movie?'

'Yes, it is. And that's the other reason I'm calling. We've had some trouble with filming at an Indian restaurant in Southall and desperately need to find another location. Do you think you can help us out?'

'Sure, anything for you, babe. Listen, since I'm away, why don't you have a word with my dad and tell him precisely what you're looking for? I'm sure he'll be happy to assist. You made quite an impression on the old boy!'

'Oh, super. Thanks! Could you please text me his number? I need to speak with him urgently because we really are in a fix.'

'No worries. I'll do it right away. But give us a bell later and let's catch up on your news, all right?'

'Thanks, doll. Speak soon. Oh, by the way, do you know Ricky Kumar?'

'Ricky Kumar … now, why is that name so familiar?'

'He's the son of that old actor, Kapil Kumar. I'm acting in this film opposite Ricky. Hunky six-footer—seriously good-looking—I thought you might know him.'

Gautam suddenly recalled where he had heard the name. Ricky was that scumbag Bollywood brat who had blatantly lied about seeing him snort coke at Pink Paisley. Gautam was both jealous and angry.

'For fuck's sake, Meneka—that bloke's a complete tosser! He's been talking all sorts of bollocks about me! I'm sorry, but I'll be damned if I allow him to come anywhere near one of our restaurants. Take my advice and stay as far away from that knob head as possible.'

Meneka listened patiently as Gautam ranted for another ten minutes, denouncing the young actor as the epitome of evil. She was inclined to believe that Ricky had, in fact, seen Gautam doing drugs in Delhi, as he didn't seem the type to fabricate stories. But she decided to remain quiet and finally hung up on Gautam, promising to meet him upon his return to London. She then informed Kapil that the Goyals had declined assistance and that Gogi should look for another location.

Meneka had set her sights on Ricky Kumar and it was clear to her that she had to keep the temperamental Goyal scion as far from the sensitive young actor as she possibly could.

That evening, Ricky was pleasantly surprised to find Meneka at the door of his hotel room.

'Hi Ricky, I thought I'd drop by to check how you're doing.'

'That's very kind, thanks, Meneka. Umm ... won't you please come in?'

'Yeah, sure. Actually, I've brought some Rescue Remedy cream to apply on your injury.'

'Oh, please don't bother. The doc says it's only a bruise—nothing serious. I'll live. But thanks anyway.' Ricky smiled, touched by Meneka's concern.

'Look, this is just a harmless flower essence extract, but it works wonders. Let me rub a little bit on your shoulder. I swear it will speed up the healing process. Come on, off with your shirt.'

Ricky looked at Meneka and started to redden. But she was trying to be helpful, and he didn't want to make a fuss. He allowed his statuesque co-star to take him by the hand and sit him down on the bed. He didn't protest when she began to slowly unbutton his shirt. Meneka took a small dab of ointment on her finger and began rubbing it gently around his angry bruise.

'You know, I wanted to thank you for making me feel so

safe when that mob attacked us today,' she cooed, running her hands over Ricky's bare chest. 'It was amazing to see you brave the crowd like that.'

It struck Ricky that his relationship with this woman could proceed in any direction he desired. He could either put on his shirt and politely show her out the door or allow Meneka to continue with her obvious yet seductive act and take their association to an altogether different level.

As Meneka rubbed a little more cream over Ricky's torso, he felt an electric impulse course through his spine. When his penis surged involuntarily, his mind was made up. He moved his face closer to Meneka's and she instinctively leaned towards him. Ricky shut his eyes as they kissed—gently, tenderly. As their passion intensified, his tongue sought hers and twined around it in a snaking embrace. He grabbed hold of her breast and squeezed it roughly. She responded by reaching for his bulging cock. Fully aroused, Ricky ripped open her blouse, not bothering to unbutton it as might be expected of someone otherwise so unfailingly polite. Meneka was surprised by his ardour and relieved the boy was no pussycat in the bedroom. She had initiated the seduction, but it was now vital to let Ricky have the upper hand. Most Indian men she had slept with felt emasculated when women took the initiative in the bedroom, and Meneka did not intend to make this hunky young actor feel inadequate in any way.

As Ricky cupped her bare breast and started nibbling at her nipple, Meneka moaned in delight. She deftly undid his belt and Ricky wriggled out of his jeans. Naked, he pulled down Meneka's skirt and yanked off her silk underwear. He wanted to waste no time in penetrating the inviting chasm between her legs. He positioned himself atop Meneka and as he was about to ease into her, he suddenly stopped.

'Hey, sorry—but I don't have any protection—is that okay?' he whispered.

'Yes, don't worry. I've taken care of it.'

Meneka had clearly come prepared. She kissed Ricky passionately and then, clutching his buttocks, guided his cock deep within her. As Ricky sought to find his rhythm, Meneka began to undulate under him. He thrust into her, then smoothly flipped her over and proceeded to pummel her from behind. Meneka grabbed hold of the headboard and held on tight as Ricky pounded her for a tormenting twenty minutes before bringing her to a rapturous climax. She collapsed in a relieved heap when Ricky finally came, withdrawing just in time to ejaculate all over her bare back and buttocks.

As they lay in bed, winded after their exertions, Meneka murmured, 'You're full of surprises, aren't you, Ricky boy? I want me some more of that rough love. What say? Are you up to it?'

'Yeah, I will be. Give me a few minutes?' panted Ricky, elated at having fucked after a long time.

'Awesome. Why don't you take five and I'll be right back.'

Ricky gazed at Meneka's superb body as she slid out of bed, starkers, and glided to the bathroom. He felt another powerful surge between his legs and grinned, gratified that he was ready for round two.

Suddenly a film song started playing in the hotel room. Ricky realized it was his mobile phone, and his heart immediately began to pound. He had programmed this particular caller ringtone for Rhea's number. After all these months of silence, she had decided to call when his loyalty had wavered, after he had had sex with another woman.

Ricky's mind raced to what Babaji had said. 'When the time is right, she will appear just as suddenly as she disappeared.'

The great seer had been right all along, and Ricky felt like a fool for having doubted Babaji's prophetic words. He scrambled off the bed, desperately trying to locate his phone. He rummaged through the pockets of his recently discarded jeans and finally located the handset. He fumbled desperately for the answer button and blurted out excitedly, 'Rhea! Is that really you?'

'Ricky—hi, yes! Are you okay?'

'I'm fine—where the hell have you been? I've been worried sick about you!'

'And I'm worried about you! I just saw on the news you were attacked by a mob in London this afternoon. Are you sure you're all right, Ricky?'

'Trust me, I'm absolutely fine. But why haven't you returned any of my calls?'

'Listen, I know I owe you a huge explanation. There's so much to tell. Can you possibly come to Antwerp to see me?'

'Of course I can. We don't even have a location to film in so I can be out on the first flight tomorrow.'

'Oh, that's great! I'm so relieved you're okay. I'm really looking forward to seeing you, Ricky.'

'Me too! I'll call with my flight details as soon as I have them.'

'Ricky, I have to go now. But we'll speak in the morning, okay?'

'Rhea ...'

'Yes ...?'

'I love you.'

'I ... I love you too, Ricky.'

As Ricky disconnected, he caught sight of Meneka looking down at him. Sitting naked on the carpet of his hotel room, he felt hugely embarrassed.

'Meneka, I'm so sorry—that was my old friend ...'

'Rhea Zaveri. I know who she is,' said Meneka quietly. Although she had been in New York when the incident at Scandal Point occurred, Meneka had followed the gossip about Rhea and Ricky on the Internet.

'Yes, well ... umm ... I've only just heard from her after all these months. She wants to meet me tomorrow. I'm ... I'm extremely sorry to have put you in this position Meneka, but I really love Rhea and ...'

'Don't worry, Ricky, I understand. I can't say I'm not disappointed. But perhaps it's better you got back with her before anything serious developed between us.'

'Thanks for being so understanding, Meneka. You're an amazing woman, and I really hope we can remain friends?'

'Of course we can, Ricky. Now let's get dressed, shall we? Unless you prefer we become friends with benefits?'

Ricky laughed nervously. He was wracked by guilt at having slept with Meneka and was grateful she was being so gracious about this incredibly awkward situation. But Rhea, the love of his life, had finally called, and he was going to Antwerp tomorrow to see her! It had taken an attack by an angry mob to compel Rhea to pick up the phone. Ricky had come to appreciate the fact that the universe sometimes operates in the strangest of ways. It toys with you, tests you, wreaks havoc with your life, but ultimately it is just and fair.

As Meneka put on her clothes, she noticed that Ricky had ripped the buttons off her blouse. She left her co-star's room wearing a borrowed shirt, feeling hurt, angry and humiliated by this unexpected turn of events. But Meneka had seen the look in Ricky's eyes and she knew there was no place for her in the life of the besotted young man.

Zaveri Mansion in Antwerp's fashionable Wilrijk district was a stately residence that had once belonged to Belgian nobility. The Jain merchants who arrived from India and settled here in the 1970s had been shrewd entrepreneurs who succeeded in establishing themselves as dominant players in the diamond trading industry. Along with the Jews, the astute Jains now controlled most of the gem and jewellery trade throughout Europe. And much like the Jews, they remained a close-knit, conservative community that married strictly within their own.

Kantilal Zaveri's parents rued the day they had agreed to send their son to Stanford University in distant, heathen America. Kantilal returned with not only an MBA but also sacrilegious habits like munching on Kentucky Fried Chicken and drinking Bourbon whisky. He now espoused subversive ideas like equality of the sexes and marrying for love. To his family's horror, Kantilal then eloped with Kaamiya, a meat-eating Bollywood actress with an unsavoury reputation. Despite his father's threat to immolate the new daughter-in-law and subsequently himself, Kantilal stood resolute by Kaamiya. The rebel elected to live apart from his orthodox clan and began his own firm of jewellery design and exports that soon flourished internationally.

When Rhea was born, Kantilal promised Kaamiya they would never disallow their beloved daughter from marrying the man of her dreams. Therefore, twenty-six years later, when Rhea declared she had fallen in love with Ricky Kumar, her father was ecstatic. Kanti had known Ricky since he was a baby and had fondly watched the introverted little boy grow into a handsome, intelligent young man.

When Kaamiya objected to the relationship and forbade Rhea from contacting Ricky, Rhea put up a spirited resistance and Zaveri Mansion reverberated for days with high-decibel arguments, imprecations, abuse and wailing from both parties.

Kaamiya, for her part, tried to explain to her strong-willed daughter that marrying a Hindi film hero was the worst thing any young girl could do. They are all egotistical, arrogant, temperamental, disloyal bastards who ruthlessly use and discard women, she ranted.

But Rhea refused to accept that Ricky was anything less than her soul-mate. He was kind, caring, compassionate, loyal and drop-dead gorgeous. He was also a universal object of female desire and Rhea was damned if she was going to lose out on marrying Ricky Kumar because her deranged mother considered him an unsuitable boy.

When Ricky rang the doorbell at Zaveri Mansion, Rhea ran down the ornate marble staircase and through the endless corridor lined with paintings by Flemish masters, to welcome him. The disturbing news of the mob attack had catalysed her into breaking her long silence and calling Ricky. And since her parents were away attending a wedding in India, this was an opportune time to invite the young actor home.

Ricky wrapped Rhea in a tight embrace and they stood interlocked in the doorway for an eternity. When they finally separated, she took him by the hand and led him up the marble stairs. The young actor had stayed at the Zaveris' sumptuous home several times over the years and his pulse began to race when he realized Rhea was leading him to her bedroom. Once inside, Rhea turned to bolt the door and Ricky moved closer, ready to wrap her in his arms again. But Rhea simply took his hand in hers and said, 'Please sit down, Ricky. There is something very important I need to tell you.'

Ricky began to fear the worst. Had he been summoned all the way to Antwerp only to be dumped?

'I'm sorry, but I felt it was vital to tell you in person what I recently discovered and have been keeping a secret these last few months.'

She sounded formal and rehearsed and this worried Ricky further. 'What is it, Rhea—just tell me!'

'Ricky, you should know that, after your arrest, when I fled Mumbai, my mother wanted me to cut off all contact with you.'

'Yes, I guessed as much. But why? Does Aunty Kaamiya really believe I had anything to do with drugs? Didn't you explain to her it was a police frame-up in order to extort money from my dad? For God's sake Rhea, I'm completely innocent!'

'I know that, Ricky. I also know you would never lie to me. Unfortunately, as I discovered, my mother has been lying to me all my life.'

'What do you mean?'

'All this while, she led me to believe that Kantilal Zaveri was my biological father.'

'What are you saying? Uncle Kanti is not your real dad? Then who is?'

'Take a wild guess?' Rhea looked Ricky straight in the eye.

'No, it can't be!' The horrible realization suddenly hit home.

'Yup. It seems that twenty-six years ago your dad and my mum had a fling while filming together. Mum got pregnant and, being unmarried, naturally wanted to abort the baby. But then Kantilal Zaveri came along and proposed to her. She was fed up of working in the film industry and decided to accept his offer. They ran away together, and a few months later I was born—a conveniently premature baby.'

The room was swirling around Ricky, he was glad Rhea had asked him to sit down. 'So ... that means ... you're my half-sister?'

'I'm afraid so, Ricky. And when my mum found out that we had gotten romantically involved in Mumbai, she tried every trick to get me to dump you. When everything else failed, and I insisted on running away to Mumbai to be with you, she was forced to reveal the truth.'

'No way, Rhea—this can't be true! Surely there must be some mistake. Or your mother's lying, to keep us apart!'

'I pretty much accused her of the same thing. But she showed me the paternity test she had done a couple of years ago which proves that I am, without doubt, Kapil Kumar's daughter.'

Ricky began to panic. Jumping up, he frantically began to pace the room as the full implication of what Rhea was saying started to sink into his frazzled mind.

'Oh no, this is so fucked up! Does Uncle Kanti know?'

'Nope—he thinks I'm his flesh and blood. That poor, dear man. We don't have the heart to tell him.'

'And what about my father? Surely he must know you're his daughter.'

'No, not a clue. He believes my mum went through with the abortion and conceived again after marriage.'

Ricky found himself in tears. There could be absolutely no future to their relationship now.

'Tell me this is all a nightmare, Rhea. What are we going to do?'

'There's nothing we can do, Ricky! I love you, but there is no way I will knowingly commit incest. Just the thought of what we did at Scandal Point makes me want to puke. Let's face it—you're my half-brother and that's pretty much that.'

Rhea had exhausted her quota of tears, having already wept for weeks at this aberrant twist of fate. Eventually, she had managed to develop an aura of stoicism, knowing she would have to be strong for the both of them.

'But … but shouldn't we at least tell our parents the truth?'

'And what will that achieve, besides hurting everyone involved? As far as I'm concerned, Kapil Kumar is just some hot-blooded hero who slept with and impregnated my mother. Neither was married at the time, so we can't really blame them. You and I are already victims of this mess, Ricky. Why drag anyone else into it?'

Seeing Rhea deal with the situation with such equanimity, Ricky tried hard to pull himself together.

'I … I agree. Did Aunty Kaamiya forbid you from telling me as well?'

'Yes. She was so embarrassed and ashamed of herself, which is why she wanted to cut off all contact with you and your family. But I knew I owed you an explanation. I've waited a long time to summon up the courage, Ricky. I want you to swear you will always keep this between us.'

Ricky Kumar did not intend to divulge to anyone that the love of his life was his half-sister. The sins of the father had been visited upon the son and he was reeling from shock and anguish at how malevolent the gods could be.

SEVEN

Sir Dharmesh was impressed by the presentation Gautam made in the company boardroom. His feasibility report on Thailand was exceptionally well-researched and left little doubt that undertaking this new venture made perfect business sense. Rani endorsed the project too, and applauded volubly when her brother concluded. Gautam beamed as he accepted congratulations all around and took his seat at the conference table. All eyes were now on Sir Dharmesh, who would pronounce formal acceptance of the proposal.

'Thank you, Gautam. That was a wonderful report. I think we are all in agreement that we must soon open the doors all over Thailand, hai na?'

Everyone nodded vigorously in assent as Sir Dharmesh surveyed the boardroom. 'Now that we are fully in unanimous approval, I would like to make a suggestion.'

The board members looked expectantly at Sir Dharmesh as he paused for dramatic effect. 'I propose that we make Rani bitiya the head of the Thailand project.'

Rani almost toppled off her chair when she heard her father's outrageous suggestion. 'But … but, Papa, this entire project is Gautam's baby … surely he should be put in charge!'

'Yes, Rani, I know that but Gautam is still too fresh and raw to manage such a big task. That is exactly why I want him to stay here only, with me, to gather much more experience. In the meantime, you can easily handle this important project on your own, hai na?'

Sir Dharmesh smiled benignly at Rani, who suddenly realized she had been masterfully manipulated by her father and brother. They had misled Rani into thinking Gautam would be sent away to Thailand if the proposal was approved, and Rani had given it her full support. However, here was an ingenious ploy, devised to banish her from London so the reins of the company could be handed over to the upstart.

Rani was livid at being tricked but knew she had to maintain her composure in the boardroom. 'Okay, Papa, as you wish. Though I must put on record that, in my opinion, Gautam should spearhead this assignment.'

Sir Dharmesh neatly sidestepped her protest and proclaimed, 'Of course, of course. I know you will make me so very proud! My blessings are with you. A big round of applause for hamaari pyaari Rani bitiya!'

Rani could barely fight back the incipient tears as everyone around clapped politely. A sly grin broke out on Gautam's face as he turned and thumped Rani on the back. He had adroitly outmanoeuvred his sister. Sir Dharmesh had been furious when Gautam informed him that it was Rani who had leaked the detective's information to Mukesh Menda in India. Rani, Gautam had complained to his father, had not only publicly humiliated him but also tarnished the Goyal name and reputation in the process.

Even as Rani scowled at Gautam, he exulted in the success of his machinations and looked forward to celebrating his triumph that evening with the eminently shag-worthy Meneka Kansal.

Ricky Kumar returned to London despondent. He had endured a roller-coaster of emotions these past few days and couldn't come to terms with the cruel blow fate had dealt him. In sheer desperation, he contemplated begging Rhea to ignore the fact that they shared a father and to run away and start a new life together, far from Kaamiya's censorious glare. But Rhea was clearly sickened by the thought of being romantically involved with someone she knew was her half-brother. Ricky wondered whether there was any likelihood of his having been adopted. How he wished he had been a foundling, taken in by the kindly Kumars twenty-five years ago, to be raised as their own. Why, oh why, did his randy father feel compelled to fornicate with every woman he met? Why couldn't he keep his raging bulli in his pants?

As these thoughts ricocheted through Ricky's addled mind, he heard his mobile phone ring. Glancing at the caller id, he saw it was a call from Amanda, the English girl he had met at the Suryanamaskar Spa in Goa several months ago. She had been a true friend when he was last plunged in a crisis and had counselled him wisely.

'Mandy, hi! It's good to hear from you.'

'Hiya, Ricky! I read in the papers you're here in London busy sparking off riots. So are you all right or have the coppers bunged your brown bum into jail?'

'Ha ha—I'm fine! How about you?'

'Well, been laid off these past couple of months, me boyfriend dumped me and I'm living on the dole. Other than that, life's just tickety-boo, dear!'

'I'm so sorry to hear that. Listen, I'd love to see you. Are you free to come to dinner this evening? I'm staying at St. James' Hotel.'

'Ooh, how very posh. Sounds lovely. Can't wait to see you, ducky!'

'Likewise. I'll meet you in the lobby bar at eight.'

That evening, as Ricky waited for Amanda to arrive, he caught sight of Meneka in the hotel foyer. She was dressed in a tantalizingly short red dress, killer heels and sported a carefully coiffured, just-out-of-bed look that suggested she was entirely ready to be ravished. Gazing at her, Ricky was seized by a wave of lust. Perhaps a fling with his sexy co-star was exactly what he needed at this juncture. Ricky wanted nothing more than to apologize profusely to this voluptuous woman and whisk her to bed.

As he crossed the lobby to speak with Meneka, Amanda suddenly howled his name and came bounding up to give her old chum a bone-crushing hug. From the corner of his eye, Ricky saw Meneka glance in his direction and smile as the big Brit girl continued to smother him. When Amanda finally detached herself, Ricky tried to excuse himself. Just then, he saw Gautam Goyal walk up behind Meneka, grab her by the waist, spin her around and kiss her full on the lips. Ricky gaped forlornly as Meneka returned the kiss passionately and they exited the hotel, arm-in-arm.

'You all right, love?' Amanda could see Ricky was distraught.

'I'm fine.' Ricky smiled weakly. 'Just feeling completely shafted by the universe.'

'Well then, what are we waiting for? Let's go get piss drunk and you can tell Aunty Mandy all about your woes!'

Sir Dharmesh sat in his gilded dining room in Belgravia, tucking into a nostalgia- and calorie-packed breakfast of mango lassi and aaloo pooris. Twenty identically reproduced Louis XIV chairs flanked either side of a gargantuan, floridly carved table designed to seat forty guests. The patriarch presided at one end, occupying a forty-first chair that was a foot higher than the others, so he could have the pleasure of looking down on his gora guests at the elaborate, formal dinners he regularly hosted.

The old codger was delighted when Meneka walked in with Gautam to join him at breakfast. When the vivacious girl informed him that she would be staying in London for a month, filming *Pardesi Pardesi*, he congratulated her heartily.

'This is wonderful news, beta. You will no doubt become a number one ki heroine soon. God bless.'

'Thank you, uncle.' Meneka smiled.

'By the way, Papa, Meneka's unit set off a full-blown riot while filming at an Indian restaurant in Southall the other day. She asked if we could help with one of our restaurants, but I had to decline,' smirked Gautam, as he stirred the tumbler of protein shake the butler had brought him.

'But why, betaji? We can always work out some mutually benevolent deal with the producers, what's the problem?'

'The problem is that her co-star, Ricky Kumar, is a right tosser, Papa. He's been talking shit about me in Delhi so I don't want him coming anywhere near our restaurants.'

'Arrey betaji, never mix the personal with the professional, always remember that. But, okay—if that is your wish.'

'Don't worry, uncle. I believe our location manager has found another restaurant, so we won't need to trouble you.'

Just then, Rani entered the dining room, and Sir Dharmesh greeted her chirpily. 'Good morning, Rani bitiya! Have you met Meneka? She is originally Gautam's friend, but now she is also my friend, hai na?'

Rani took one look at the exquisite brunette in her brother's pyjamas and vividly recalled meeting Meneka four years ago, in Delhi, at the launch party of Masala Magic. Rani had become rather infatuated with Meneka and prodded Mukesh Menda to introduce them. Mukesh had informed her that though Meneka was heterosexual, she was known to be sexually adventurous and wickedly suggested that she might be game for a little lesbian encounter. Rani had flirted all evening with Meneka, who initially played along but eventually left on the arm of some man she had just met.

Rani remembered something else. Mukesh had sniggered that Meneka was the daughter of the crooked politician Jagjit Kansal, who was legend for sleeping with several prominent Delhi socialites. This implied that Meneka must be the sister of Sheena, the girl Gautam had been rogering in Behramjee's clinic. This was too good to be true!

'Hello, Meneka. It's nice to see you again,' said Rani, sweetly.

'You girls know each other?' Gautam was suddenly on guard.

'Yes, Gautam. We met in Delhi a few years ago. Tell me, how is your sister, Sheena?' Rani wanted to ascertain if her hunch was correct.

Meneka now remembered the besotted dyke who had pestered her all evening at Masala Magic. She had had to pretend to chat up a male friend just so Rani would leave her alone. 'Sheena's fine, thanks,' replied Meneka evenly.

'Such a small world,' said Gautam, extremely uncomfortable that Rani had established the connection between the two sisters.

Rani grinned and decided to go for the jugular. 'So true, Gautam. First you slept with Sheena Kansal, and now you are sleeping with her sister, Meneka Kansal. It really is a small world, isn't it, Papa?'

Sir Dharmesh sputtered into his masala chai. His betaji had shamelessly bedded two sisters in quick succession! What was even more shameful was that Meneka had no problem sleeping with Gautam even though she knew he was her sister's ex-boyfriend. The morality, or rather the lack thereof, of this new generation never ceased to dismay Sir Dharmesh. However, the sage advice he had given his son now sprang to mind. 'Never mix the personal with the professional.'

Masala Magic in Delhi had remained sealed for several months despite Sir Dharmesh's willingness to grease the requisite palms. The cost of keeping this prime piece of real estate fallow for so long had begun to mount, and Sir Dharmesh was thinking of approaching the well-connected Jagjit Kansal for assistance. But since Gautam had already broken up with Sheena, the old restaurateur no longer had a direct conduit to the powerful politico. Perhaps this other daughter had come as a blessing in disguise and could prevail upon her father to help the Goyals reopen their flagship Indian restaurant? Sir Dharmesh quickly regained his composure.

'Yes, yes. You're right. It is a very small world, Rani bitiya. Meneka, did you know that Rani is soon leaving for Thailand to head a very important project for us? She may be gone for more than one year, so meanwhile I will be grooming Gautam to take over our company.'

Gautam, who had been dreading the repercussions when his father discovered Meneka's family name, was relieved by how calmly Sir Dharmesh had taken the matter in his stride.

Meneka, smarting at having been rebuffed by Ricky

Kumar, suddenly developed a new respect for Gautam. If he was going to head the mighty Goyal empire, then Gautam was a far better catch than Ricky, a mere actor whose fortunes depended every opening weekend on the whims and fancies of the cinema-going masses. It was just as well Ricky had gone back to Rhea Zaveri.

Ricky Kumar awoke for the second time in his life with a punishing hangover. The bender he had gone on with Amanda was, perhaps, exactly what he had needed to unburden his heavy heart. But now, his pounding head made him severely regret the excesses of the night before.

The last time around it had been Preeti, his ministering angel, who had plied him with an elixir to help ease the pain. Preeti was, however, back home in India, having wrapped her portion of filming, and Ricky wondered if he had made a huge mistake in not pursuing a relationship with that good-hearted girl. He missed having Manju by his side to counsel and comfort him in this time of despair. But his mother was far away in Rishikesh, meditating at Babaji's ashram.

Meneka had meanwhile found comfort in the arms of his nemesis, and Rhea, his soul mate, was unattainable.

The Kumars had known Rhea for twenty-five years and considered her a family member, little realizing she was Kapil's own daughter. Ricky wondered if that was the reason Kaamiya had kept sending Rhea every year to stay with them in Mumbai—so she could spend time with her real father?

Ricky groped for the phone at his bedside and dialled housekeeping for a couple of Alka Seltzers. He staggered to the bathroom and caught sight of himself in the massive mirror.

Under the harsh fluorescent glare, he looked bloated, unkempt and undesirable. Staring at his reflection, Ricky resolved to forget about all his woman troubles. It was vital to focus on his career, even if it meant putting his love life on hold for the next couple of years.

Suddenly the doorbell shrilled, jangling Ricky's frayed nerves. When he blearily answered the door, instead of a housekeeping maid, he found Amanda.

'Sheesh ... what happened to you, mate? Rough night?' Amanda chortled.

'Mandy, hi. What are you doing here?'

'Don't tell me you've forgotten? We made a lunch date, love.'

'Oh lord—really? What time is it?'

'I've got a quarter to one.'

'I'm so sorry, Mandy. I don't think I've ever slept in this late in my life.'

'Well, that's what comes of drinking till four in the morning, ducky. That was quite a piss-up, eh? I'm impressed. You matched me shot for shot all evening.'

'And yet you're up and about, fresh as a daisy, and I'm feeling shattered.'

'Don't be so hard on yourself, Ricky. I can drink most lads under the table. Now go get showered and take me to lunch. All this talk is making me thirsty,' guffawed Amanda as she thwacked Ricky on the back.

Lathering himself under the rejuvenating steam shower, Ricky felt blessed he had a straight-talking friend like Mandy to stand by him in his hour of need.

But Amanda Hardy was there with an ulterior motive. One that would have enormous ramifications for Ricky and his entire family.

Jagjit Kansal had waited patiently for the phone call from Dharmesh Goyal regarding the reopening of Masala Magic. After all, it was Jagjit who had engineered its shutting down several months ago, and it was he alone who could miraculously ensure that its giant teakwood gates swung open once again. The public interest litigation filed by the urban conservationist was merely a ploy devised to obtain an order of closure from the court. The order could be lifted only if the complaint was revoked. Otherwise the matter would drag on for several years before coming up for hearing.

Ved Kapoor, the litigious conservationist who had Masala Magic shut down was, in fact, an old crony of Jagjit Kansal. He had successfully filed cases against dozens of quasi-legal businesses throughout Delhi only so the crafty politician could extract hefty sums of money from the desperate owners. It was a simple yet lucrative extortion technique, one that Sir Dharmesh had not yet encountered in his many years of running a restaurant chain.

'Of course, Goyal saab, anything I can do to help will be a pleasure. No, no, please do not worry about money at this stage. Let's first get the job done then, we shall see. After all, Gautam and Sheena, and now Mini, are such good friends. I can only try my level best. The rest is up to the Almighty.'

Jagjit hung up and smiled to himself. He had been a little worried when, all this while, Sir Dharmesh had refused to reach out for help. In the interim, that junkie Gautam had callously dumped his older daughter after having stayed under his roof and enjoyed his hospitality for weeks in Delhi. Worse, he had embarrassed Jagjit by dragging Sheena into the eye of a media storm. And now, he had the gall to sleep with his younger daughter in London. Jagjit Kansal was determined to squeeze every rupee he possibly could from Sir Dharmesh before he would allow Masala Magic to reopen.

'I swear I will do double to Dharmesh Goyal what his son has done to both my daughters!' he said to himself.

Kaamiya Zaveri kept close tabs on Rhea to ensure she was not in contact with Ricky Kumar. In his heyday, Kapil Kumar had been a flamboyant, formidable life force and Kaamiya had willingly jumped into bed with him, knowing that she would only ever amount to another fling for her Casanova co-star. Kaamiya's mentor Sultan Habib was already a bent old man when he took her as his mistress and catapulted her to stardom by producing films featuring her in the lead. Feeble Sultan had no real use for Kaamiya except as a trophy to flaunt among his peers. The amorous, virile Kapil was an exciting diversion for the hot-blooded heroine, then in the prime of her youth.

Kaamiya had successfully concealed the true identity of Rhea's father for a quarter century. She felt no real guilt at her subterfuge, since she knew it was in everybody's interest, particularly her own, to keep this fact well hidden. She had never imagined her daughter would one day become sexually attracted to her half-brother. But when she discovered the truth, the only recourse was to tell Rhea the truth. Born wealthy, Rhea had grown up with the luxury of being able to afford a sense of morality, unlike her impoverished mother, who had tenaciously traversed the path to success the only way she knew how: on her back.

Kaamiya was fearful that after the drug scandal, her daughter would have to settle for some less-than-desirable suitor. Her billionaire husband, a man of foolish principles, was adamant he would not pay one naya paisa in dowry to prospective in-laws, maintaining that Rhea herself was the greatest treasure he could give away.

Kantilal Zaveri was acutely aware Rhea had not sprung from his loins. Having discovered at an early age that he was sterile, Kanti was thrilled when his blushing bride claimed to have been impregnated by him a few months after marriage. The wealthy jeweller had resolved that Rhea would be raised as his own and found no reason to tell his wife he was on to her lie. After all, as Kanti had learnt from the worldly Kaamiya, sometimes a little discretion is far more prudent than full disclosure.

Contrary to all expectations, filming on *Pardesi Pardesi* proceeded without any further hitches and the unit wrapped in London barely a week later than originally scheduled. Kapil Kumar was both ecstatic and amazed he had managed to bring in his maiden venture only slightly over budget. As is customary at the end of every film, a wrap party was to be hosted by the producer, to give the cast and crew a chance to let their hair down after months of hard work.

Shivani Mehta, publicist par excellence, planned a lavish celebration in London to announce the successful completion of the film. The guests included local dignitaries besides the who's who of the Brit-Asian community. A posse of the Indian film press was being especially flown in, and a sizeable number of the local media was also invited to cover the mega Bollywood bash.

'Shivani baby, the food will be totally Indian, the champagne French and the whisky Scotch, ya!' proclaimed Kapil Kumar, feeling magnanimous after having acquitted himself so admirably.

Manju Kumar also arrived from Mumbai to join in the festivities, bringing with her Preeti Bhasin. Now that filming had been completed, Manju hoped Ricky would start showing some romantic interest in his stunning co-star. Shivani had already fed the Indian media several spicy stories of their alleged romance, and it was in everybody's interest that the on-screen duo actually become an item.

Meneka was determined to make a grand entry at the wrap party on Gautam's arm, knowing it would garner widespread attention and announce to the world they were officially an item. She also felt enough time had passed to let Sheena finally know her former boyfriend was the new man in her life.

A few months ago, whilst studying in New York, Meneka had become rather envious when her sister gloated that she had snagged Gautam Goyal, one of the world's most eligible bachelors. She had initially been put off by Gautam's bad boy, druggie reputation and had only slept with the notorious playboy to best Sheena. Gradually, though, she had found herself genuinely drawn to the charismatic, arrogant billionaire who happened to be extraordinarily gifted in the sack. Meneka had one month in London to get Gautam to fall in love with her and assiduously devoted herself to the task. She had spent every moment of her spare time with the Goyal scion, staying most nights at his Belgravia residence and reporting the next morning on location directly from there.

The upscale nightclub Pascha was the venue selected by Shivani for the wrap party and the entire place was had been redone to resemble an Indian village, replete with brightly coloured buntings, earthen pots, a bullock cart and waiters dressed in shiny silk kurtas of different hues. Bollywood was putting its best foot forward, and the Londoners lapped it up with gusto.

A boisterous Bhangra band got everyone in the mood and Preeti and Ricky were dragged onto the dance floor to shake a leg to one of the energetic tracks from their film. Seeing the vivacious couple boogie to the throbbing beat, the invitees began to clap and whistle, encouraging the duo to twist and twirl with greater abandon.

Kapil Kumar grabbed Manju and began to energetically wiggle around her, much to the delight of the crowd. Present as Ricky's guest, Amanda too was in her element as she started a Bollywood conga line that began to balle-balle and feistily serpentine around the nightclub.

As the jubilant evening wore on, Meneka tried repeatedly to get Gautam to dance with her, but he refused to join in the celebrations. He was already in a bad mood, having been emotionally blackmailed into attending the party, and kept glowering as Ricky Kumar basked in the limelight, the undisputed star of the evening.

Gautam knocked back another whisky as a new track began to boom on the mega-watt music system. It was the steamy, sexy cabaret number that marked Meneka's entry in the film and suddenly all eyes were on her. Meneka knew this was her opportunity to shine.

She shimmied seductively onto centre stage, and the crowd cleared. Meneka oozed oomph as she slinked and slithered to the suggestively choreographed number and snaked her way to where Ricky was standing. The assembled guests roared in approval as she sensuously gyrated before her handsome co-star who began to blush as she swayed dangerously close to his crotch. Meneka grabbed Ricky by the collar and led him to the dance floor where she continued her orgasmic dance of seduction.

Considerably inebriated by now, Gautam watched his girlfriend shamelessly throw herself at the Bolly brat he had grown to despise. Furious at having to endure such public humiliation, he staggered onto the dance floor, intending to drag Meneka out of the nightclub. He yanked the gyrating actress's hand, but she resisted, reluctant to leave when she was the cynosure of the crowd. It became apparent to all present that Gautam was getting belligerent as Meneka struggled to free herself from her drunken boyfriend.

When Ricky protested Gautam's manhandling of Meneka, the seething Goyal scion spun around and viciously punched him in the face. Even as the guests gaped in consternation, Ricky recovered from the blow and charged, letting out a volley of expletives.

The rage Ricky Kumar had bottled up for years against Gautam Goyal came bursting forth in an unstoppable torrent. He toppled Gautam to the ground and started raining blows on him with all his might. Gautam was not only drunk but also overwhelmed by the power Ricky packed in his fists. Unable to defend himself, Gautam almost passed out as the furious actor pummelled him in full view of the assembled media.

Amanda and Kapil tried to hoist Ricky off the profusely bleeding restaurateur, but it took four bouncers to finally restrain him. Meneka was aghast and rushed to tend to Gautam, screaming for an ambulance. Preeti and Manju were in tears, horrified by the turn of events.

The only person from the unit who was thrilled at the way the evening had ended was Shivani Mehta. This public fracas would be worth millions in free publicity. The tabloids in India and England could have a field day publishing juicy stories about the fierce rivalry between the two hunks who had literally come to blows over Meneka Kansal—the ultimate Bollywood femme fatale.

Sir Dharmesh was livid his son had been brutally assaulted by some Bollywood hero and wanted to file criminal charges against Ricky Kumar. However, numerous camera crews had filmed the incident, which established that Gautam had initiated the brawl by punching Ricky in the face. The media leapt to the young actor's defence and painted him as a hero for standing up to the obnoxious, whisky-addled Goyal scion.

Gautam had already informed Sir Dharmesh that Ricky had been fabricating tales about seeing him snort drugs in Delhi. The anxious father was keen the actor did no further damage to his son's already tarnished reputation. Through Meneka, Sir Dharmesh sent word to Kapil Kumar that both families should call a truce, and neither should initiate legal action against the other.

Meneka sat by Gautam's bed, gazing at her lover as he slept, sedated after being discharged from hospital. Ricky had not only battered Gautam's face and chest but also gashed his eyebrow, which had required several stitches. She was afraid that Gautam would be furious with her for refusing to leave the party early. She knew he had been festering all evening, but she had been determined to enjoy her moment in the spotlight. The ambitious girl had eventually got more than she bargained for and was being sullied in the media as a scheming temptress who had two-timed Gautam Goyal with Ricky Kumar. Hankering for fame, Meneka had instead acquired tabloid notoriety overnight and didn't quite know whether this newfound publicity would help or harm her.

As he recuperated at home, Gautam cursed himself for letting his jealousy get the better of him. He considered himself an emancipated chap but he wondered if his overdeveloped ego could tolerate seeing his girlfriend continue to romp on and off screen with other men.

Meneka had got under his skin like no other girl, and he had begun to care for her deeply. But Gautam wasn't sure he could allow himself to be attached to someone who could hurt him so deeply. Emotional vulnerability was not a virtue in his eyes and he was loath to accept he was fast falling in love. So he told Meneka it was imperative that she go home to allow them both some space.

Meneka was devastated. But her pride would not allow her to beg. Also, she believed she now knew the truth about Gautam Goyal: that he was an intensely damaged man incapable of loving anyone but himself.

EIGHT

Mid-June, the monsoon hit Mumbai with potent fury and washed clean the city that never sweeps. A year's worth of accumulated garbage, grime, mulch and muck ran in greasy rivulets down the nullahs and bystreets and inveigled its way into the city drains. Ever so slowly, the sludge oozed towards the Arabian Sea and disgorged itself into the water. It was little wonder that Mumbaikars abstained from seafood during the rainy season, when the filth of the city provided fodder for the fish that inhabited its coastline.

The lashing rain, marshalled by powerful gusts, vanquished the feeble, futile resistance offered by waterproofing defences. Nothing in Mumbai, it seemed, was impermeable; the water invaded homes through roofs, terraces, windows, walls, cracks and crevices. The great irony of living in a city like Mumbai was that the poor pined for water in their homes for eight months of the year and suffered a surfeit the remaining four.

Waman Dixit, clad only in striped underwear, cursed the rain gods as he splashed about, valiantly bailing the water that flooded his one-room tenement in Dadar's Manjrekar Chawl. His wife and three daughters had gone on a pilgrimage to Shirdi over the weekend, and Waman had been looking forward to a little quiet time when he could finally watch, undisturbed, the pirated porno DVD he had bought outside Chinchpokli railway station. But each year, during high tide, the city sewers choked, unable to drain the relentless downpour. The water levels then rose and engulfed the metropolis, bringing trains, traffic and all semblance of normal urban life to a squelching halt. Waman's modest abode, located in a low-lying area, was annually submerged. Plastic bucket in hand, the hapless fellow waged a battle to keep the water level from rising to the point where it would swamp the 42 inch LED TV he had proudly purchased from the settlement amount received in lieu of his broken nose.

The Kumars returned from London in early July to discover their Pali Hill bungalow had sprung several leaks. The damp had seeped through the walls and desecrated the ersatz Michelangelo fresco that stretched across the palatial living room. Large bubbles had appeared on the figures of both Adam and God, who seemed covered in unholy blisters as they reached out to each other in that sublime moment of mortal creation. Restoration was pointless until the monsoon receded, so the Kumars were forced to live with the sight of this maculated mural till October. Mercifully, Kapil's den had escaped the ravages of the rain and the ageing hero retreated to his velvet-shrouded sanctuary to commence post-production work on his film.

In August, Kapil summoned Shivani Mehta for an important meeting. Ricky was also asked to be present. Kapil continued to gloat about how admirably his son had stood up to that drunken lout in London.

'Well done, Ricky boy! Arrey, what a terrific thrashing you gave that Goyal bugger! I don't think he will ever forget what happens when you try and mess with the Kumars, ya?'

'Thanks, Papa. I'm not proud of what I did, but he really

had no business manhandling Meneka like that,' said Ricky, modestly.

'Arrey, he punched you in the face and you gave it back to him, good and proper. That's what being a man is all about! Isn't that right, Shivani baby?'

The marketing whiz nodded. 'Absolutely, Kapilji. Ricky, in the eyes of the world, you are a hero. Plus, you were standing up for a woman's honour, so that makes you a true knight in shining armour to your female fans.'

Ricky blushed. He had been trying to play down his infamous showdown with Gautam but felt exhilarated at finally having been able to avenge himself.

'So, Shivani baby, I have asked you here today because I have had another amazing marketing brainwave!'

Shivani froze. She dreaded these meetings at Casa Kumar where Kapil came up with bizarre ideas and suggestions.

'I'm thinking there is no point in simply remaking a carbon copy of *Pardesi Pardesi*. We must give today's modern audience something new. A minty fresh twist in the tale—so they are completely entertained in the theatres and get total paisa vasool!'

'I see. So what is it that you propose, Kapilji?'

'I propose to change the climax of the film, Shivani baby!'

'And what change, precisely, do you suggest, Kapilji?'

'I suggest that instead of Sonia dying at the end, it is Gauri who should get killed by the villain!'

Both Shivani and Ricky wailed in protest at this exceptionally ludicrous suggestion. Kapil was obviously suffering another bout of lunacy.

'Papa, how can you kill off the heroine of our film? The audience will never accept that!'

'Ricky's right, Kapilji. Why do you want to tamper with the ending? The shooting has been successfully completed, now let's just finish the post-production and quickly release the movie to cash in on all the hype we have generated.'

'Shivani baby—don't you get it? That is exactly what I am doing! I want to milk the fact that our Ricky boy has become a hero to Meneka in real life by beating up her villain of a boyfriend.'

'Yes, Kapilji, but what does that have to with the climax of your film?'

'Arrey, the public is now expecting to see Meneka and Ricky together in real life and also in reel life. So, if we show in our film that Meneka dies in the end, the fans will get very upset! It is much better to show that Preeti, I mean Gauri, died by sacrificing her life for Bhola and her last wish is that he must marry Sonia and live happily ever after!'

Kapil's perverse line of reasoning made sense in the light of recent events but Shivani was not convinced that radically changing the film's climax was such a bright idea.

'I hear you, Kapilji, and you make an interesting point. But I would prefer to do a focus group test to determine how audiences will react to the heroine dying at the end.'

'Screw your hocus-focus group, Shivani baby! Nobody on earth can predict how an audience will react. Otherwise, every single film would be a super-duper hit at the box-office! In film-making you have to go only by your gut instinct. You have to feel the pulse of the public in your balls!' declared Kapil.

Ricky decided it was time to speak up. 'Papa, this is such a drastic step. The times may have changed, but even today's modern audience is ultimately looking for moral order in the universe. Why should an innocent be punished for no fault of her own? Good must eventually triumph over evil, otherwise only anarchy will prevail and then …'

'Ricky boy, have you totally lost your marbles? Why are you jabbering all this bullshit philosophy funda to me?' thundered Kapil. 'This is a fucking Hindi movie, and I am the motherfucking king of Bollywood! I know exactly what my audience wants, and maa kasam, I will give it to them—otherwise my name is not Kapil "Platinum Jubilee" Kumar, ya?'

Preeti Bhasin was disappointed when she was informed that her character was being bumped off in the end. Nevertheless, the sweet-tempered girl sportingly acquiesced to her director's demand that she die in a hail of bullets instead of Meneka. The debutante actress delivered an emotional speech as she lay gasping in a pool of fake blood. She teared up as she extracted a promise from Bhola that he would marry Sonia and name their daughter Gauri in memory of one who had loved him truly. It was an excruciatingly melodramatic scene, but Preeti brought a level of sincerity and pathos to her performance that had even Kapil bawling copiously.

In London, Sir Dharmesh summoned Gautam to announce that Jagjit Kansal had finally made good his promise. The authorities had lifted the order against Masala Magic, and the relieved restaurateur wanted his son to oversee its grand reopening in Delhi.

'Apna manager Nazareth says the competition has become very great these last six months, betaji. I think so those Walia fellows must have definitely used their influence to shut down our place. Their Pink Parsley is doing zabardast business, and two other restaurants have also recently opened up. You must throw a shaandaar party and invite all the who-the-who of Delhi to show everyone we are back with a bang!'

'Don't worry, Papa. We'll give Delhi an evening they'll never forget!'

After months of working at the head office, Gautam was itching to prove himself in the field. He also looked forward to seeing Meneka, whom he had brusquely expelled from Belgravia six weeks ago. Gautam knew he had left the girl in limbo and owed her an answer, either way, regarding the future of their relationship.

Meneka didn't quite know what to expect when Gautam called to say he would be arriving soon to spend a fortnight in Delhi. Her implicit faith in her ability to get men to dance to her tune had been jolted. She was plagued by a morbid fear that the infamous playboy had had his fill of her and moved on to his next conquest.

When they finally met at the Imperial Hotel near Connaught Place, where Gautam was staying, Meneka was affable but restrained. She was glad his injuries had healed; even the gash above his eye had barely left a scar. She listened politely as Gautam bragged about the grand reopening party and how he intended to floor all of Delhi society with his panache.

'Well—here's to us, babe!'

Meneka smiled sardonically. 'Is there really going to be an us, Gautam? As far as I can see, there's only you in this relationship. You arbitrarily sent me away from London and now you're here only because it suits you. In two weeks you'll be gone again, and I will be back exactly where I started.'

Gautam looked at her guiltily. 'Look, I know I behaved poorly but please, trust me—this separation has done me a world of good, babe. I don't want us to spend any more time apart.'

Hope suddenly sprang in Meneka's heart. 'And it took you six weeks to come to this conclusion?'

'Yes. But now I know you're definitely the woman for me.'

'Well, I'm not so sure you're right for me, Gautam.' Meneka tried hard to play it cool.

'Listen to me, Meneka Kansal. I fell for you because you're a no-nonsense straight talker with fantastic knockers to boot. I want us to get hitched and spend the rest of our lives shagging our brains out. What do you say?'

'Wow, Gautam Goyal—did you just propose to me?'

'I suppose I did.'

'You're one fucked up son-of-a-bitch, you know that?'

'So, is that a yes?'

Meneka grinned and pushed Gautam, toppling him onto the bed. She flopped on top and tenderly kissed him, whispering, 'You seriously want to make an honest woman of me?'

'Of course, babe. What sort of man do you think I am?'

'Oh, I think you're a total shit. But I'll marry you anyway!'

Babaji was a humanist who worked with missionary zeal to pursue secular ideals. Recently, the savant had drawn up an ambitious plan, dubbed Project Pavitra, to build a multitude of toilets across India so its poorer citizens could defecate with dignity in the privacy of a covered lavatory. Millions of villagers, even inhabitants of small towns and cities, performed their daily ablutions in the open, at the edge of rivers, lakes and ponds. This caused the proliferation of a number of waterborne diseases and also resulted in widespread water pollution. The womenfolk suffered the most as they were forced to evacuate their bowels either before dawn or under cover of night so they could shield their modesty from the gaze of passersby. The need of the hour, Babaji declared, was to build hygienic, low-cost toilets and septic tanks that could effectively process the tonnes of human excreta generated every day. Successive governments had failed to provide such basic infrastructure to the people, and it fell to private organizations to take up the slack.

Over the past one hundred years, the wealthy and pious Zaveri clan had built many temples and hostels for Jain pilgrims across India. About a decade ago, through the good offices of Manju Kumar, Kantilal had come into contact with the dynamic spiritualist from Rishikesh who preached that charity should not discriminate between religions. The Antwerp-based billionaire was impressed by Babaji's teachings and became one of his chief disciples and fundraisers, helping to facilitate the building of schools, hospitals and orphanages that cared for all denominations of society.

Kanti pledged financial support for Babaji's Project Pavitra, promising also to canvas donations from other NRI philanthropists to help realize this noble objective. He also encouraged his daughter to get involved with the mission, aware that she required a distraction to get her mind off Ricky Kumar.

'You know, Rhea, it's so sad that in India, while we worship our sacred rivers as mothers—calling them Ma Ganga and Ma Narmada—we don't think twice about bathing and washing and urinating in them. Apart from building toilets, I feel we must also create a national public awareness campaign to curb water pollution. Why don't you take up the responsibility of creating such a media drive? After all, you have a major in marketing and this will give you a chance to do some community service and also better understand our great and complex country.'

Rhea was elated her father wanted to entrust her with such a challenging task. She craved an opportunity to do something meaningful with her life and expensively acquired degree. Besides, she was tired of Kaamiya's constant imprecations to meet with eligible suitors and grateful for the opportunity to get away. For she had resolved never to fall into the trap of marrying a man in order to get over another.

In the ten years he had been divorced, Jagjit Kansal had little occasion to climb the flight of steps at his Golf Links bungalow to the floor above where his ex-wife Nina and daughters resided. Meneka had, however, requested a family conference to discuss Gautam's proposal and Jagjit felt it pertinent to honour his paternal duty.

'How very ironic,' the politico thought to himself. 'I wanted to engineer an alliance between Sheena and Gautam but that rascal broke one daughter's heart and has now asked for the other's hand in marriage.'

Nina Kansal, attired in a cleavage-flaunting blue spandex ensemble, looked particularly unfortunate that evening, even by her own abysmally low standards. Fate, it seems, had finally favoured Nina. She had recently met with an elderly widower, Mayank Thawani, whose enterprising forefathers had migrated to Kenya a century ago and prospered immensely there. Mayank practically owned half of Mombasa and could sire no heirs, an unfortunate result of a hunting accident in the Serengeti. A single old man in possession of a large fortune, he was precisely the sort of candidate Nina had been hoping to snare all these years. She was keen to marry the aged billionaire and move away from Delhi as quickly as possible before some other gold-digging skank got her talons into him.

Sheena sat beside her mother and stared sullenly at Meneka, who looked annoyingly radiant and flushed with joy. Barely recovered from her despondency, Sheena had been shattered to learn through the tabloids that her sister was having an affair with her ex-boyfriend. Recently, the embittered young woman had started using art as a medium to articulate her angst. Her pain had found poignant expression on canvas and she had produced several moving self-portraits that reflected her inner turmoil—it helped that she depicted herself in the nude. Her collection of powerful, provocative paintings had begun to attract many an amateur enthusiast besides serious afficionados of art.

'Thank you all for being here for me,' beamed Meneka. 'Gautam wants to host our engagement bash at Masala Magic, which is going to reopen in two weeks because Dad used his incredible clout. Yay, Dad!'

Jagjit bowed, acknowledging his part in the Masala Magic imbroglio. He had intended to extract a hefty sum from Sir Dharmesh for the favour but he could hardly expect to demand money from his daughter's prospective father-in-law. Instead, a substantial part of his ill-gotten gains would probably have to be given as a dowry. He wondered what figure the Goyals would expect for taking one girl off his hands for good.

'So, Gautam is planning to combine your engagement with his restaurant opening and have one big party, is that it? Clever boy—two birds with one stone!' Jagjit marvelled at how shrewdly his future son-in-law intended to create a buzz around Masala Magic, knowing full well that all of Delhi's elite would make it a point to attend the engagement bash of the daughter of such an influential politician.

'Yes, Dad—isn't it a great idea? And then we will fly to London and have another engagement party there, which obviously you all have to attend. You too, Sheena.'

Sheena was damned if she was going to attend a function where everyone would snigger at her for having lost Gautam to the beauteous Meneka. She yearned to confront Mini and demand an apology for the humiliation and hurt she had caused. But she didn't have the will or the courage to stand up to her unscrupulous sister and so she nodded noncommittally.

Meneka continued to prattle. 'Great! Now, the dress code is strictly formal. So, Dad, black tie or bandhgala for you and Mum, please control the urge to wear one of your usual tacky outfits and cover up in a sari, okay?'

'Don't you dare try and tell me how to dress! I will wear exactly what I like,' snapped Nina. Mother and daughters regularly squabbled on matters sartorial.

'Just don't embarrass yourself or any of us, Mum. Like it or not, you're the mother of the bride. So you may as well look the part and conduct yourself with some dignity for a change.'

'Shut up, Mini, or I'll give you one tight slap!' Nina was fearful her Mombasa-based beau would be less inclined to marry her when he discovered she had a grown-up daughter who was getting engaged. 'And why do you want to get married, anyway? Your career in Hindi movies will be finished even before it has begun.'

'I don't enjoy playing second fiddle in films, Mum. It's much better to walk off into the sunset with a real-life billionaire than some fake filmi hero,' Meneka retorted. The decision to quit acting had been taken quickly and without regret now that Gautam had promised to keep her in luxury for the rest of her life.

Jagjit approved wholeheartedly. 'It's a very sensible decision darling. Much better to secure yourself financially from an early age. Later on, who knows what kind of husband you will get? Only a divorcee or some dirty old letch. And very often, a combination of the two.'

Meneka smirked as she looked around. She had a crooked politician for a father, a painted tart of a mother and a deluded druggie older sister. Meneka Kansal was glad she would soon escape the clutches of her dysfunctional family and live the jet-setting highlife she had always envisioned for herself.

'Shivani baby, I have some horrible news! That bloody Kansal girl is getting engaged to that Goyal bugger even before our film's release! Now, how can I possibly show Ricky marrying Meneka in my climax?'

The spin-doctor was amazed by this new development. Obviously, the opportunistic Meneka had decided to jump at the offer to marry the heir to the Goyal fortune and no longer gave a hoot about her film career. This meant the marketing and publicity strategy for *Pardesi Pardesi* would once again have to be re-tooled. Being a consummate professional, Shivani managed to keep her calm.

'Don't worry, Kapilji. Under the circumstances, it's probably wiser to stick with the original ending. We can project Preeti and Ricky as a golden couple and hope the public will forget about the Meneka fiasco.'

'Arrey, but how do you expect me to forget that I have pumped over a crore of rupees into this fucking re-shoot?'

'Just be grateful you got away cheap, Kapilji. Trust me, it's probably for the best. These sorts of unconventional endings never go down well with Indian audiences.'

'I suppose you're right. But that girl has no bloody business getting engaged to the same fellow that Ricky bashed up. It's totally unethical behaviour, ya?'

'Totally unethical, Kapilji.' Shivani nodded, relieved

the bizarre climax had been scuttled thanks to Meneka's impending nuptials.

Sir Dharmesh vehemently opposed the idea of Gautam marrying Meneka Kansal. The Goyal patriarch, with his overdeveloped sense of nostalgia for the motherland, longed for a traditional, demure daughter-in-law who would press his feet and bear him many grandsons. Meneka was too free-spirited for Sir Dharmesh's liking, but his son was adamant that this girl was his soul-mate. Afraid the hot headed Gautam would rebel if he put his foot down too firmly, Sir Dharmesh finally agreed to the match on condition that Meneka gave up her career as a film actress. No Goyal bahu could ever be seen cavorting on screen wearing skimpy clothes and romancing filmi heroes, he prescribed. Of course, Gautam too wanted Meneka to quit acting and he was elated when she readily acceded to his demand.

After the stupendous success of the Masala Magic party in Delhi, Sir Dharmesh hosted another lavish engagement bash back home in honour of the happy couple, inviting the 'who-the-who' of London society.

Meneka was familiar to readers of various scandal sheets as the sexy starlet over whom Ricky Kumar and Gautam Goyal had publicly come to blows. Her engagement to the notorious playboy, who also happened to be her sister's ex-boyfriend, made for deliciously scurrilous reading and ensured masses of press coverage. Gautam was unfazed by the gossip and even Sir Dharmesh somehow managed to retain his composure. The media frenzy surrounding his family ensured Masala Magic was constantly in the news, and the pragmatic restaurateur concluded there really was no such thing as bad publicity.

Sir Dharmesh regretted that Rani had not made it to either celebration. She had requested to be excused from attending her brother's engagement, as she was inordinately busy setting up six restaurants across Thailand. Although Rani had been away from home for several months, she had diligently sent in weekly progress reports to reassure her father that things were on track and all deadlines were being met.

Gautam was determined to make every effort to ensure his betrothal to Meneka was hailed as the wedding of the century. Several Indian billionaires based in the UK and US had shot to international prominence overnight thanks to the massive public and media interest in their mega-nuptials. Gautam convinced his father that the publicity and goodwill they would generate from hosting a grand wedding would yield rich dividends.

'Why don't we hold your wedding at Versailles, betaji?' the patriarch suggested. Sir Dharmesh had become fascinated with the court of Louis XIV ever since his interior designer had famously titivated his Belgravia residence to resemble the Sun King's ornate palace.

'Uncle Lakshmi has already beaten you to that, Papa. Let's think of a fresh location.'

'Then, what about somewhere in Rajasthan? After all, that is the land of your glorious four fathers,' said Sir Dharmesh, holding up his fingers to indicate the number of generations of Goyal traders who had plied camel caravans across Rajputana.

'Oh, please! Every second B-lister is getting married in Jaipur, Jodhpur or Udaipur. No, we need a virgin venue, Papa.'

The Goyal scion summarily rejected Goa, Thailand, Bali and Las Vegas when Meneka piped up, 'Hey—how about the

Maldives? I haven't heard of any wedding that's been hosted there on a really lavish scale.'

Gautam was enthralled by his fiancée's suggestion. 'That's a great idea, babe! They say it's sinking and will soon disappear into the ocean. So let's do it while we can—let's get married in the Maldives!'

The Goyals engaged the services of London's foremost event planners to orchestrate a wedding of enormous magnitude in the tiny island nation. Guests would be flown in from all over the world on charter jets and accommodated in various premium hotels that had sprung up in the middle of the Indian Ocean. International chefs, decorators and entertainers would be contracted to work their magic to ensure that it became a truly memorable extravaganza. Strategies were drawn up to sell exclusive documentary and photo rights to the highest media bidder. Bollywood stars would be compensated handsomely for attending and dancing at the various wedding functions, pretending, of course, to be close friends of the family.

Meneka and Gautam flew to the Maldives to vet the venues shortlisted by the wedding planners. The picture-perfect archipelago with its sapphire skies, placid cerulean waters, pristine soft sand beaches and luxurious retreats seemed an ideal locale where they could exchange intimate wedding vows with a thousand hand picked guests in attendance. Incredibly, everything on these emerald isles was imported from elsewhere: the thatched cottages from Bali and the flowering plants from Thailand; even the spotless white sand was from neighbouring countries like India and Bangladesh. The Maldives faced the threat of being inundated if the sea level rose by so much as a metre and its hapless citizens were constantly in danger of becoming climate refugees.

Unperturbed by these upheavals, Meneka and Gautam made themselves into a poster couple for Maldives tourism as they sunned on the beach, flaunted their buff bodies in designer swimwear and snorkelled in tranquil waters that teemed with a fascinating array of tropical fish. At night, they dined on Kobe steaks flown in fresh from Japan, and toasted their impending union over a bottle of Cristal in the privacy of their exclusive water villa. This secluded suite, built on stilts in the resort's azure lagoon, was a honeymooner's delight, affording the lovers the liberty of taking a midnight skinny-dip in temperate waters that sparkled in the silver moonlight. With options to windsurf, parasail, jet-ski, scuba dive, golf, play tennis or simply lounge in a shaded cabana and contemplate the turning of the earth, it wasn't difficult to comprehend why tourists flew in from around the world and paid astronomical tariffs for the privilege of being transported to a state of ataraxia.

One morning, Gautam woke in the early hours to the sound of retching emanating from the bathroom. He rushed to find Meneka doubled over the sink, vomiting violently. He immediately called for the hotel doctor, who administered an anti-nausea shot and prescribed a series of tests.

Once her queasiness had subsided, Meneka curled up in bed and moaned, 'Oh man, I really hope I'm not pregnant!'

Gautam froze. He had stopped wearing protection because Meneka had assured him that she was taking care of it. The Goyal scion was ambivalent about the idea of siring a child. He knew what a problematic son he had been and feared a similar fate awaited him as a parent. Also, if Meneka were pregnant, she would either have a significant baby bump or already have delivered at the time of the grand wedding in the Maldives. Either scenario would be unacceptable to Sir Dharmesh, who would undoubtedly rather die than allow such shame to attach to the family name.

Seeing her fiancé's face blanch, Meneka managed a weak laugh. 'Relax, Gautam, I was only joking. It's probably a case of food poisoning.'

The couple flew from Male to Delhi to spend a couple of days discussing the details of the wedding with Jagjit Kansal who, as father of the bride, was expected to contribute substantially towards funding this lavish jamboree. The astute politico was hoping the strategic alliance with the Goyals would catapult him to an altogether different stratum of power brokering and expected eventually to double his investment through garnering key international contacts.

Meneka was keen they stay at her Golf Links residence, but Gautam was anxious to avoid bumping into Sheena. She had chosen not to attend either the Delhi or London engagement party, and Gautam was grateful an awkward situation had thereby been avoided.

The day after she arrived in Delhi, Meneka went to visit her gynaecologist in Chanakyapuri. Dr Khaitan was a sprightly sixty-two-year-old who had helped deliver both Sheena and Meneka at her eponymous maternity home. Having concluded her examination, the beaming sexagenarian congratulated Meneka and said she looked forward to bringing the next generation of Kansal babies into the world before finally hanging up her well-worn stirrups. Meneka was stupefied and tried hard to conceal her dismay at this unexpected development. She certainly did not want this child and knew that Gautam didn't either.

That evening, back at their suite in the Imperial Hotel, Meneka gently broke the news to her fiancé.

'I'm so sorry, Gautam. I really don't know how this could have happened. But, don't worry, I'm going to take care of it. If it's okay with you, I'd prefer to have the MTP done in London.

Delhi is too damn incestuous and someone is bound to find out and spread the word.'

'Of course, babe. Don't stress. I'll handle everything back home,' said Gautam, relieved that Meneka was as keen as he was to drop the baby. It wasn't the first time he had knocked up a girl and he knew a private clinic in Hounslow where they could carry out the procedure discreetly. It had taken all of Gautam's powers of persuasion to get his father's consent, and nothing, particularly not an unwanted pregnancy, could be allowed to jeopardize this precious union.

Rhea Zaveri spent an exhilarating month journeying across India. Basing herself in Delhi, she travelled to pilgrimage sites like Haridwar and Rishikesh, to the cascading Cauvery and the meandering Krishna, to timeless Varanasi and bustling Indore, researching and collating information on the various causes of water pollution. The majesty of the Gangotri glacier, where the eternal Ganga originated, mesmerized her. And in Amarkantak, in the heart of central India, she visited the legendary kund from where the Narmada, wilful maiden daughter of Lord Shiva, reportedly sprang.

Rhea was dismayed to see that both pilgrims and pandits polluted these water bodies every day by floating thousands of toxic aluminium diyas in them, ironically as an offering of salutation.

She also observed that the poor, who could not afford the high cost of cremating their dead, often immersed charred corpses into India's sacred rivers, hoping that the consecrated waters would purify the deceased and ferry their souls to salvation. Defecating, laundering and bathing by the riverbanks significantly exacerbated the problem and it was alarming how poisoned these once pristine rivers had become due to the human and chemical waste that was daily dumped into them. Through her travels, Rhea understood that there were no easy answers to these vastly complex issues and felt awed by the task her father had entrusted to her. She worked out that rather than create one nationwide public awareness communication, as she had originally planned, it was better to produce a series of smaller territory-specific campaigns where local celebrities could each make an appeal to the people of their region to refrain from contaminating their water sources. Aware that cricket and cinema were the two primary obsessions in India, she sought to rope in cricketers and film stars to endorse her drive.

Ricky Kumar was in the midst of a photo shoot for a leading fashion magazine, part of Shivani's publicity initiative for the impending release of *Pardesi Pardesi*, when he received a phone call that made his heart flutter. Rhea had been incommunicado after their fateful meeting in Antwerp and Ricky had often contemplated calling her, but he had restrained himself.

When Rhea explained that she required his assistance with roping in celebrities to endorse her campaign, Ricky immediately agreed. He also suggested that she engage the services of a media professional who could help guide her in the project and offered to introduce her to his friend Tarun Roy, who ran a mid-sized advertising agency in Delhi.

Rhea had deliberated calling Ricky at all, questioning the wisdom of resuming contact with the man she had such strong feelings for. However, after the initial awkwardness melted away, it seemed she was talking to an old friend, one who remained sincere, helpful and good-hearted as ever.

Upon his return to London, Gautam learnt from Sir Dharmesh that Rani would be arriving the next day. The biannual board meeting of Masala Magic was scheduled in a week's time, and Rani obviously wanted to assert her presence at company headquarters. Gautam wondered if his sister still harboured old grudges or whether time had mellowed her.

The next morning, Gautam sat with Sir Dharmesh in his office going over the wedding expenses. Halfway through, his father's executive assistant buzzed to say his next appointment had arrived and was waiting outside.

A slightly built man with a thin pencil moustache and slicked back hair was ushered into the office and Sir Dharmesh rose to greet him. Gautam excused himself and was about to leave when he realized the visitor looked vaguely familiar. Nattily dressed in an expensive pin-stripe suit, he walked up to the Goyal patriarch and extended his hand.

'Hello, Papa. It's nice to see you again.'

Sir Dharmesh recoiled in shock and fell back into his gilded throne when he recognized the visitor to be his daughter, Rani.

'Bitiya, what is the meaning of this? And why are you dressed in this funny way?'

'Papa, I'm wearing this suit because that's exactly how smart young executives dress these days. Isn't that right, Gautam?' said Rani, delighting in teasing the Goyal men.

Gautam scanned his sister from top to toe and sneered. 'What bloody stunt are you pulling now, Rani?'

'It's no stunt, Gautam. Papa always wanted his first-born to be a male. So here I am.'

'Rani, stop this nonsense and go change your clothes immediately!' Sir Dharmesh was in no mood for frivolity.

'Papa, I can certainly change my clothes, but that won't

change the fact that I'm now a man,' said Rani, with a gleam in her eye.

'What? What? What do you mean you're now a man? What rubbish bloody nonsense is this? Bullshit bloody bakwaas, haan, haan?' The patriarch had a tendency to sputter when he was worked up.

'Papa, I went through several surgeries in Bangkok. I had my breasts removed and my jaw reshaped. I've had multiple hormone treatments and I've also got myself a penis. So, for all intents and purposes, I am your son—just like you wanted.'

Gautam gaped in horror and Sir Dharmesh began to panic. 'Please, please stop joking with me, bitiya Rani. It's very bad manners to fool with your papa this way.'

'I'm so sorry Papa, I didn't mean to offend you. If you like, I can show Gautam my new cock to prove that I have, in fact, changed my gender.'

Sweat streamed down Sir Dharmesh's face as he clutched at his heart and began to hyperventilate. 'Hey Bhagwan … I want to die, I want to die …'

Gautam rushed to his father's side and lunged at the intercom to speak with his assistant. 'Ruby, call Dr Batra. I think Papa is having a stroke.'

As he loosened his father's tie, Gautam roared at his transgendered sibling. 'Rani, what the bloody hell do you think you're doing? You're not a man—you're a fucking freak! Get the fuck out of here before I beat the living daylights out of you.'

Rani smirked and replied with a hiss, 'I'm not going anywhere, Gautam. Like it or not, Dharmesh Goyal's first-born child is now a man. I've come home to stake my rightful claim to the company I helped build. And there is absolutely nothing you can do to stop me, little brother. Oh, by the way, my name is no longer Rani. From now on, you can call me Rana!'

NINE

On Diwali day, *Pardesi Pardesi* opened to packed houses across the country. The hype surrounding Ricky's debut and the return of Kapil Kumar succeeded in bringing excited audiences to the cinema halls. No other producer dared compete against such a keenly anticipated film and the Kumars were assured a bumper opening weekend at the box-office.

However, actually watching *Pardesi Pardesi* unfold on screen caused the audience's enthusiasm to dip considerably. Kapil Kumar had made the movie the only way he knew how. The eighties style of film-making with jerky zoom shots, slack editing, stilted dialogue and melodramatic music score was difficult to digest for viewers accustomed to watching slickly produced films in the new millennium. Some of them heckled and hooted to express their disappointment, others walked out in disgust.

> '*Pardesi Pardesi* is a putrid, pointless remake that neither amuses nor entertains. In this pathetic comeback vehicle, Kapil Kumar reclaims his status as the leading ham of Hindi cinema. Let us hope Kumar's directorial debut doubles also as his swan song!'

The film critic at the *Post* wasn't in the mood to mince words or to oblige Shivani, who had sent him an oversized Diwali hamper in hope of a favourable review.

The cinema pundits and paying public were in tacit agreement that Ricky Kumar's first outing as an actor had fizzled. He was criticized for his poor dialogue delivery and patchy performance and, especially for being unable to pull off the simple village character convincingly. He did come in for some praise for his portrayal of the suave don, but the final verdict was that though the much-hyped star son showed some promise, he had a long way to go before becoming a full-fledged hero who could shoulder an entire film.

Meneka was appreciated as the vampy Sonia, but it was apparent that she would henceforth be typecast. It was unlikely that any producer would risk giving such an overtly sexy actress a role as a conventional Hindi film heroine.

Preeti Bhasin, on the other hand, captured the nation's heart with her earnest and lovable performance as Gauri, the buxom village belle. The magical combination of oomph and innocence she exuded marked her as a future A-list heroine.

The mechanics of the modern Indian box-office are such that the opening week's collection can sometimes prove adequate to recover a film's cost of production. Kapil Kumar—actor, director, producer and presenter of *Pardesi Pardesi*—was relieved he had only lost face and not hard cash at the end of his cinematic blunder. His ego may have suffered a brutal beating at the hands of the Indian public, but his bank balance was mercifully intact.

'Thank God I can celebrate Diwali and not mourn my diwaala,' joked Kapil, surrounded by his cronies who had assembled at Casa Kumar to offer condolences at the film's early demise and to drown their sorrows collectively in Scotch.

Shivani Mehta was disappointed that, despite all her stratagems, neither was the film a hit, nor was her young client hot property with advertisers any longer. The spin doctor had endured Kapil Kumar's insanity for nine months in the hope that Ricky would eventually become her golden goose but now had nothing to show for her troubles.

Ricky Kumar took the failure of his launch vehicle exceptionally hard. The adoring masses had gone to the cinemas to witness the birth of a superstar, but instead of fireworks on screen, all they had got was a damp squib. Ricky became a target of ridicule, not only for disappointed fans but also for Kapil's many detractors, who sniggered that neither father nor son possessed an iota of acting talent.

Ricky realized his professional and personal life were both in a shambles. Rhea was unobtainable and Meneka was betrothed to Gautam Goyal. Preeti Bhasin's career had skyrocketed and she had a swarm of producers clamouring to sign her. The wounded actor longed to escape Mumbai where every day cruel media reports reminded him what a complete loser he was.

Manju Kumar experienced the agonizing pain only a mother can feel, seeing her child flounder helplessly in troubled waters. She urged Ricky to spend a month at Babaji's ashram to help heal his injured spirit. She was pleasantly surprised when Ricky readily agreed and left the next morning for Rishikesh.

Babaji received Ricky with open arms and set him to work tending the vegetable garden.

One morning, down on his knees weeding the tomato patch, Ricky heard his name being called. He turned and squinted up to find Tarun Roy grinning at him.

'Tarun! Hey, good to see you, buddy! What brings you here? Are you also a disciple of Babaji?'

'No, not exactly. To tell you the truth, I hadn't even heard of him until Rhea told me about all the good work he's been doing. Which reminds me, thanks so much for introducing us, Ricky. She's such a great client—super bright and receptive to ideas—I'm really enjoying working with her.'

'Oh, I'm delighted things are working out. So, is Rhea here as well?'

'Yes, very much so. We both got in from Delhi this morning to make our initial campaign presentation to Babaji.'

'That's great! I'd love to see her ... er ... I mean ... it!' Ricky blushed at his little slip, but the prospect of seeing Rhea again made his heart gambol.

Tarun laughed. 'Absolutely! Love to show it to you. By the way, Ricky, yaar ... may I ask you something personal?'

'Sure.'

'Umm ... I know Rhea and you were seeing each other—about a year ago—at the time of your ... er ... drug bust ... but since you're obviously not together any more, would you mind if I ... umm ... you know ... tried my luck?'

Ricky was nonplussed. Tarun had been several years his senior at school, and the house captain he had looked up to. A clean-cut, bright and reliable chap, he had exuded self-confidence and had no trouble attracting female attention despite his average looks and modest height. He had become one of the youngest national creative directors at a leading advertising agency before quitting to start his own firm in Delhi a couple of years ago. Now this boy wonder was asking him for permission to pursue Rhea? Ricky wanted to sock him in the face for his impertinence. But he managed to mumble his acquiescence and Tarun gave him a wink and a thumbs-up in gratitude.

Rhea had just emerged from her cottage when she

caught sight of Ricky in conversation with Tarun. She had followed the reviews of *Pardesi Pardesi* and gone to watch it on the opening night in Delhi. She had felt extremely sorry for Ricky, who deserved a better debut than Kapil's filmic atrocity. Quickening her pace, she strode over to where Ricky stood and ran the last few metres to envelop him in a hug, the intensity and length of which surprised even her. Ricky, his hands and clothes muddy from working in the soil, took a deep, intoxicating whiff of her. Rhea always, always smelled of mandarins.

'Ricky, it's so good to see you! How are you?'

The concern in Rhea's voice was unmistakable, and Ricky managed a half-smile as he replied, 'Honestly? I've been better ... you know ... but I'll be fine. Thanks for asking.'

Rhea nodded in understanding. 'It's good you came here. I've heard so much about this place from my father. It's such an oasis of calm.'

'Yeah. Spending a month or so here with Babaji will do me a world of good. So, congratulations. Tarun tells me you guys have cracked a strategy for your campaign—that's wonderful!'

Rhea smiled, happy to change the subject. 'Yes, we have. And thanks again for putting me in touch with Tarun. He's an absolute genius!'

Tarun beamed and put an arm around Rhea, 'Nyaah—let's just say you inspire me. It's rare to find such an erudite and vivacious collaborator. We make a great team.'

Rhea blushed, suddenly feeling self-conscious. She disentangled herself but Ricky, already despondent after the failure of his film, felt miserable knowing he was responsible for having introduced his soul-mate to this smarmy upstart. He wanted nothing more than to bellow his lungs out at the gods and curse them for so cruelly sporting with him. But there was nothing he could do other than smile politely and pretend all was right with his world.

The next morning, Rhea and Tarun left for Delhi. Ricky was grateful not to have her around. Her presence was a constant reminder of how profound his loss had been.

After he had spent a week of blissful quietude at the ashram, Ricky was summoned by Babaji to his cottage. The guru sat the dejected actor on a charpoy and said softly, 'Son, I realize you came here seeking refuge from the real world. I am aware your soul aches and your self-confidence is low. But, if you recall, I told you a long time ago that you must first learn to fall before you can truly rise. It's time now for you to return; to confront your demons and learn how to conquer them.'

Ricky was devastated. 'But ... Babaji, I'm not yet ready to go back. I ... I simply don't have the stomach for it.'

'That's where you're wrong, Ricky. I see the fire within you. You have talent, intelligence and also resilience. What you lack is the will to hone your craft. You must work hard to transcend your limitations, otherwise you will remain mediocre for the rest of your days.'

Ricky knew the savant was right. 'Babaji, can't I please stay a few weeks more?'

'No, son, your true place is not here in my ashram but back home in Mumbai. You have tasted failure, now it's time to discover how sweet success can be. Go pack your bags and meet me at the gates in half an hour. I will take you to the airport.'

It usually took three hours negotiating the winding mountain roads to reach Dehradun airport. Ricky sat beside Babaji in the back of an SUV, looking forward to chatting with the wise man on the long drive ahead. To his surprise, the vehicle turned into a small airfield located barely twenty minutes away. Babaji alighted and smilingly asked the intrigued young actor to board the two-seater aircraft that stood on the narrow airstrip.

Getting behind the controls of the compact plane, Babaji instructed Ricky to buckle himself in. Within minutes, they were taxying down the rustic runway and were soon airborne.

'Wow, Babaji, you're full of surprises.' Ricky gazed in wonder at the snow-clad peaks that glistened below in the mid-day sun.

'I find it easier to visit all my schools and orphanages across the country this way.' Babaji winked at Ricky, who shook his head in amazement.

'Listen to me, son. I need you to soar. I want you to spread your wings and leave all your doubts and insecurities behind. You have to conquer your fear of heights and reach for the stars. Promise me you will strive to better yourself.'

This past week, the guru had sought to teach his young disciple one basic truth of life: that there is no mantra for success besides hard work and dogged determination.

'I will make a success of myself, Babaji. I swear to you, I will,' Ricky responded.

'I'm glad. One final piece of advice, son,' said Babaji, turning to face Ricky. 'Please don't allow your heart to play games with your head. Stay focussed and in the present. Otherwise, all you will do is scuttle your dreams.'

Gautam ensured his sibling was kept away from their father's hospital room while the old man recuperated post the massive myocardial infarction he had suffered. Dr Batra's orders had been explicit: Sir Dharmesh should not be subjected to any further stress. Gautam was convinced a visit from his deranged sister, who now thought herself a man, would give the Goyal patriarch another, and this time quite possibly fatal, heart attack.

To Gautam's dismay, a week after being discharged from hospital, Sir Dharmesh asked to meet privately with his troubled daughter back in their Belgravia home.

The Goyal first-born sobbed and pleaded with the patriarch. 'Don't you get it, Papa? I am not some abomination or sick, twisted pervert. I am your flesh and blood. My whole life I have only seen disappointment in your eyes that I wasn't born a boy. Mummy died trying to give you the son you desperately wanted, and when Gautam was born, you showered all your love on him and forgot all about me. I worked day and night to help build our company, Papa, but you ruthlessly shunted me off to Thailand just so Gautam could take over. Yes, I was hurt, humiliated and angry with you, but that is not why I decided to change my sex. I did it because I was unhappy as a woman. I felt trapped and suffocated in my female form. I wanted to break free. I am now truly liberated, Papa. I am now Rana Goyal, your son!'

'Bitiya, please, I beg of you, please don't say such terrible things. You are Rani, Rani Goyal—my bitiya rani—you cannot be anything else for me. I will show you to the best doctors in the world. I will spend whatever amount is necessary to cure you. But please, please stop saying you are this Rana person!' For the first time in his life, Dharmesh Goyal wept in front of his daughter and pleaded with her to see the error of her ways.

After the tears and many impassioned arguments, father and child arrived at a settlement. Sir Dharmesh grudgingly agreed to respect the fact that his obviously disturbed daughter considered herself a man. The patriarch would henceforth address his first-born as Rana, provided she went to see a psychiatrist who could counsel her and help establish her true sexual identity. At his father's insistence, Rana agreed to move back home and after a fortnight of high drama, an uneasy calm returned to the Goyal household.

Gautam knew Sir Dharmesh felt personally responsible for having sent his daughter over the edge. The old man was convinced Rani would never have taken the drastic step of altering her gender if her father and brother had not conspired to oust her. The younger Goyal was nervous; if his guilt-ridden father genuinely accepted Rana as a son, the first-born could very well lay claim to the lion's share of Masala Magic. Gautam knew the tenacious Rana would fight him tooth and nail for control of the Goyal empire and his succession to the throne was now no longer a given.

On returning from Babaji's ashram, Ricky engaged the services of a tutor who could help improve his Hindi diction and limited vocabulary. The young actor realized that if he wanted to make a career in Bollywood, he had better learn to speak the language fluently and berated himself for not having paid attention to this crucial failing before embarking on his first film.

Most Indian movie stars cultivate a distinct style of dialogue delivery. Fans associate them with this style and mimick it affectionately. Ricky decided to work with a dialogue coach who could teach him how best to modulate and project his voice. He observed that the most challenging roles in Hollywood were often awarded to British actors who had years of experience in theatre and a commanding voice with which they engaged audiences. After considerable research, Ricky located a senior drama coach in London who was willing to take him under his wing for an intensive six-week course in acting and voice training.

Kapil Kumar privately scoffed at the idea of Ricky going to London to learn how to become a better Hindi film actor, but he said nothing. The debacle of *Pardesi Pardesi* had humbled Kapil. A more experienced film-maker might have been better suited to helm Ricky's launch vehicle and to coax a convincing performance from the inexperienced young actor. *Pardesi Pardesi* became the biggest turkey of the year. It was the front-runner at the Bollywood version of the Raspberry Awards, with nominations for Worst Direction, Worst Film, Worst Comeback and Worst Remake of All Time.

Lord Yama had recently come to Belgravia, astride his black buffalo, to ferry Sir Dharmesh to Parlok and eternally reunite him with his beloved Sakshi. However, the aged restaurateur had evaded the ride, thanks to the timely intervention of Dr Batra.

Sir Dharmesh stared disdainfully at the bowl of muesli and skimmed milk that lay before him. Vivek Batra may be a trusted friend, but he was also clearly a sadist, prescribing these ridiculously bland firangi food items to a man whose entire health, wealth and reputation were built on piquant desi fare.

Flanking the patriarch at the breakfast table, Meneka, Gautam and Rana helped themselves to another round of sizzling aaloo parathas that had freshly emerged from the family's industrial-size kitchen. Sir Dharmesh stared longingly at the glistening ghee-soaked paratha his first-born was devouring and felt a twinge of anger, knowing that the only reason he was forbidden such wholesome culinary delights was because of the heart attack engendered by this child's unholy return.

As Meneka reached for a bowl of yoghurt, she felt a sudden lurch in her stomach and a wave of nausea overwhelmed her. Struggling to keep down her breakfast, she rose from the table and rushed to the adjacent powder room to upchuck into a bejewelled commode.

Rana looked up quizzically at Gautam and then at his father. Sir Dharmesh paused for a moment before asking, 'What's the matter, betaji? Is Meneka bitiya okay?'

Gautam was nonplussed. Meneka's abortion had taken a backseat thanks to Rana's dramatic return and Sir Dharmesh's resultant hospitalization. The faintest baby bump had appeared on Meneka's well-toned tummy and she was anxious to be rid of it at the earliest. Gautam had assured his fiancée he would schedule an appointment in the coming week and accompany her to the clinic in Hounslow.

'I'm sure she's fine, Papa. Must be something she ate.'

'Are you sure, betaji? Because if there is any good news you are hiding from me, I will be very upset, haan.'

The look of surprise on Gautam's face prompted his father to favour him with a benign grin.

'Yes, betaji, if Meneka is by any chance pregnant, I will be most happy to become a dadaji, ASAP. After all, god only knows how many weeks or months I have left on this earth.'

Gautam's mind began to race. If his father was pining for a grandchild, and Meneka already had a bun in the oven, it would give him a much-needed edge over Rana. After all, his transgendered sister, despite her recently acquired penis, was incapable of providing the old codger with a babbling baby. Gautam knew he would have to discuss this with Meneka. Perhaps her pregnancy was a blessing from the heavens after all.

Gautam had a hard time convincing his fiancée that it was in their best interest to keep the baby that was growing inside her. Meneka had little desire to become a young mother. She feared her freedom would be curtailed by the presence of a sprog who might also suckle and disfigure her magnificently pert breasts. She did see the wisdom, though, in consolidating their place in the patriarch's recently operated-upon heart. Dr Batra had informed the family that Sir Dharmesh's triple bypass would only help to extend his life for a short period as the cholesterol he had consumed over the decades had clogged his arteries beyond repair. Succumbing to both emotional blackmail and material considerations, Meneka finally relented.

When the couple came clean to Sir Dharmesh, the dadaji-to-be was ecstatic. 'Arrey, fantastic news, betaji! Heartiest congratulations to you two and thank you for this godly gift you are giving me.'

'I'm so relieved you're happy, Papa. We were a little worried you might disapprove of Meneka getting pregnant before the wedding,' beamed Gautam, squeezing Meneka's hand tenderly.

'Don't you worry, betaji. Most people think I am some old-fashioned fuddy-wuddy. But to me, family is much more important these days than what this bloody hippocratic society has to say. You think I don't know what people are whispering about Rani behind my back? Calling her "chhakka" and "hijra" and god knows what all else bakwaas bloody nonsense, hain? I say damn them all and let us be one big, happy family, kyon Meneka bitiya?'

'Absolutely, uncle. I couldn't agree with you more.'

'Arrey, no more of this uncle-wuncle business. From now, you will only call me papa, okay?'

'Yes, Papa,' said Meneka blushing, as she stooped to touch her new father's bunion-afflicted feet.

Tears welled up in Sir Dharmesh's eyes as he gave her a hug. 'Bless you, bitiya. May you prosper and produce one hundred sons.'

Ricky landed at Heathrow in the first week of December and faced the brunt of an early and exceptionally punishing winter. He was used to visiting London in April, when the weather was balmy. Ricky was now experiencing, for the first time, how miserably numbing his favourite city could feel. The icy, biting wind and freezing rain went through his jacket and chilled his bones.

Ricky had leased a cosy studio flat in Chelsea, and all day he worked with his acting coach in Hampstead. In the evenings he occasionally went with Amanda to the Barbican or the West End to watch the stalwarts of the English stage tread the boards. Babaji had taught Ricky there are no short cuts to success and the young actor was determined to diligently work at improving himself. He spent many long winter evenings talking to Amanda about his heartbreak, aspirations and insecurities. Amanda proved a good listener. Perhaps too good a listener, as Ricky Kumar would some day find out.

The Goyals took a collective family decision not to tone down the scale and scope of the wedding celebrations. Meneka was due to deliver a few months before the festivities and Sir Dharmesh, a changed man, was amenable to the idea of flaunting his new grandchild to his guests in the Maldives.

Meneka busied herself with preparations for her big day and solicited Gautam's opinion on which fashion designer she should award the privilege of executing her elaborate wedding lehenga. Indian bridal couture is an extremely lucrative business for desi designers who look forward to the wedding season. During these months, hordes of wealthy clients descend on their glossy boutiques to purchase heavily embroidered trousseaus at exorbitant prices. Meneka was well aware these designers, most of whom she knew personally, would fall over themselves for the opportunity to dress her.

As they surfed the website of a couturier famed for his ebullient zardozi workmanship, a thoroughly bored Gautam noticed that a barrage of emails, all personal news alerts, had sprung up on his computer. This usually meant grim tidings because he was only ever in the news for the wrong reasons. As he clicked on a link highlighting Meneka's and his name, a scowl creased his brow.

The link opened to a website, *Meow, Meow with Mukesh Menda*, which had been recently launched by the catty columnist in India. The scandalmonger, buoyed by the popularity of his Delhi-centric column, now operated a salacious, no-holds-barred site that reported racy celebrity chatter targeting the Indian diaspora.

> Exclusive, red hot *taazaa khabar*, my gorgeous *golgappas*! *Suna hai ki* Meneka Kansal, the sexy vamp of mega flop movie, *Pardesi Pardesi*, is PREGNANT!
>
> Yes, you read this shocking good news here first! It seems this *chikni chameli*, who was all over the news for cheating on her billionaire boyfriend (and now fiancé) Gautam Goyal with wannabe hero (and now full-time zero) Ricky Kumar, is keeping her pregnancy a top secret!

> Obviously, this *teekhi mirchi* has to keep the news quiet because even though she is engaged to richie rich Gautam, her wedding is many months away! Yes, yes—this jet-set *jodi* were planning a *shaandaar shaadi* in the Maldives, but now they may just have a shotgun *shaadi* instead! Tee-hee, my tangy *tamaatars*!
>
> A bitchy birdy also whispered in my ear that the real father of Meneka's child is Ricky Kumar, *apna faltu filmi*, who apparently impregnated the sexy starlet when they were shooting together in London for their disaster flick. My feathered friend also swears the Kansal *kudi* is trying to pass this baby off as Gautam's because she wants her Baba/ Barbie to inherit all the Goyal billions. I refuse to believe such nasty rumours, of course, but *bhagwaan jaane* what the truth is, *hain na,* my luscious lambchops?
>
> I only hope the child is genuinely Gautam Goyal's; otherwise this former *chhammak chhallo* will have to go back to jiggling her booty in Bollywood and singing, *Meneka badnaam hui*!
>
> Meow, meow, my precious pussies!

Gautam was livid. 'That turd burglar has obviously written this as revenge for my debagging him in the loo of Pink Paisley. I swore I'd post a picture of his tiny willy on the net if he wrote any more shit about me. Now I'll teach him a lesson he'll never forget!'

'Gautam, just ignore him! He's simply trying to create a controversy to popularize his pathetic website. Let's not give him or his silly allegations any importance, okay?' counselled Meneka calmly, even as her mind tested and instantly rejected the possibility of having been knocked up by Ricky Kumar. The time Ricky and she had slept together, she had been on the pill. Moreover, Ricky had had the good sense to withdraw in time.

But Gautam was enraged at the thought of people gossiping about his fiancée being impregnated by Ricky Kumar, a man he thoroughly despised. Convinced his venomous sibling had once again instigated Mukesh into writing slanderous things about him, Gautam burst into Rana's room.

'Rani, Rana—whatever the fuck you are—I know you put Menda up to this filthy stunt and I swear I'm going to destroy the both of you!'

'What's the matter, Gautam? What stunt are you talking about?' Rana seemed perplexed by his brother's outburst.

'You're messing with the wrong guy, you sick fuck! How dare you drag Meneka into our fight? Have you no shame?'

'Gautam, please calm down and explain what it is you're accusing me of. I honestly don't have a clue what you're babbling about.'

'This is about you using every dirty trick to make my life a living hell! Why did you tell Mukesh Menda that Meneka is pregnant with Ricky Kumar's child?'

'What? I haven't told anyone anything. I've been busy dealing with my own problems, Gautam. You've got to believe me.'

'I know you're raging with jealousy, you twisted pervert! But don't you dare spread these lies about us or I'll cut off your new cock and ram it down your throat!' Trembling with rage, Gautam turned and strode out of his brother's room, slamming the door behind him.

Rana Goyal shook his head in amazement and then a wide grin bloomed on his recently rechiselled face. After ensuring Gautam was well out of earshot, he picked up his mobile phone and called Mukesh Menda in Delhi.

The British gutter press had a field day reviving and playing up the old story of Meneka having two-timed Gautam Goyal with Ricky Kumar. The juicy premise that a sexy Indian starlet had cheated on her billionaire playboy fiancé and was now pregnant with a Bollywood film actor's baby, was such sensational fodder for the tabloids that they outdid one another in coming up with cheeky front-page headlines.

'Sexpot Starlet knocked up by Tricky Ricky?'

'Bad boy of Belgravia cuckolded by Bolly bombshell!'

'Hurrah for BollyWoody!'

When Amanda informed Ricky it was all over the news that he had got Meneka up the duff, the young actor was mortified. But Amanda seemed to have found new respect for him.

'Well done, you randy little scamp. I didn't know you'd been rogering Meneka! She's a total hottie!'

'Oh, for Christ's sake, Mandy. I admit I did sleep with her, once, in my hotel room. But that's when I received that call from Rhea. So I immediately asked Meneka to leave. And that was the end of that.'

'Cor! I don't know too many blokes who would kick a totty like that out of bed!'

'Yes, well, I guess I'm the one schmuck who did, because I thought Rhea wanted to get back with me,' said Ricky, wistfully.

'So, let's see. You shagged Meneka once and haven't shagged Rhea ever. But you're the one who's been shafted in the end! Am I right, love?' Amanda chuckled at the irony, but Ricky was not amused.

'I think I had better call and check how Meneka is doing. Perhaps we should issue a joint press statement denying these ridiculous rumours.'

The young actor missed having Shivani at hand to assist with the professional damage control. He dialled Meneka's mobile and when it was finally answered, he was stupefied to hear Gautam's voice at the other end.

'Ricky Kumar, you have some nerve calling my fiancée in my home.'

That entire morning Gautam had been inundated with emails and phone calls from the press, asking for a quote regarding Meneka's alleged infidelity. A call from Ricky Kumar, the man responsible for all his troubles, was the last thing the Goyal scion wanted.

'Gautam, is that you? Is Meneka with you in London? I'm in town too, and just read all the rubbish that's being written about us.'

'Oh yeah? Well, we don't need you getting involved. So sod off, you meddling twunt. And don't you dare call back again!'

Ricky bristled at being spoken to in this manner but attempted to stay calm. 'Gautam, this gossip is affecting all our reputations, so I think it's best we combine forces and squash it collectively.'

'I'm going to fucking squash you, you useless piece of turd!' erupted Gautam. 'You're nothing but a fucking loser, Ricky Kumar! Your film is a massive flop and you've been exposed to the entire world as a talentless twat! So bugger off and leave us the fuck alone.'

The diatribe hit a raw nerve with Ricky. 'You're the fucking loser, Gautam! You're nothing but a lowlife junkie and a wastrel who has achieved absolutely nothing in life. You pride yourself on being a playboy and a ladies' man? Yet, your fiancée was desperately throwing herself at me! I pity you, Gautam Goyal!'

Overhearing Gautam's outburst, Meneka came rushing

out of the bathroom. 'Gautam, give me the phone! Let me speak with Ricky.'

'Nothing doing, I'll be damned if I allow you to speak with that scumbag while you're living under my roof!'

'Gautam, you're behaving like a child. Just shut up and give me my phone!'

'Why? So you can make plans with him to humiliate me further? Why don't you fuck off and move in with him? But no, you want to marry me for my father's money, don't you, you gold-digging whore?'

'Gautam, you've gone completely mad! We can discuss this later—but right now, give me my bloody phone!' As Meneka lunged for her mobile, she accidently scratched Gautam's cheek with her sharp nails. He winced in pain and instinctively lashed out at his fiancée, striking her hard across the face. Meneka fell to the ground with the force of his blow.

Realizing what he had done, Gautam rushed to Meneka's side. 'I'm so sorry, babe. I … I didn't mean to hit you.'

'Get away from me! You're a fucking animal!' Menka shrieked.

'Please, Meneka—listen to me—I know I lose control when I get jealous, but that's only because I love you so much! You know I trust you, but I can't deal with the fact that you've been with this bloke!'

'Gautam, I've told you a dozen times. Ricky has always been in love with his childhood sweetheart, and there was never any question of anything happening between us. Please trust me, Gautam—otherwise this will destroy us all!'

Gautam was instantly remorseful for having lashed out at her. He knew Ricky Kumar was capable of fabricating stories. The actor had blatantly lied before about seeing him snort coke. Was Ricky also lying about Meneka throwing herself at him, he wondered. He desperately wanted to believe his fiancée and put all doubts behind him. However, the pressure from the media was beginning to get to him. The best way to squash these rumours, Gautam decided, was to prove conclusively that the baby was his.

The weary monarch of Masala Magic shifted uneasily on his faux French throne. He was wondering if it had been worth spending a lifetime building an empire and a name for himself when, in his golden years, his reputation lay in tatters. His disturbed daughter had changed her sex and thought herself a man and his ex-junkie son's fiancée was quite possibly pregnant with a Bollywood actor's child. Having had a recent intimation of mortality, Sir Dharmesh felt compelled to ask himself if there were any real reasons left to live. But the old man knew that it was imperative to salvage the vestiges of the Goyal family honour before he died. Otherwise his tormented soul would never find eternal peace.

The wizened restaurateur had heard of several floozies who had deliberately got themselves impregnated by the scions of wealthy families and successfully blackmailed these gullible young men into marrying them. Sir Dharmesh summoned Meneka to his office and sat her down.

'Meneka, beta, as you know, even Sita maiyya was accused of being unfaithful to Lord Ram. But she happily went through an agniparīksha, a trial by fire, you know, to prove her innocence to the world. Now, this pregnancy of yours is causing us a lot of embarrassment …'

Meneka quickly interjected. 'Yes, Papa. I'm extremely sorry, but you have to believe that …'

Sir Dharmesh held up his hand to silence her. 'You will appreciate, beta, that now it is not a case of believing. It is about getting concrete hard proof that this child is definitely Gautam's and no one else's,' he said sternly.

'Of course, I ... I understand. Just tell me what I need to do?'

'Arrey, nothing much, bitiya. All we have to do is a simple paternity test.'

'I'm more than happy to do that, Papa.'

Meneka's confident tone reassured Sir Dharmesh. 'Very good, bitiya. Dr Batra will arrange for the test tomorrow morning at the hospital. Then, when we get the proof, we will file a case of defamation against all these dirty, filthy presswallahs and force them to publicly apologize for their lies. Now, you go and get some rest. You must be very stressed out with all this bakwaas nonsense, hai na?'

Meneka left Sir Dharmesh's office feeling relieved that her future father-in-law was willing to give her an opportunity to clear her name. She hoped that, with a bit of luck, the baby would be a boy and then Sir Dharmesh, thrilled to have finally become a dadaji, would shower both his love and his riches on his gurgling grandson.

Tarun Roy was a Renaissance man. Not only was he a gifted copywriter and marketing wunderkind, but he was also passionate about Indian classical music and mythology. Together, he and Rhea created a unique media campaign designed to generate awareness on the evils of water pollution. Rhea was amazed at the ease and skill with which Tarun had charmed some of the country's finest classical singers to each record a soul-stirring salutation to the major Indian rivers. He used the songs as an underlay to emotive visuals, and intercut them with celebrity endorsements to create a series of captivating public service films that appealed at once to the head and the heart.

Babaji was impressed when the duo showed him the fruits of their endeavour and explained that they planned to release these short films in local cinema halls, on the Internet and various TV channels.

'This is remarkable work, you two. Thank you so much for your efforts.'

'It has been a real pleasure, Babaji. Now let's just hope it manages to do some good.' Tarun smiled.

'Oh, I'm confident it will. Even if it inspires one soul to effect genuine change, this entire exercise would be well worth the energy you both have expended. Kanti should be proud of you, Rhea. Has he seen the films as yet?'

'No, but I'll show them to him when he comes down for the launch of your project, Babaji. He wanted me to seek your approval first. He says he's happy to keep writing cheques as long as you're happy with the work we've done.' Rhea laughed.

Kanti, Babaji's indefatigable champion, had not only personally underwritten the cost of the campaign but also collected a substantial amount by way of international donations to help realize his guru's dream of building public toilets in India. A symbolic ground-breaking ceremony in Rishikesh, on the banks of the Ganga, was scheduled to take place in a fortnight to launch Project Pavitra. The national media was expected to attend as a host of luminaries had promised to be present to lend support to the cause.

'Why don't we premiere these films at the project launch,

Babaji? That way we can generate some buzz around them before the public release,' suggested Tarun, the astute ad man. Rhea look at him appreciatively and suddenly found herself drawn to the multitalented maverick. She was aware Tarun had a crush on her and was glad he was being such a gentleman, allowing her time to get over the pain of having loved and lost Ricky Kumar.

A week before Christmas, Ricky received a call from a weeping Meneka. She begged him to let her come over to his Chelsea flat. Between sobs, she managed to convey that Dr Batra had brought over the paternity test reports that morning, which established that Gautam was not the father of her unborn child. Her fiancé had been too shattered to speak. Sir Dharmesh had tersely informed her she should vacate the Goyal home and consider her engagement to his son cancelled.

After Meneka had cleared out of Belgravia, Sir Dharmesh attempted to console his devastated boy. 'Betaji, if this child is not yours, obviously this chaalu ladki has slept with that Ricky Kumar or some other third, fourth or fifth fellow! Better we found out now, before she brought some haraami into our home, hai na? But don't you worry—this time I will find you a proper virgin from Rajasthan. Then you can settle down and quickly make me into a dadaji before I die, okay?'

Numb with shock, Gautam nodded. Despite all that had been said and written about Meneka, Gautam had believed his fiancée when she claimed the baby was his. Returning to the room he had shared with Meneka for several months, Gautam gazed at the row of empty wardrobes that, until an hour ago, had been stocked with her belongings. Her clothes, lingerie, shoes, lotions, perfumes, magazines, laptop … all gone, leaving no trace of her ever having been here. As tears began to stream down his face, Gautam slowly closed the doors of every wardrobe in his room and shut himself off from the world.

Bewildered and distraught, Meneka arrived at Ricky's door. The young actor hugged his former co-star, who was shivering not only from the chill outside but also because her world had suddenly turned upside down. Meneka's face was wan from having wept all morning and she looked defeated.

'My whole life has been ruined, Ricky! Gautam and his family want nothing more to do with me.'

'Don't worry, Meneka. I'm here to help. Do you need any money … a place to stay? I can sleep on the couch, you know.'

'No, thanks—that's not a problem. It … it occurred to me that since Gautam is not the father, that must mean … I'm carrying your child, Ricky!'

Ricky was stunned. 'My … my child? Are … are you sure, Meneka? I mean … we did sleep together … once ... all those months ago. But I remember telling you I didn't have any protection and you … you assured me that it was all right. Even then I took precautions, you know and … umm ...'

'Yes, yes, I know all that. I'm not blaming you, Ricky. But I thought you should know that the only other person I was sexually active with during that period is you. So there really is no doubt that you are the father of my child.'

'Oh, I see. I'm … I'm extremely sorry about this, Meneka … I obviously never meant to put you in this position,' said Ricky, flustered but genuinely contrite at the thought of having knocked her up.

'What am I going to do, Ricky? I'm going to be the laughing-stock of the whole world!'

'Umm … I don't mean to sound insensitive, but can't you … you know … umm … see a doctor and umm …'

'Have an abortion? You think I haven't thought about that already? It's too late, Ricky! It's neither safe nor legal to get it done at this stage,' wailed Meneka.

'Of course … of course. Please forgive me, I'm obviously not thinking straight,' said Ricky, trying awkwardly to comfort her.

'That's all right, Ricky. I understand. It's a difficult time for us all. I just hope you intend to do the honourable thing and marry me.'

Ricky was aghast. 'Marr … marry you? Meneka, marriage is a very serious step. And frankly, please don't get me wrong … how can we even be sure this baby is mine?'

'I know it is, Ricky. It has to be! Listen, if you're not willing to take my word for it, why don't you come down to the hospital tomorrow and submit to a paternity test? Either way, we will both have an answer. But if it's proved that you are the father, you will marry me, won't you, Ricky? Otherwise, I … I simply won't be able to survive the shame.'

Seeing how distraught she was, Ricky nodded. He obviously did not want to be coerced into marrying this troubled woman but he had been brought up by his mother to do the right thing. He knew that if, seized by lust, he had been reckless enough to get Meneka pregnant, he had to shoulder the responsibility of raising the child with her. Ricky Kumar figured the universe was once again up to its old tricks, but he really had no option other than to play along.

'All right, Meneka. Why don't you set up the appointment for tomorrow? I give you my word of honour. If this is my baby, I will stand by you.'

Soon after their return from Babaji's ashram, Tarun invited Rhea to his apartment in Gurgaon one evening, promising to cook her a Bengali meal. Making every effort to impress, he conjured up a fiery mustard Hilsa and a delicately flavoured daab chingdi, prawns simmered in tender coconut. His kosha mangsho, a melt-in-the-mouth mutton delicacy, had Rhea begging for seconds and she devoured several delectably fluffy luchis before protesting she could eat no more. Pairing the meal with an exquisite Pouilly-Fuisse he had saved for a special occasion, Tarun regaled Rhea with hilarious, self-deprecating stories of his early misadventures in advertising.

Rhea knew she was being wooed with a view to being seduced that evening. It had been almost a year since the infamous incident at Scandal Point and she had not been intimate with anyone since. She wondered now if it was finally time to get on with her life.

Standing on the small balcony of Tarun's apartment, Rhea gazed at the twinkling city lights, as the strains of a lilting thumri wafted from the music system in the living room. Returning from the kitchen, Tarun quietly curled an arm around Rhea's waist and offered her a drag from the joint he had just lit.

'Thanks, but this will be wasted on me.' Rhea smiled.

'That's the whole point, isn't it—to get wasted?' said Tarun. 'Go on, take a hit.'

'No, seriously, I know it sounds really lame, but I don't know how to inhale.'

'Seriously?'

'Seriously! I tried several times in college, but I couldn't get the hang of it. So, I finally gave up and prefer sticking with alcohol now.' Rhea giggled, tipsy from the wine Tarun had plied her with.

'You really don't know what you're missing. My guru Bob Dylan, the Babaji of rock and roll, has commanded, "Everybody must get stoned".' Tarun took a deep drag and then, drawing Rhea close, kissed her on the mouth, gently releasing a cloud of sweet smoke into her lungs.

Rhea gasped as the marijuana entered her system. But, rather than recoil, she took hold of Tarun's face and kissed him back. Tarun reciprocated with ardour, elated that his patience and elaborate efforts were paying off.

Steering Rhea into his bedroom, all aglow with candles in anticipation of a successful seduction, Tarun eased her onto the bed, nuzzling her neck and breasts as he attempted to get her out of the flowing red kurta she had bought especially for the evening. Eventually managing to undress the petite target of his affections, Tarun pulled off his own clothes and reached within the bedside drawer for his stash of condoms.

'Tarun, wait, wait ... I'm so sorry ... but I don't think I can go through with this.'

Tarun was startled by this coitus interruptus before he had even had a chance to enter her. 'What's the matter, Rhea?'

'I'm really sorry, Tarun, but I need more time. It's not that I don't want you ... I do ... but I can't ... not yet, anyway.'

'It's Ricky, isn't it? You're in love with him? I knew it!' Tarun was both jealous and insecure that he didn't measure up to the hunky actor.

'No, Tarun, it's so much more complicated than that. It's not Ricky—it's me. You just need to be patient. I need to clear my head a bit.'

'Okay, sure, I understand ... you take your time. It's not like I'm going anywhere,' said Tarun, trying to muster as good-natured a face as he possibly could.

'Thanks, Tarun. You're a really special guy. I promise I'll make this up to you someday.' Rhea smiled as she scooped up her kurta and embarrassedly walked away to get dressed.

Tarun Roy, advertising maverick and ladies' man, peered down at his limp penis and sighed. This was what the boys back in college called a complete KLPD.

On a bleak winter morning, the day before Christmas, Ricky Kumar bundled himself into a double-breasted cashmere overcoat and hailed a taxi to Tower Bridge Hospital. The paternity test results were due that day and Ricky hadn't managed to sleep a wink the previous night, fearful of what strange new twist fate had in store for him.

The weather had taken a turn for the worse and there was a blanket of treacherous sleet on the roads that had slowed traffic to a crawl. Frustrated and stifled in the back of the gridlocked cab, Ricky couldn't take the agonizing wait any longer. Impulsively abandoning the taxi, he trudged the last half kilometre, shivering and often slipping on the icy footpath that hugged the Thames. Ricky looked up at the ominously grey Tower of London that loomed ahead, portending doom. It seemed to him that much like the prisoners once incarcerated there, he too was on his way to a sentencing and could soon face the executioner's axe.

Ricky met Meneka in the hospital foyer and they wordlessly went up to the third floor to collect the dreaded DNA test results. Nervous and numb with cold, Ricky fumbled with the sealed envelope. Meneka, on edge herself, impatiently grabbed it and ripped it open. Ricky's heart was pounding as he scanned

Meneka's face, searching for a clue as to which way the scales had tilted. Her impassive expression betrayed nothing as she handed him the printout and walked away.

A quick glance at the results was enough to assure Ricky he had been absolved of responsibility. He wanted to yell in triumph, but seeing Meneka slumped in a chair and beginning to cry, he controlled the impulse to rejoice and went over to comfort her instead. Knowing he ought not to leave her alone when she was despondent and friendless, Ricky insisted she come back with him to his Chelsea flat.

Once home, Ricky made the distraught girl a cup of tea and gently broached the subject of the paternity test. 'Listen, Meneka, I know all this has been extremely tough on you. But obviously someone else is the father of your child. If you don't want to talk about it, that's fine, but please know I'm here if you need a friend.' Truth be told, Ricky was rather curious to learn who had knocked her up.

Meneka looked at Ricky and smiled wistfully. 'Thank you, Ricky. I really appreciate all that you've done. I'm so ashamed of myself. But, you know, after we finished filming in London, Gautam started behaving really strangely. He seemed so distant and cold and insisted I go back to India to give our relationship some space. I was convinced he was dumping me just as he had done with my sister. I felt vulnerable and insecure at that stage and it was then that I found comfort in the arms of another man.'

'Well, that's perfectly understandable, Meneka. Gautam should have been more sensitive to your feelings,' said Ricky supportively, even though he disapproved of Meneka's bed-hopping ways.

'I only slept with this man once, but now it's apparent that I'm pregnant with his child. My life is a complete mess, Ricky!'

'Don't worry, Meneka, everything will be all right. Does this chap know you're pregnant?'

Meneka shook her head and began to cry. Ricky put his arm around her. 'Look, why don't you tell this fellow you're carrying his child? Perhaps he would like to share the responsibility of jointly raising it or he may even want to marry you?'

'Yes, that's exactly what I was thinking. And I'm sure you'll help me, Ricky,' Meneka said.

'Me? Really? How can I help? Do I know this person?'

'Of course you do, Ricky. After all, he's your father.'

'My … my father? You … you slept with my father?' Ricky was dumbfounded.

'Yes, Ricky. It was a terrible mistake, as I realized immediately. But there is no doubt now that Kapil Kumar is the real father of my baby.'

'Meneka, this is outrageous! I don't believe a word you're saying. How can you even suggest that my father is the father of your child? That's disgusting!'

'I know it's hard to believe, Ricky, but I swear it's the truth. Kapil Kumar had sex with me in my hotel room in Mumbai when I came down for the dubbing of our film.'

'Look, Meneka, I promised I would stand by you if this baby was mine. But now, when the results have proven otherwise, you're accusing my dad of getting you pregnant. Do you have any idea how ridiculous your lies sound?'

'Don't you dare accuse me of lying, Ricky,' Meneka snapped. 'I swear Kapil Kumar is the father of this child. And I'm prepared to prove it in court if I have to!'

Ricky was appalled. He decided it would be prudent to calm her down. 'Listen, Meneka, I know you've had some terrible news and are very upset. So tell me, what is it that you want? Are you looking to get some money from my father?'

'Oh please! My own dad has more money than you can imagine. No, I just want you to do the honourable thing and marry me, Ricky.'

Ricky was flabbergasted. 'Meneka, that's out of the question! I was willing to consider it if the baby proved to be mine. But these wild allegations will simply not hold up ...'

'You think I'm naïve enough to make such a claim without hard evidence? I have a video recording of your father having sex with me in Room 512 at the Land's End Hotel in Mumbai, Ricky. Now what do you have to say? Are you willing to do the right thing and marry me, or do you want me to make the video public?'

'Meneka, are you blackmailing me into marrying you? That's crazy! You've lost all perspective. You really should think twice about what you're saying.'

'Think about it, Ricky,' Meneka pleaded. 'We can get married and raise this child together as our own. No one will ever know it's your father's. Admit it, we were instantly attracted to each other and would have definitely ended up together if it weren't for Rhea. And you two have obviously broken up, so there's no reason for us not to marry.'

Meneka leaned into Ricky and tried to kiss him on the lips. Ricky recoiled and jumped up.

'Meneka, I think you had better leave now. I'm sorry, but there is no way I will be coerced into marrying you.'

Meneka rose with a snarl. 'Screw you, Ricky! I thought you were different from other men, but you're no better than all those pigs who think they can simply use and discard women at will. I'm giving you a week to make your decision. Either you publicly admit this child is yours and marry me, or I'm going to send a DVD of your dad doing me doggie-style first to your mother and then to every news channel I know! The choice is yours, Ricky boy, because at this point I honestly have nothing to lose!'

It dawned on Ricky then, that he was dealing with a sociopath. This amoral girl was both disturbed and desperate and, therefore, all the more dangerous. Ricky Kumar knew he would have to play his cards carefully to keep Meneka Kansal from wreaking havoc on the Kumar clan.

Gautam loathed himself for having made the mistake of letting his guard down and allowing Meneka a place in his heart. His devious fiancée had ruthlessly betrayed and cuckolded him, and now he was hurting. He sat alone in his room, draining a bottle of Lagavulin. But no matter how much alcohol he consumed, the stabbing ache in his soul refused to subside. The former junkie knew he required something stronger than whisky to dull his pain. After battling the temptation for several hours, he succumbed and made a call to his old supplier, who readily agreed to make a delivery at four o'clock that morning.

Drowsy with all the narcotics that now coursed through his bloodstream, he finally managed to fall into a deep sleep.

Late that evening, an incessant pounding on his bedroom door jolted Gautam awake. He roused himself and staggered to the door to find Rana standing outside.

'What the fuck do you want?' Gautam snarled, convinced his sibling had come to gloat at his misfortunes.

'Papa wants to see you, Gautam. He's worried you haven't eaten since yesterday and insists you join us downstairs at dinner.'

'I'm not hungry—so naff off and tell Papa I'll see him

tomorrow.' Gautam tried to shut the door, but Rana prevented him from doing so.

'Listen, Gautam. There can be nothing better for me than to have you fall back into your old ways, now that you're such a lovelorn wreck. But I think it's important you pull yourself together. The night guard showed me the security camera tapes, so I know you met with a dealer outside the gates early this morning. I haven't told Papa about this as yet, but I swear I will if you ever do it again.'

'What the fuck do you care what happens to me? You're just here to grab control of the company. Well, congratulations—your plan worked perfectly. I don't know how you managed to get the information, but it turned out Meneka was pregnant with some other bloke's kid after all. So you outplayed me brilliantly, and now you've won because I don't want anything any more. You can have it all, Rana. Just leave me the fuck alone!'

'Gautam … you should know it wasn't I who gave Mukesh Menda that information. It was Sheena Kansal.'

'Sheena! But … how could she have known?'

'I don't know the details, Gautam. But I did call Mukesh in Delhi to find out who was behind the leak. It seems Sheena found out through their family gynaecologist. And since she wanted revenge for what Meneka and you did to her, she gave Mukesh the scoop and swore it was Ricky and not you who was the father of the child.'

A wave of despair swept over Gautam. All these machinations and devious plots of revenge and retribution were taking a heavy toll on him. He longed for nothing more than to escape this miserable existence where every move and counter-move had to be carefully calibrated in order to vanquish one's foes and ensure personal success. He had been happier as a narcotic-addled playboy who drifted through life without a care in the world. He had worked hard to give up his drug habit but found only pain and unhappiness when he emerged from rehab into the real world. Sobriety, in his opinion, was an overrated state of being. It was perhaps better to stay sedated, in a perpetual stupor, and let life pass by in a carefree haze. Gautam resolved to escape the vicissitudes of love and career and opt instead for a life of quiescence, so he could nurse his wounds and recover from the anguish of having once loved Meneka Kansal.

Ricky Kumar sat in Amanda's council flat in Peckham, tipsy after all the mulled wine he had imbibed over their raucous Christmas lunch. The warm, intoxicating brew, infused with spices, lemon, lime and alcohol, tasted exactly like 'Xmas in a glass', as Amanda's loquacious mother had promised it would. After the other guests had tottered home and the merrily pickled mother had been tucked into bed, Ricky helped Amanda clear the dishes and then collapsed on the red sofa-bed that dominated the tiny living room to have a heart-to-heart.

'What the hell do I do now, Mandy? I'm so damn confused.'

'I think she's having you on, Ricky. Do you think that tart is deluded enough to believe you'll actually marry her?' slurred Amanda.

'I honestly don't know! But I'm afraid she's so desperate she may end up doing something reckless.'

'And how do you even know your dad is the father of her sprog? A promiscuous girl like that could have slept with half of Delhi and London! Has she shown you this sex tape of hers yet?'

'No. And frankly, I don't ever want to see it! Knowing my dad, I'm sure he wouldn't have passed up the opportunity to sleep with Meneka. So he could very well have got her pregnant.'

'Oh, there's no question Kapil would have been all over her in a trice. Why, he even tried to shag me when I was staying at your place in Mumbai.'

'What? Why didn't you tell me?' exclaimed Ricky, suddenly jolted out of his inertness.

'Oh, he was so clumsy about it all—pretending to drop his towel accidentally after coming into my room one evening. I just pointed at his wobbly old knob and laughed. He was so embarrassed, he turned and fled and never tried anything again,' chortled Amanda.

'I'm so sorry, Mandy. My dad is incorrigible!'

'That he is, ducky! Listen, why don't you have a paternity test done to ascertain if he is the father of Meneka's baby? Because if he isn't, there really is nothing to worry about, is there, love?'

Ricky knew Amanda was right. All he had to do was gather proof his father was innocent and confront Meneka with the evidence. But if Kapil had, in fact, impregnated Meneka, Ricky Kumar would once again have to pay a hefty price for the sins of his father.

TEN

The collapse of the Soviet Union had proved a blessing for Dharmesh Goyal. He had realized, to his delight, that a number of stunning Eastern European ladies were making their way to London to find employment, many choosing to work as companions to Britain's wealthiest men.

After his wife's death, Sir Dharmesh had developed an affinity for natural blondes, the younger the better, and exulted in having his pick of the finest Ukrainian, Estonian and Latvian women that money could procure. For many years, he had a discreet arrangement with a buxom old Russian aristocrat who specialized in introducing the freshest faces from across the former U.S.S.R. to lonely gentlemen of means.

The Goyal patriarch had been advised by Dr Batra to abstain from vigorous activity after his triple bypass. However, the arrival of Tatiana Pudrova, a barely seventeen-year-old beauty from Minsk (who was touted to be a real minx in bed) severely tested, and finally defeated, the good doctor's edict.

The assignations with the post-Glasnost girls were carried out at a luxurious house in St. John's Wood, which was fitted with all the conveniences any hot-blooded lord of the realm could desire—a spacious jacuzzi, mirrored walls and ceilings, slippery satin sheets and an oversized bed on which several young women could simultaneously be accommodated. In addition, there was a startling array of lubricants, paddles, whips, chains, dildos, vibrators, hoods and assorted erotic paraphernalia with which these upstanding gentlemen could indulge every conceivable fetish.

Sir Dharmesh was partial to a good spanking now and then, and relished being tied up and fellated by two of the lovely ladies concurrently.

Tatiana Pudrova was everything the Russian madam had promised Sir Dharmesh she would be. Her natural bouncy breasts, blow-job lips and cascading blonde hair sent the old man into paroxysms of joy as she sucked and fucked him till his Viagra pill ran out of juice. Not satiated after having been serviced by the delectable Tatiana for over an hour, Sir Dharmesh popped another little blue pill and waited for the wonder drug to work its magic.

When he achieved another erection, he sent for Sascha, his favourite dominatrix, to join the maddeningly young Tatiana and him for another round of uninhibited rumpy-pumpy. The blonde duo set to work on Sir Dharmesh and managed to arouse him into such a frenzied state of ecstasy that his cholesterol-clogged ticker could not hold out any longer.

Sir Dharmesh suffered a fatal heart attack while enjoying his fifth orgasm of the evening. It was ironic that he died whilst engaged in a sex act identical to his age. Some felt sixty-nine was far too young for such an illustrious man to have passed away. Nevertheless, Sir Dharmesh departed this corporal world that fateful day a happy, happy man.

'Ricky boy, that bloody bitch is babbling all bullshit! I swear I never ever slept with her!' Kapil vehemently denied Meneka's allegation. 'Arrey, she just wants to hog free publicity by claiming to be pregnant by the legendary Kapil Kumar. You don't worry about all this, I will handle her.'

Pacing his father's den at Casa Kumar, Ricky sensed Kapil's indignation was all bluster. The more Ricky thought about it, the more likely it seemed that the veteran actor must have seduced Meneka at a point when she was not only on the rebound from Gautam but also keen to consolidate her Bollywood career.

'Don't lie to me, Papa! Meneka showed me the tape that she made of the two of you at the Land's End Hotel,' bluffed Ricky.

Kapil was shocked. 'She showed you the tape? But ... but ... she swore to me she wouldn't! That bitch has no ethics whatsoever, I tell you!'

'Papa, you swore a moment ago that you hadn't slept with Meneka and are now admitting that you did! How dare you lie to me like this?' shouted Ricky.

Kapil looked sheepishly at his son. 'I didn't lie to you, Ricky boy. All I said was, I never slept with Meneka. I only had sex with her, then I left. So, technically, I wasn't lying, ya?' He tittered nervously.

'Papa, you're disgusting! Aren't you ashamed of what you've done?'

'Come on, Ricky boy, don't get upset. Arrey, even apna Bill Clinton tried this logic and almost got away with it. After all, boys will be boys!' Kapil winked at his son in an attempt to dismiss his tryst, but Ricky was in no mood to back down.

'Papa, you've got Meneka pregnant and now she's going to have your baby. And she's going to tell the whole world about it if I don't marry her! For fuck's sake, why can't you keep your dick in your pants, you filthy old man?'

It was the first time that Ricky had shouted at his father and Kapil was rattled by his wrath.

'Arrey, what am I supposed to do if a sexy woman throws herself at me? I'm just a man, not some mahatma! Meneka invited me to her hotel room after dubbing one day and said she had always been a huge fan of mine. Then, out of nowhere, she offered to give me a back massage and started unbuttoning my shirt. Obviously, at that point, I knew she was ready, willing and able. So I bonked her. It's that simple.'

'What's so simple about it? And why didn't you wear any protection? You can't go around sleeping with women and not think about the consequences, Papa!' Ricky was apoplectic.

'Ricky boy, I swear I asked her about that, but she said she was wearing a diagram or something, so there would be no problem. Now, obviously my seed is so potent it must have got her pregnant in just one shot. How is that my fault?'

'Nothing is ever your fault, is it? You do exactly as you please, with whoever you please, and refuse to accept responsibility for your actions. You're pathetic, Papa!' roared Ricky.

Kapil realized it was time to come clean before Manju heard the commotion and walked into the den.

'Ricky boy, please calm down and listen to me. First that bloody girl not only seduced me and then she also blackmailed me!'

'Really now? So, what did she do, Papa? Did she force you to have sex with her over and over again?'

'No, no, nothing like that. But she called me the next morning and said she had made a video recording of me bonking her. She threatened to show it to Manju and you if I didn't change the climax of *Pardesi Pardesi*.'

'What! And is that the reason you re-shot the end of our film?'

'Ya—that loony bin insisted she wanted the audience to see her marrying the hero in the climax. So, I was forced to spend over a crore to re-shoot, only because I didn't want Manju and you to find out I had made this stupid mistake. But then, when that Goyal fellow proposed to her, she immediately got engaged to him and forgot all about the film. She's a completely unprincipled crackpot, I'm telling you!'

'Papa, why didn't you tell me about this earlier? We could have done something about it together.'

Kapil moaned at his own folly. 'I'm so sorry, Ricky boy. All my life I have been taking care of Manju and you. I thought I had handled this matter, but the bitch is now threatening to ruin your life because of something that's my fault! I've made a big bloody booboo!'

Kapil sounded genuinely penitent and Ricky found himself feeling sorry for the randy old coot. He was also amazed at how icily calculating Meneka had been. She had not only successfully seduced Kapil and blackmailed him into changing the climax of the film, but she was also coercing Ricky to marry her.

'Papa, we desperately need to figure out some way to stop her. Otherwise all hell will break loose.'

'Ya, Ricky boy. This Kansal babe fucked us both—good and proper!'

Later that afternoon, Ricky slipped into his parents' bathroom. Snapping on a pair of latex gloves, he picked up his father's well-worn toothbrush and replaced it with an identical one. He then sealed the used toothbrush in a small zip-lock bag and couriered it to Amanda in London. The lab technician at Tower Bridge Hospital had assured them that it would provide them with sufficient evidence to conduct a conclusive paternity test. Ricky knew his duplicitous dad was quite capable of faking a genetic sample, so it was vital to discreetly source his DNA. Ricky first needed to confirm his father was indisputably the father of Meneka's child before he could plot his next move. Now that the wheels had been set in motion, all he could do was wait patiently for the results.

The young actor had read in the papers that Preeti Bhasin had signed a prestigious new project opposite one of the leading Khans of Bollywood. Ricky called his former co-star to congratulate her on her meteoric success. Preeti was delighted to hear from him and insisted that Ricky visit her on set as she was filming close by at the Mehboob Studios in Bandra.

Sitting in her vanity van, surrounded by make-up man, hairdresser, assistants and minders, Preeti was now every inch a Bollywood star. Ricky felt a pang of envy at seeing how her career had skyrocketed whilst his own floundered in a sea of uncertainty.

Ricky had recently begun to wonder again if he had made a mistake in not following his mother's advice and wooing Preeti when he had the chance. Now, when she was well on her way to becoming a leading Bollywood heroine, it might seem opportunistic to latch on to her stardom. But perhaps this talented, sweet-natured, earthy girl was the right woman for him after all?

As he waited for Preeti to finish her make-up, Ricky began to fantasize about marrying the former flight attendant just as his own father had married his stewardess mother. Preeti and he could settle down and produce films and babies together, living happily ever after in tinsel-town. As Ricky spun a fairy tale in his mind, a young assistant director entered the vanity van to inform Preeti she was required on set.

'I'm so sorry, Ricky. The shot is ready. But please wait for me. I'll be back soon.'

'Of course, no problem,' said Ricky, prepared to wait as long as necessary for the lovely Preeti.

'Oh Ricky, I want you to meet Prashant Sethi, he's our second A.D.' Preeti gestured to the young assistant, who smiled warmly as he shook Ricky's hand.

'Pleasure to meet you, Prashant. So, have you been working in the industry a while?'

'Yes, sir. This is my fourth film as an A.D. But I hope to become an independent director someday soon.' The fresh-faced young man sounded polite and self-confident.

'Prashant has written a fantastic script, Ricky. You really must read it,' chirped Preeti.

'I'd love to, Prashant. Feel free to drop it off at my place anytime,' said Ricky graciously.

Preeti leaned into Prashant and kissed him tenderly on the cheek. 'See darling, I told you—everyone wants to work with you.'

Prashant blushed and excused himself. When he had exited the vanity van, Preeti turned to Ricky and squealed excitedly, 'So, what do you think? Isn't he a wonderful guy? I only met him a few weeks ago and it turns out he's also from Chandigarh and has come to make it in Mumbai, just like me. I'm so happy, Ricky!'

Ricky managed a smile as he hugged his former co-star. 'He does seem like a wonderful guy, Preeti. And you're a truly remarkable girl. I wish you both every happiness. Now, I really must run, I forgot I have to be somewhere soon.'

Madame Menshikov, the Russian brothel keeper, demanded a substantial sum from the brothers Goyal to maintain a tactful silence on the indelicate details of Sir Dharmesh's death. Rana paid off the enterprising old woman and arranged for his father's body to be cremated in London. The Goyal patriarch had often expressed a desire to have his ashes immersed in the Ganga at Haridwar and it fell to his children to carry out his last rites in India.

Gautam had sunk deeper and deeper into a vortex of narcotic abuse and refused to heed Rana's pleas. 'Papa gave us everything, Gautam. We owe it him to fulfil his last wishes. You have to roust yourself from this stupor and make the journey to India with me.'

'You go. You are his older son. You can perform all the rituals. You don't need me, Rana,' said Gautam wearily.

Rana knew the drug-addled Gautam was reluctant to leave the sanctuary of his room in Belgravia. He was glad, though, that his younger brother was finally acknowledging him as a man.

After the first heart attack, Sir Dharmesh had drawn up his final will and accorded an equal share to both his children. Rana realized that, in the end, his notoriously chauvinistic father had been fair to both his offspring. Now, with Gautam wallowing in a drug haze, the field was wide open for Rana to take over the company. However, in his last days, Sir Dharmesh had extracted an oath from his first-born that he would take care of Gautam and guide him wisely. Rana knew he would have to honour this promise for the rest of his life.

Ricky Kumar studied the paternity test report that Amanda had emailed him from London and burst into his father's den.

'Papa, we need to talk!'

Kapil, who had been occupied all day surfing inter-racial porn sites, hastily slammed his laptop shut and turned to face his son.

'What is it, Ricky boy?'

'I've just received the results of the paternity test!'

'What bloody test are you talking about?'

'The one I had done in London to ascertain if you are the father of Meneka's baby.'

'What? How? Since when did you become so bloody devious, Ricky boy?'

'Since I realized what a horny old goat you are, Papa! You lie, you cheat, and you cause havoc in people's lives ...'

'Arrey, I know all that—just tell me what the report says. Is Meneka going to become my new bahu or not?'

'No, she's not. You're off the hook, Papa! Apparently the baby is not yours either.'

Kapil Kumar whooped with joy and did an impromptu jig around his son. Clambering atop his desk, Kapil looked heavenward and, perhaps inspired by the material he had been perusing on the Internet, bellowed with all his might, 'Free at last, free at last. Thank God Almighty, I'm free at last!'

Ricky smiled, shaking his head at his father's theatrics. Kapil Kumar was many undesirable things: a liar, a philanderer, a chauvinist and an egotist. The one thing he was not was the father of Meneka Kansal's baby.

Leaving his father dancing atop his desk, Ricky returned to his room and called Meneka in Delhi.

'Meneka, hi. It's me. I want you to know I had my dad's DNA test carried out at the same hospital in London where we got ours done. The results prove my father didn't get you pregnant either. So, it's got to be someone else, I'm afraid.'

'Oh, really? And you expect me to take your word for it? Do you think I am that naïve, Ricky?' snapped Meneka.

'No, I don't. So, you're welcome to come down to Mumbai, take a swab of my dad's DNA and conduct an independent test to satisfy yourself. Bottom line is, I refuse to be blackmailed into marrying you, Meneka. And if you want to send my mother a recording of you having sex with my father, please go ahead because there is nothing I can do to stop you. I just hope you come to your senses and do the right thing. Good luck, Meneka.'

As Ricky hung up, Meneka hurled her phone across the room in a terrible rage. She knew, in her heart, that Ricky Kumar was telling the truth. She had seduced Kapil and blackmailed him into changing the climax of the film at a point when she was desperate to establish herself as a Hindi film heroine. It was unlikely that fleeting fumble of a fuck with the ageing actor could have resulted in a pregnancy, particularly when she had taken ample precaution.

Despite all her threats, Meneka had no intention of making her sex tape with Kapil public. It would prove a monumental embarrassment if the masses saw the wheezing old actor pummel and paw Meneka clumsily from behind and collapse on top of her in a heaving mess within seconds. Meneka knew she did not have the stomach for a full-blown scandal that cast her as a conniving slut, foolishly impregnated by a man old enough to be her father. She had only been anxious not to carry this baby to term alone, without any emotional support, and had hoped the conscientious Ricky would succumb to coercion and agree to marry her.

Meneka, who had spent the better part of her life manipulating men into giving her what she wanted, was at a loss, now that her plans had backfired. She had once aspired to marry Ricky Kumar but ended up falling in love with Gautam Goyal. Gautam was her soul-mate but somehow, due to her own insecurities, she had doubted his intentions. The web of deceit and blackmail she had spun to entangle others had ensnared her. Though she had hankered all her life to be famous, Meneka knew that all she had achieved was fifteen minutes of shame. She had no career, no lover, and was carrying a baby whose father's identity was wholly unknown.

A knock on the door snapped Meneka out of her ruminations. It was her mother. Nina had heard the phone smash against the wall separating their rooms and had come to investigate whether her troubled daughter was okay. Mayank Thawani had recently proposed to Nina and she was ecstatic; many months of assiduously withholding sex had paid off. The randy geriatric was in heat and keen to whisk his bride away to Mombasa, where he could ravish her at leisure in the many rooms of his mansion.

'Are you all right, Mini?'

'No, mum—I'm not! Everything was going so well for me and now, suddenly, I can't seem to catch a break. It's so unfair!' Meneka collapsed on her bed and started to sob.

Nina sat down and gently stroked her daughter's back, something she hadn't done since the divorce eleven years ago. 'Don't worry, Mini. Everything will be all right. Once I get married to Mayank, you can come to Mombasa and quietly have your baby there. If you want, I will raise this child as my own. I know I haven't been a very good mother to you, darling, but perhaps I can be a better one to my grandchild. What do you say?'

Meneka looked up at her mother, surprised. Nina Kansal had been driven to desperation when Jagjit and she got divorced, leaving her to raise two teenage daughters whilst he philandered with a multitude of young women. Demoralized, insecure and alone, the once respected Nina had been relegated to an object of social ridicule as she indiscriminately sought companionship in the wrong places. Meneka could see now that her mother was not the cold-blooded troll she was painted to be, just a despondent divorcee suffering a severe mid-life crisis. It dawned on her that she too could head down the same path and end up an embittered woman whose rampant promiscuity would eventually prove her undoing.

Now that Nina had been offered a second stab at happiness, her insecurities had evaporated. She was offering to make amends for her misdeeds by adopting her daughter's illegitimate child. Meneka could only be grateful for her mother's largesse.

Rana Goyal had to employ all his powers of persuasion to convince Gautam to accompany him to Haridwar in Uttarakhand, where the peripatetic Ganga wends her way through the Himalayas to traverse the plains of north India. There, at the sacred Brahmakund Ghat, to the accompaniment of vedic chanting, the two brothers solemnly immersed their father's ashes in the holy river to ensure his soul passed directly to heaven.

Both siblings stripped to the waist to take a dip in the hallowed waters, which were reputed to cleanse a lifetime of sins. Gautam noticed the scars on Rana's chest and realized they were from the double mastectomy he had undergone to enable the transition from woman to man. After the ritual bathing, as they sunned themselves on the timeless riverbank, he felt closer to Rana than ever before. It had become obvious that it was futile to fight him. It was wiser to combine forces and forge a formidable team that could jointly nurture their father's legacy rather than dissipate it with their rivalry.

Sitting in these serene environs, united in their grief, Gautam turned to his brother and said softly, 'You know, Rana, Papa spent his life playing us against each other. He probably thought he was making us tougher and more competitive in the process. I want you to know I respect you and will not fight you any longer. You will always be my brother, but I hope, someday, you will also become my friend.'

Rana replied, 'Gautam, they say a dip in the Ganga is meant to purify our bodies and wash away our sins. But you also need to go back to Mumbai and purge yourself once again. I have spoken to Dr Behramjee, and he is willing to take you in. Tell me, are you ready to make the commitment?'

Gautam looked at his brother and nodded. Performing their father's last rites had given him a much-needed sense of closure, but this day also signified an important new beginning.

The next morning, the two brothers flew to Mumbai and after depositing Gautam in Dr Behramjee's care, Rana met with the Mumbai manager, Waman Dixit.

Dixit was shocked to see his old employer's daughter dressed as a man. He, however, heartily welcomed the return of Gautam Goyal to Mumbai. As his dear friend Senior Inspector Madhukar Bobde's grandmother used to say, 'The fruit of patience is most delicious.'

The day Gautam Goyal arrived in Mumbai, Ricky Kumar and his mother flew to Delhi and from there took a bumpy Fokker flight to Dehradun's Jolly Grant airport, intriguingly and eponymously named in honour of an obscure British colonial. There they engaged a private taxi to ferry them to the picturesque little town of Rishikesh where, on the banks of the Ganga, Babaji was scheduled to flag off Project Pavitra, his nationwide campaign to build toilets for the poor. Ricky's irremediable father had flatly refused to accompany them, saying he thought it ridiculous to travel halfway across the country to witness the digging of a shit pit.

Ricky was relieved he had succeeded in keeping the reasons behind his recent woes from his mother, not ever wanting her to learn what a philandering rogue her husband was. He was afraid Meneka might leak her sex tape in revenge and regularly monitored his phone to check if any scandal involving Kapil Kumar had erupted on the Internet. Also on his mind was the possibility that since the last time he met them, Rhea and Tarun might have hooked up together.

A buzz went around the media enclosure that Ricky Kumar had arrived from Mumbai. Even though his debut film had flopped, Ricky was considered a bona fide Bollywood star by the gaggle of local journalists, who hared off to collar him for an interview.

Kantilal Zaveri was delighted that his daughter had stepped up to the task entrusted to her. He was flush with pride; his only child had grown into a diligent and conscientious young adult. His wife, much like her erstwhile lover, Kapil, had no interest whatsoever in Babaji's exalted activities and considered such spiritual and philanthropic pursuits utter hokum. She had been perfectly happy to let her husband do his thing as long as he didn't expect her to get involved with his infantile plans for saving the planet. She only grew alarmed when Kanti began to indoctrinate their impressionable daughter. Rhea had already spent several months away from home, and her mother feared the naïve girl would become some sort of Babaji groupie, choosing to spend the rest of her days bathing lepers in India rather than settling down with a nice billionaire in Belgium. She had accompanied her husband to Rishikesh, with the intention of coaxing her headstrong daughter back to civilization at the earliest.

A marigold-festooned stage had been erected by the scenic riverbank where the ground-breaking ceremony would soon commence. The public service films Rhea and Tarun had produced would also be premiered here. Rhea walked behind the pandal to find Tarun, who was busy ensuring the powerful backlit projector that would beam the films onto a large screen was working perfectly. A jittery Rhea was expected to join Babaji on stage and give a speech outlining the purpose of their water pollution campaign.

'I'm so bloody nervous, Tarun. Why don't you speak instead of me?'

'No way, Rhea. This is your baby and you're going to be great. Just calm down, breathe easy, and relax …'

'That's easy for you to say! I've only ever spoken in college debates, never in front of the national media. Oh god, I could really use a drink right now.'

'Yeah? Well good luck finding booze in this holy city,' snorted Tarun. 'But you know what's available in abundance?' He produced a crumpled reefer from his jacket pocket and held it up with a flourish. 'This!'

'Where did you get that? Don't tell me you brought it on the plane?'

'No way. I bought it off a local sadhu this morning. A hundred bucks for a whole bagful of weed. Can you fucking believe it?'

'Put it away, Tarun, someone will see you!'

'Chill, Rhea. It's cool to toke in these parts. Marijuana isn't considered a drug by the locals—it's a transcendental medium, a pathway to meditation. Everybody smokes dope here.'

'You've got to be kidding me!'

'No, not at all. Even Lord Shiva is believed to smoke up, sitting cross-legged in Mount Kailash. Which is a great excuse for some sadhus to remain perpetually stoned.'

'Are you absolutely sure about this, Tarun?'

'Absofuckinglutely, trust me. Boom Shankar, baby!' Tarun jauntily lit the joint and took a deep drag. Having vetted its efficacy, he nodded in approval. 'Man, this is some serious shit! Come here—you've got to take a hit—it'll totally calm you down.'

Inhaling again, Tarun leaned over and gave Rhea a lengthy blowback, sending the potent smoke billowing into her lungs. After a couple more hits, Rhea realized Tarun was right. She felt light-headed and relaxed, completely ready for the world.

Unbeknownst to the toking duo, they were standing directly in the path of the backlit projector and the invitees milling about the venue were treated to a scandalous curtain raiser as two giant silhouettes repeatedly kissed on the big screen adjacent to the stage.

Ricky was engaged in an interview with a supari-chomping reporter from Dehradun, when he heard the commotion. He turned crimson when he looked up and recognized the dark phantasms snogging on screen. Politely excusing himself, he darted backstage to warn the blissed-out couple that they had inadvertently become the evening's opening act.

The rest of the evening played out according to plan, but an apoplectic Kaamiya had found the perfect excuse to whisk Rhea back to Antwerp the very next day. Through the nine-hour flight she berated Kanti for his part in ensuring their daughter would die a spinster. No self-respecting billionaire, she moaned, would ever want to marry a shameless tramp who also happened to be a depraved drug addict.

Rana Goyal had instructed Waman Dixit to engage the services of a detective to keep a close watch on his brother in Mumbai. Dr Behramjee was emphatic that he would not tolerate any shenanigans this time. He was already peeved by the callous manner in which Gautam had behaved with his favourite ex-patient, Sheena.

The day after Gautam checked into rehab, Dixit summoned detective Virendra Dhadda and Senior Inspector Madhukar Bobde to a meeting. The trio met at Dixit's favourite dive bar in Dadar, Night Lovers, and ordered a quart of whisky each along with several plates of masala paapad, paneer manchurian and everyone's favourite, Chicken 65.

'Bhau, paaji, I have asked you here tonight because, as you know, that chutiya charsi has returned to the Bawaji's clinic in Breach Candy.'

'Oye, I'm not surprised that munda has gone back on drugs after what all happened to him! At one time Gautam Goyal was world-famous for being a major laundiabaaz. But, by god, that Kansal kudi ghoomaoed him properly, hain? Jaisi karni, vaisi bharni!'

Detective Dhadda was abreast of the gossip surrounding Gautam, courtesy the Hindi press, which had breathlessly reported the cuckolding.

'Arrey, who cares why the fuck he has come back! The important thing is he is finally here, in aamchi Mumbai. Now we must act quickly, kai Waman?' Inspector Bobde was determined that this time Gautam would not get away scot-free.

'Correct, bhau! His poor papa died of a heart attack after seeing what shame his madarchod mulga brought on the family. Now I hear this bhadwa has inherited half of his father's wealth, so we can squeeze his balls fully for at least a few crores.'

'Waman, shall I just thoko a case on him for breaking your nose? Once that angrez ki aulad gets my danda up his gaand, he will happily pay whatever we ask to be released from police custody.'

But Dixit had already accepted substantial monetary compensation from Sir Dharmesh for his broken nose and also signed a letter exonerating Gautam. 'Nai re, bhau, let's think of some other, better way of making money from the gandoo.'

Detective Dhadda was struck by an ingenious idea. He had read all about the legendary enmity between Ricky Kumar and Gautam Goyal. Ricky had not only beaten up Gautam at a party in London, but also had an affair with Gautam's fiancée. Worse, the handsome actor was rumoured to be the real father of Meneka's baby. Dhadda had, in his possession, explicit photos of Ricky Kumar receiving oral sex from some NRI girl. The detective was sure Gautam would gladly pay five crores for these pictures to exact revenge on his bitter rival. Though Dhadda had demanded ten crores from Kapil Kumar in exchange for the photos, his lawyer had negotiated the detective down. Dhadda was convinced Hotchand Fatwani had quietly pocketed the other five crores and felt quite justified in recovering this sum from Gautam.

He briefly wondered if it was necessary to involve Dixit and Bobde in his plan. He had successfully blackmailed Kapil Kumar on his own and didn't require these money-grubbing jokers to broker the deal with Gautam. After considerable soul-searching, the private dick concluded he might as well give his partners in crime a small portion of the proceeds. After all, there was such a thing as honour among thieves.

One of the perks of being born into a filmi family was that many producers were willing to give a failed star son a second chance at becoming a hero, convinced his daddy's box-office charm would rub off some day. Several such actors, some of whom had delivered as many as a dozen consecutive flops, were considered more bankable than a fresh face who did not have the heft of a famous father's name to provide ballast in Bollywood.

A brave new breed of young film-makers who wanted to defy convention and bring an independent edge to local cinema had recently emerged in the Indian film industry. International art-house cinema informed their sensibilities and even though some of these youngsters ripped plotlines from foreign movies, it was gratifying that their sources were more esoteric, like Korean and French films, rather than mainstream Hollywood blockbusters.

At Preeti's behest, Prashant Sethi approached Ricky with an intelligent, gripping script for a noir film, *Fareb*, set in Mumbai. Downhearted after witnessing the recent shadow play in Rishikesh, Ricky jumped at the opportunity to immerse himself in the role of an edgy, urbane reporter who gets embroiled in the conspiracies of guileful politicians, unscrupulous media barons and the Mumbai underworld. He looked forward to applying the new techniques he had learnt from his drama coach in London and diligently attended script readings and acting workshops to prepare for the part that would mark his second coming as a Hindi film hero.

The reinvigorated actor was unaware that Preeti had exerted her newfound influence in Bollywood and convinced an astute producer to sign both Prashant and Ricky by agreeing to waive her considerable fee. The sympathetic actress was sure all Ricky required was a decent script and a passionate director to showcase his innate talent. Besides, Preeti was delighted to have an opportunity to repay Ricky for the faith he had once so generously reposed in her.

Napping in his room between counselling sessions one afternoon, Gautam was woken by Sister Fonseca, who announced that he had some visitors. He was annoyed to find the obsequious office manager and a burly turbaned man waiting for him outside in the sun-soaked veranda of the sanatorium.

'Hello, Gautam baba! How are you keeping these days? Myself, Waman Dixit. You remember? Last time we met, you broke my nose. Here only, one year ago?'

'Yeah, I remember, Dixit. And I am sorry. I was obviously not in my senses at the time.' Gautam was groggy from sleep but knew he ought to be civil to this unctuous man.

'Arrey, please don't apologize and make me shameful, Gautam baba. I am very sorry you are losing your daddyji. He was a top-class man, ekdum top-class.'

'Thank you, Dixit. So, what brings you here? Has Rana sent you?'

'No, no … we … actually, we are wanting to discuss something fully personal and private with you. This is my very good friend, Shri Virendra Dhadda, who is number two detective in all Mumbai.'

Dhadda proffered a chunky, ring-bedecked hand to Gautam. 'Very pleased to make your acquaintance in person, sirji. I have read so much about you, so it is big honour to finally meet you.'

'Cheers, mate. Now, what do you want to discuss?'

'Gautam baba, detective Dhadda is having some sexy photos, which we think may be of very much interest to you,' Waman whispered conspiratorially.

'Look, Dixit, I'm really not interested in any porn you may be ...'

'Oye, sirji, please take one look only and then decide if you are interested or not.' Dhadda gave Gautam an exaggerated wink and held out the large manila envelope he was carrying.

Gautam perused the incendiary contents and said coolly, 'All right, how much?'

'Sirji, for you, no bargaining. Only one last, full and final price, five crore rupees.'

Gautam snorted. 'Five crores? Are you barmy? I'll give you five lakhs.'

'Arrey, sirji, what are you saying? What will my poor children eat in five lakhs, hain?'

The negotiations lasted a considerable time while both parties arrived at a mutually agreeable amount. Gautam assured Dixit the money would be arranged upon his release from rehab and the pictures could then be handed to him. As Messrs Dixit and Dhadda jubilantly exited the sanatorium, Gautam Goyal revelled in the knowledge that he had Ricky Kumar precisely where he wanted him.

ELEVEN

Gautam Goyal was glad he had chosen to enter rehab at a point when the narcotics he had begun consuming in London had not yet taken over his system. Motivated as he was to kick the habit and begin life anew, Gautam was a model patient who impressed the sceptical Dr Behramjee with his focus. He also earned the admiration of nurses and ward boys by helping to counsel other inmates worse off than him.

Now, almost at the end of his month-long stint, Gautam sat in the counselling room, patiently outlining the basics of the twelve steps of narcotic rehabilitation to a rebellious seventeen-year-old whose sponsor he had recently become. The young punk reminded Gautam of himself, full of angst and attitude, spewing venom at the world, uncomprehending that the cause of his numerous problems lay chiefly within himself.

The ward boy, Munna, popped into the room with a message that Dr Behramjee had sent for Gautam. He was to go to his private quarters. Never having been asked there before, the intrigued inmate strode past a frail security guard who unlocked a massive iron gate to allow him access to the sanatorium annexe, where the doctor resided alone in his cavernous bachelor pad.

A creaking servant, flaunting stained teeth and a spotless

uniform, received Gautam at the gate and escorted him slowly through Behramjee's labyrinthine mansion, first laboriously ascending a flight of steps flanked by yellowing marble busts of beaky ancestors, philanthropists all. They negotiated the ginormous living room, taking a circuitous route between Art Nouveau rosewood bureaus and filigreed side tables, past overstuffed chintz sofas, and wove their way through a maze of rattan-knit Bombay fornicator chairs that lay randomly scattered for no other purpose than to thwart smooth passage across the hall. The doddering retainer finally ushered Gautam into Dr Behramjee's private study and withdrew with a bow, straining to pull shut the large stained-glass doors that depicted the prophet Zarathustra radiating light and love.

The good doctor, dwarfed by his massive mahogany desk, waved Gautam in. 'Mr Goyal, come in, come in. I have a wonderful surprise for you.'

Sitting in front of Behramjee was a guest who rose to greet him. 'Hello, Gautam, it's good to see you again.'

'Sheena!' Gautam was shocked. 'I ... I didn't expect to see you here!'

'Young Ms Kansal has come to invite me to the opening of her exhibition at the Jehangir Art Gallery tomorrow,' beamed Dr Behramjee. 'And she has also graciously presented me with one of her captivating paintings,' he said, gesturing to a large canvas that rested close by. 'When I informed her you were in residence, she said she would love to see you again. So, I'm going to give you two youngsters some privacy and go on my rounds.'

Dr Behramjee left the room with a twinkle in his eye, hoping he had played Cupid by reuniting the former lovers.

'I'm sorry to have surprised you like this, Gautam. But when Doc B told me you were here, I knew I had to see you.

I … I suppose you must have figured out by now it was I who put Mukesh Menda up to writing all that stuff about Meneka and you?'

'Yeah, my brother told me. He said you'd found out through your family doctor. But … it doesn't really matter, Sheena. I suppose we're even now. Though I don't regret what I did to Mukesh—that tosser deserved what he got.'

In an effort to convince Mukesh to post the story, Sheena had lied to the scandalmonger, telling him that she had managed to delete his naked pictures from Gautam's phone. When the Goyal scion posted graphic photos of the shrivelled scribe online in retaliation for his scurrilous writings, Mukesh 'Meow Meow' Menda was mortified. The catty columnist suddenly found himself the laughing stock of the nation and was now better known by the epithet 'Chilly Willy'.

'Look, I'm truly sorry, man. I'm really ashamed of what I did. I was just so angry at the time, and I guess, also jealous of Mini and you. I know it's because of my actions you guys broke up and …'

'It's all right, Sheena.' Gautam shrugged. 'I'm glad I found out sooner rather than later that Meneka had been cheating on me. I suppose I should be grateful to you that I didn't end up raising Ricky Kumar's bastard as my own.'

'That baby isn't Ricky's, Gautam. The paternity test proved that in London. Didn't you know?'

Gautam was surprised. 'No … I didn't. I guess when I found out the baby wasn't mine, I really didn't give a shit whose it was.'

'Yeah, Mini doesn't seem to know either. I guess she wasn't really discerning about who she slept with. It's been a bit of a problem with her.'

Gautam was bitter but curious about what had become of

the girl who had broken his heart. 'So, is Meneka with someone now? And has she dropped her sprog yet?'

'Nope. I don't think there are too many takers, even in Delhi, for a heavily pregnant girl, you know? But she's due in a couple of weeks, so she's in Mombasa.'

'Mombasa? What the Dickens is she doing there?'

'Well, since it was too late for her to abort, my mum—who's recently married and settled in Kenya—suggested she have the baby there. Dad really doesn't want to deal with the shame of his unmarried daughter delivering in Delhi.'

Jagjit Kansal had once nurtured high hopes for Meneka, but she had managed to besmirch his sullied name even further. Jagjit's goons had succeeded in keeping the media on a leash for years, but since the floodgates had opened, there had been no stopping the torrent of bad press that engulfed the once feared politico.

'I see. So, what does Meneka intend to do with her kid?' asked Gautam.

'Mum and I have both told her that we'd like to raise her baby if she doesn't want it. Man, I really do hope she decides to give it to me.'

'You want to raise this baby—on your own? That's … great!'

'Yeah, I thought, why not? I think I'll make a totally awesome mom, and frankly, if I can have a child without the hassle and heartache of marrying some jerk, that's ideal, don't you think?' Sheena winked at Gautam, favouring him with a knowing smile.

'Wow, I didn't realize I'd turned you off men for good.' Gautam winced.

'Don't flatter yourself, man. It's just that I'm so much happier being single. Later on, who knows? If I find a nice guy, I may settle down. But right now, I'm done with the lot of you.'

Gautam nodded, relieved Sheena had found her equilibrium.

'You know, I'm glad we met because I meant to call you after I got out of here,' said Gautam.

'Oh yeah? Why is that?'

'I ... I guess I'm pretty serious about following Doc B's twelve-step rehab programme this time. So I needed to apologize to you and ask forgiveness for having ended things the way I did. I behaved like a right tosser, despite everything you did for me!'

'Oh, I forgive you, man. So, chill. I bear you no grudges now. I mean, till a few months ago, yeah, I prayed every day you'd die a slow and miserable death.' Sheena laughed. 'But then I realized we were too different to have worked out as a couple. So, now that we've both forgiven each other, we're good, right?'

Gautam smiled wistfully. 'Yes, we're good. Thanks, Sheena. I'm glad we buried the past. So, you're painting and exhibiting now? That's brilliant.'

Gautam walked up to look at the canvas that Sheena had presented Dr Behramjee. Her nude portrait of herself, raw, tormented, convulsed in grief, was both disturbing and beautiful. Her brush strokes seemed a flurry of stabs and gashes. There was no doubt that he had hurt Sheena deeply, this painting being a manifestation of her anguish.

Gautam was aware he had not asked Sheena's forgiveness for entering into a relationship with her sister after having dumped her. Perhaps it was implicit in all that he had said so far and there was no need to articulate the guilt he felt. But he knew that, as Dr Behramjee said, in order to be exorcised from the past, it was imperative to seek complete absolution.

'I ... also wanted to apologize about hooking up with

Meneka. I didn't know at the time she was your sister, and then it was too late—I had already fallen for her.'

'Yeah, Mini has that effect on men, Gautam. I mean, it's understandable you guys were so attracted to one another. You're the same, you two. Two friggin' peas in a pod.'

'Well, that didn't turn out very well, did it?' retorted Gautam.

'Mini messed you up pretty bad, huh? What happened? You got your heart broken and started snorting again?'

'Yeah, I guess I took her two-timing rather personally. I know I was weak and sought the easy way out. But look at you. You remained focussed and found your path. That's ace, Sheena. Well done, you!'

'Thanks, man. Listen, I have to run. Got to get to the gallery by six. But it was great to see you again. You be good, okay? And this time, stay clean.'

Sheena gave her old boyfriend a hug and, as she was leaving, turned and called out, 'You know, Mini's not a bad kid, Gautam. She's only about as messed up as you and me. Just messed up differently, that's all.'

Ricky Kumar ran for his life, weaving through a maze of cargo containers stacked high in the Mumbai dockyards. A bunch of thugs armed with sickles and hockey sticks chased after him, intent on murder. Breathless and desperate, Ricky attempted to give his pursuers the slip by ascending a rope ladder to clamber aboard a docked ship. He had managed to scramble halfway up when he lost his footing on the slippery rungs and fell onto the filthy jetty floor below, landing with a thud. Ricky writhed in pain even as the goons pinned him down and their leader unsheathed a jagged chopper and raised it menacingly over his head. The terror in Ricky's eyes was palpable as he prayed for a miracle to save him ...

'Cut!' shouted Prashant Sethi, pleased he had finally canned this arduous tracking shot on the fifth take. The debutant director was shooting *Fareb* in cinema verite style and wanted his lead actor to perform his own stunts in order to achieve as much on-screen authenticity as possible. 'That was fantastic, Ricky. Why don't you relax for a few minutes while we set up the next shot?'

Exhausted but satisfied by his exertions, Ricky hobbled away to flop into a flimsy folding chair that stood close by. His earnestly efficient spot boy proffered a bottle of water and attempted to deflect the unrelenting sun by holding an oversized umbrella over the hero's head. The city's fleeting dalliance with winter had come to a brusque end and the weather had turned sultry and oppressive. The muggy heat had made everyone's skin clammy and saturated their clothes with sticky perspiration. The stench of dead fish wafted in intermittently, and the humid sea breeze added to their misery. Prashant Sethi's maiden venture could not afford the luxury of air-conditioned vanity vans, so the film's hero sportingly sweated it out in the open with the rest of the unit.

The spot boy informed Ricky that some foreign-sounding sahab called Gautam Goyal had called on his mobile and requested an urgent call back. Several months had passed since he had last had contact with Gautam and Ricky wondered what the volatile Goyal scion could possibly want with him. When Gautam requested a ten-minute meeting that afternoon, and even offered to drive down to the docks, an intrigued Ricky agreed.

A flock of seagulls had zeroed in on a lone fisherwoman balancing a basket-load of freshly caught pomfret on her head. They repeatedly dive-bombed her, impudently lightening her precious burden. Seeing the hapless woman trying to fend off the aerial marauders with one hand, Ricky dispatched his spot boy to assist her. As the Man Friday gambolled away, whooping and waving his big, black umbrella at the birds, Ricky noticed Gautam's car approach. The young actor steeled himself, apprehensive of once again coming face to face with his old foe.

'Ricky Kumar, thank you for agreeing to see me!' boomed Gautam, lowering the window at the back of his Mercedes. 'You look like you really need to cool off. Would you like to get in?'

The chilled, plushly upholstered interiors of the vehicle seemed enticing, but Ricky, drenched in grimy sweat though he was, resisted the temptation. 'If you don't mind, let's take a walk, shall we?'

'Sure, why not? Bit of sun will do me good, I suppose.' Gautam alighted, holding out the envelope he had brought with him. 'Here, these are some close-ups I acquired recently. Go on, take a look.'

Ricky took one glance at the graphic photos and was stupefied. He knew that if these were made public it would cause enormous embarrassment to the Zaveris and his own family. 'How ... where did you get these?'

'That's irrelevant, Ricky. What's important now is what I intend to do with them, isn't it?'

'Do what you want, Gautam! But I'm not going to succumb to any bloody blackmail,' snapped Ricky.

'Relax. I have no desire to make these public. I mean, when I bought them a few weeks ago, I intended to post them online—to humiliate and punish you for all the grief you've caused me. You see, I thought Meneka had cheated on me with you—that she was pregnant with your child. So, naturally, I wanted revenge. But now I know that's not true. So, I'm prepared to hand these pictures over to you, Ricky. But first I'd like you to give me an explanation for one niggling question that's been bothering me all these months.'

'What is it you want to know?'

'Why the fuck did you spread those vicious lies about seeing me toot in the loo at Pink Paisley? I was in there taking a sodding dump. But you told everyone I was back on drugs, didn't you?'

Ricky knew Gautam was right. He had wilfully sullied the ex-junkie's reputation. 'I … I'm sorry about that, Gautam. I was in shock at seeing you after all those years.'

'Where the fuck do you even know me from, you lying twat? I've lived in London my entire life and I'd never laid eyes on you till that night in bloody Delhi.' Gautam's infamous temper was on the boil.

Ricky looked Gautam calmly in the eye. 'So, you really don't remember me, do you?'

'No, I don't! So, would you please remind me?' snarled Gautam

'Fifteen years ago, when you were a senior at Eton, you … you sodomized me on the very first day I entered school. I was only ten, but you had your friends strip me and hold me down in the dorm and then you raped me. You fucking raped a ten-year-old boy, Gautam Goyal!'

The terrible secret Ricky had kept pent-up finally came to the fore. For years, he had stayed awake nights plotting how, one day, he would avenge his humiliation at the hands of the bully. Today he had the chance to confront him with the truth.

Gautam was shocked. 'I … I honestly had no idea. I'm sorry, Ricky.'

'Are you, really? I realized I must be only one of your many victims, Gautam. So it's no surprise you don't remember me. But I never forgot you. How could I? I was bleeding, sobbing, traumatized by what you had done to me. But I was too ashamed to tell anyone.' Ricky tried hard to restrain the tears that sought to stream down his face. He didn't want Gautam to have the satisfaction of seeing him cry again.

'Look, Ricky, I'm sincerely sorry for what I did. But you have to know this was a common practice in school in those days. I went through the same ordeal when I joined … and I suppose I tried to avenge my own humiliation by buggering other boys.'

'Don't you dare try to mitigate your actions, Gautam! I've lived with the memory of that day for fifteen years. You're the scum of the earth, and I will do whatever is in my power to destroy you!' Ricky was trembling with rage, his old wounds freshly gouged.

Gautam knew it was up to him to make amends. 'Listen to me, Ricky—we have both suffered because of this enmity—and we can continue our feud till only one of us is left standing. But I've just come out of rehab, and I'm determined to make a fresh start. Please accept my apology and my offer of a truce right now.'

'And is that why you came here today? So you could wave these photos as a white flag before me?' snorted Ricky.

'Yes, I did. Look, Ricky, the photos are yours to keep, regardless of whether you choose to forgive me or not. But I am trying to pick up the pieces of my fucked-up life. So, the decision is yours, because I can't bloody well force you to absolve me of my sins, can I?'

Ricky was conflicted. Gautam stood before him, emotionally naked, asking forgiveness at a point when every pore of his being craved revenge. He turned away and stared out at the grey sea, awash with bilge from the ships harboured in the docks. He realized it must have taken a lot for the notoriously arrogant Gautam to suppress his ego and come make amends. Ricky knew he had avenged himself in London by thrashing Gautam in full public view. Gautam had not only lost face but also subsequently his fiancée who, no doubt, he had once loved dearly. His tormentor had suffered for his crimes, fallen back into drug abuse and was now asking for atonement. Ricky made his decision. He turned and held out his hand in an offer of reconciliation. And Gautam was glad to grasp it, finally putting an end to their vendetta.

Heading back to his Walkeshwar penthouse through the congested, enervating streets of mid-town Mumbai, Gautam knew there was much in his past he had to atone for. But making amends with Sheena, and now Ricky, were vital steps on the road to recovery. He realized that receiving forgiveness was strangely more gratifying than any pleasure he could have derived delivering retribution. It dawned on him that he was now a changed man and perhaps ready to make the journey home.

Amanda Hardy had a vested interest in collating as much information as she possibly could about Ricky Kumar and his family. In the course of her research, the garrulous Brit made a startling discovery that prompted her to pick up the phone and dial him in Mumbai. The young actor was pacing his room, rehearsing his lines for the next day's shoot, when he received Amanda's call.

'Hiya, Ricky! How's the new film coming along?'

'Great, thanks. It's been hard work, Mandy, but we wrap in less than a fortnight. I'm thrilled with the way it's shaping.'

'That's grand, love. Now listen, you remember when I sent you those paternity test results from Tower Bridge Hospital?'

'Sure, what about them?'

'Well, I was going through the lab report a couple of days ago, and I noticed something rather odd. There wasn't any commonality between Kapil's and your DNA.'

'Really? And should there be any?'

'Yeah, absolutely. If Kapil's your dad, you should share a common genetic strain. So, I asked the lab to run the tests again, and I've only just got the results.'

'And …?'

'Well, based on this report, it seems there's no way that Kapil Kumar is your biological father.'

'What? How can that be? Are you sure about this?'

'The lab did check twice, and if the samples you sent me are genuine, then yeah, Kapil's not your daddy, ducky!'

Ricky's heart began to pound. 'So, if he's not my father, who is?'

'How the hell would I know? Shouldn't you be asking your mother that question, love?' Amanda chuckled.

'Yes, yes, you're right, Mandy—speak later, thanks, bye!'

Ricky raced through the passage leading to his parents' bedroom. When he didn't find his mother there, he bolted down the stairs to the kitchen, but she wasn't there either. As he yelled for his mother in the massive living room of Casa Kumar, he suddenly heard the tinkling of a little bell and realized she was in the pooja room, where she performed her elaborate daily rituals to propitiate a multitude of deities.

'Mamma, I need to talk to you!'

Seated before a marble statue of Lord Ganesh, his mother raised a finger to her lips to signal that Ricky needed to keep silent until she had finished her prayers.

Kapil Kumar had taken off with his cronies for a week-long golfing vacation in Bangkok, even though none of this motley group of middle-aged men actually played the game. Ricky waited what seemed like a lifetime for his mother to complete reciting her mantras. She then performed an aarti in front of the deity and insisted on smearing a vermilion tilak on her son's forehead. Ricky was festering for an answer, and when his mother finally allowed him to speak, he blurted out. 'Mamma, I know Kapil Kumar is not my dad. Please, please tell me who my real father is?'

'What nonsense are you talking, jaanoo? Of course Papa is your real papa. Who else can it possibly be?'

'You tell me, Mamma. The DNA tests from London prove he is not my biological father. I beg you, please tell me the truth—was I adopted?'

'Absolutely not, Ricky! You are my real son. I gave birth to you at Breach Candy hospital twenty-six years ago. Why are you suddenly talking all this rubbish about being somebody else's child?'

'Think, Mamma, think! Is there any way at all that Kapil Kumar is not my natural father?'

'I'm sorry, Ricky, but Kapil is your papa and I am your mamma, and you cannot believe some stupid medical test that says you are not our son.' Manju began to cry, distraught at Ricky's irrational rant.

Seeing his mother in tears, the distressed actor calmed down and hugged her tenderly. 'I'm so sorry, Mamma. I didn't mean to upset you. It's just, these past few days, I've been under a lot of stress and when I got a call about those silly lab reports, I freaked out. Of course there has to be some mistake. Who else but Manju and Kapil Kumar could have produced such a handsome son, haan?'

Through her tears, Manju smiled at Ricky. Then she turned away and was silent for a moment before looking back at him. This time, her expression was calm and steady.

'Ricky,' she began tentatively, 'there is something I suppose I should share with you.'

'What is it, Mamma?'

'I ... I was involved with another man, an airline captain, at the time when I first met Kapil.'

'Oh, really? And you think he could be my natural father?'

'I honestly don't know, jaanoo. You see ... your papa and I had a very difficult courtship. He was forever chasing after other girls, which bothered me very much. It was difficult for me to accept that he flirted with his heroines while claiming to be in love with me.'

Ricky had a lot to say about his randy father's peccadilloes but decided it was wiser to let his mother speak instead.

'So ... at one point I felt I had had enough and decided to break off my engagement to Kapil and I ... I went back to my old boyfriend.'

'The airline captain?'

'Yes, but Kapil became very jealous when he heard I was involved with Bhushan again. So, he landed up at my house one day and asked my father for my hand in marriage. He swore he was a changed man and would never look at another girl.'

'And that's when you agreed to marry him?'

'Yes. Kapil was going away to Europe for three months on a film shoot and wanted me to come along with him. My father wasn't prepared to let me go until we were married. So, the next morning, we went to a mandir and exchanged garlands to keep my family happy.'

'Wow, Mamma. How very filmi of you!' Ricky smiled at his mother, who blushed at the memory of her roller-coaster romance.

'So, then, what happened to your old boyfriend?'

'He ... he was heartbroken that I had again left him for Kapil. He quit his airline job and left Mumbai for good.' Suddenly, Manju fell silent.

'So, you think there's a possibility you could have got pregnant by this man?'

'Jaanoo, if those medical reports are correct and you are not Kapil's son, the only other person I was ever intimate with was Captain Bhushan Prakash. I think you have a right to know that.'

Ricky tried valiantly to keep his hopes from surging. He had faced such bitter disappointment this past year that he felt it prudent to not become too optimistic now.

'Thanks, Mamma. I appreciate your telling me all this. So, do you have any idea where I can find Bhushan Prakash? Or have you lost touch with him?'

'I ... I do know where you can find him, jaanoo. He lives near Rishikesh.'

'Really? So do you ever meet him when you visit Babaji's ashram?'

'Ricky ... Bhushan Prakash is Babaji.'

As the aged jeep, with its disbelief of a suspension, rattled through the ashram gates, Ricky took several long, deep breaths of the fortifying mountain air and prepared for his meeting with the man who could be his biological father.

The savant soon sent for Ricky, inviting his anxious young disciple to join him for a walk through the apple orchard that surrounded the picturesque property.

'I know you have come with several questions, son. Feel free to ask whatever you want.' Babaji's disarming smile put the nervous lad at ease.

'Thank you, Babaji. My mother told me you were once an airline captain and that you quit your job and became an ascetic?'

'Yes, Ricky, I was very much in love with Manju, so when she decided to marry your father, it broke my heart. I felt disillusioned with the world and longed to escape the life that reminded me of her. I sought refuge in the mountains, and that is where I studied with many masters. I spent years absorbing the Upanishads, the Vedas, the Gita; I studied yoga, ayurveda and philosophy. And then, in trying to escape myself, I ultimately discovered my true self.'

They made their way down a narrow path flanked by drooping branches laden with cherubic Himachal apples.

'And today you're doing such extraordinary work all across India. You truly are an inspiration, Babaji.'

Babaji smiled and shook his head. 'No, son. In fact, it is I who am constantly inspired by the goodness that exists within people. I merely channelize other people's contributions to the needy. At some point, we all require a guide to show us the way.'

'I am so grateful you reminded me there is no substitute for hard work, Babaji. Last time, I came here looking for some mystical solution to all my problems, but you sent me right back to Mumbai,' said Ricky, remembering his own naïveté.

'Yes, I had to send you away because I knew you only came seeking asylum from yourself. It was important to throw you back into the ocean of reality because if you did not learn to swim, you would have sunk into an abyss of escapism. I, myself, almost made that mistake once, as you now know.'

'I understand, Babaji. And thank you for being so patient with me.'

Babaji stopped in the midst of a small clearing and gave Ricky an enigmatic smile. 'I see a lot of myself in you, son. Now, Manju tells me you think I may be your natural father. So, would you like a sample of my DNA?'

Ricky nodded, grateful that Babaji had been so forthright. This learned yet unassuming man, who advocated decisive action and plain speak in daily life, seemed the perfect embodiment of his own teachings.

The next morning, Ricky went to seek Babaji's blessings and to bid his guru goodbye. Babaji enveloped him in a deep embrace and sent him on his way, imparting a final piece of sage advice. 'Ricky, I will be very proud if it turns out you are indeed my son. But please know, no matter what the outcome, Kapil Kumar will always be your father.'

Having spent more than five weeks away from London, Gautam was glad to be home on the midnight flight into Heathrow. He awoke early the next morning and, after a light breakfast, went to meet Rana, who was already at work at the company headquarters. Walking into the florid office that had until recently been occupied by Sir Dharmesh, Gautam felt a wave of grief overcome him.

Rana rose from his swivel chair to greet Gautam with a warm hug. The throne Sir Dharmesh once proudly sat on had been moved to a corner beneath a large framed portrait of the departed tycoon, symbolizing his formidable presence in the lives of those who had inherited his legacy.

'It's good to see you, Gautam. You're looking really well. I hear you've been an exemplary patient at the clinic!'

Gautam smiled. 'So, you've been keeping tabs on me, have you? Just like Papa used to?'

Rana nodded. 'I had to. Behramjee warned me he wasn't going to brook any nonsense from you this time. And, by all accounts, you acquitted yourself admirably. Well done!'

'Cheers, Rana. And thanks for arranging to send the dosh to Dixit. I really appreciate that.'

'Hey, no problem. It's your money after all. But why did you need so much cash transferred to Mumbai? Was that weasel blackmailing you or something?'

'Nyaah—I needed to settle some old debts, that's all.'

'Well, I'm glad to have been of assistance. Sit down, won't you? I have something important to share with you.'

Gautam sensed the change in Rana's tone and took a seat across from his brother at their father's imposing Baroque desk.

'About a fortnight ago, while we were busy sorting out Papa's affairs, I discovered a concealed cabinet at the bottom right corner of this desk. Though we searched everywhere, I couldn't locate the key. Finally, I had to summon a locksmith, and when we eventually opened it, I found, among other papers, this particular document.' Saying this, Rana removed an envelope from a drawer and handed it to Gautam. Inside was a paternity test report from Tower Bridge Hospital. Gautam looked at it disbelievingly, for it showed that his DNA was a perfect match for Meneka's baby. Rana allowed his brother a moment to digest the ramifications of the document.

'But … how can this be?' said Gautam, trembling. 'I saw the test results myself, and they clearly stated there was no match between me and the child Meneka is carrying. So does this mean …?'

'That Papa lied and showed you a fake test result? Yes, Gautam, I'm afraid that's exactly what he did.'

'But … why?'

'Well, obviously he disapproved of Meneka thoroughly and only agreed to let you marry her because you were so bloody adamant. But then, it seems he learnt from his people that it was Jagjit Kansal who had orchestrated the closure of our restaurant in Delhi. Apparently this is Kansal's modus operandi to extort vast sums from desperate restaurateurs.'

'And I walked straight into that tosser's trap, literally begging Papa to ask Kansal for help!'

'Yeah, for years that crook has been taking some of the biggest players in the business for a right royal ride. Naturally, Papa was livid when he learnt how Meneka's dad had manipulated him and he bided his time, waiting to get revenge on the Kansals.'

'Wow. And I thought I was the vindictive one in the family! But how do you know so much about all this? Were you in on it too? Tell me the truth, Rana.'

'Of course not! Two weeks ago, when I found the paternity test report, I went and confronted Dr Batra. He admitted that Papa had begged him to fudge the results so he could get the Kansals off his back for good. Papa was convinced that Meneka and her father had you wrapped around their little finger and were planning to usurp Masala Magic after his death. So Batra finally gave in and played along.'

'That's sick! Papa destroyed my relationship with the only woman I've ever loved because of his own fucking agenda and insecurities?'

'Don't be too harsh on him, Gautam,' said Rana, gently. 'I don't think Papa knew what true love really is. He was too preoccupied with building his empire to submit to that experience. I think you, perhaps, were the greatest love of his life, and he felt he needed to protect you in the long run. I'm not saying I condone what he did, but I think we should at least try and understand his motivations.'

Gautam was seething with rage but he knew his brother was right. Sir Dharmesh had run his business and lived his life the only way he knew how: by alternately playing benevolent patriarch and ruthless despot. It became obvious to Gautam that he also had himself to blame for the loss of Meneka. Despite having initially begged her to keep the baby so he could curry favour with his father, he had abandoned her when it was too late to abort. Feeling cuckolded and betrayed, he had severed all ties with her, little realizing his raging jealousy had obfuscated his judgment.

The valuable life lessons recently learnt at Dr Behramjee's clinic sprang to mind. Gautam knew he now not only had to find it in his heart to forgive his father, but also seek absolution from the woman he once loved.

Turning to his brother, Gautam asked, 'Rana, have you any idea if Brit nationals require a visa for Mombasa?'

Ricky Kumar tried calling Rhea repeatedly on her international mobile number, but an infuriating pre-recorded Belgian voice insisted she was currently unavailable. Ricky then called Tarun Roy in Delhi, hoping he would know of her whereabouts, but the ad-man dejectedly informed Ricky that Rhea had broken off their relationship shortly after that fateful evening in Rishikesh and he hadn't heard from her since.

Desperate, Ricky dialled the Zaveri residence in Antwerp, and after several long rings, Kaamiya answered.

'Hello, Aunty Kaamiya, this is Ricky. May I speak with Rhea, please?'

'Ricky, Rhea is dead!'

Ricky was stunned. 'Oh my god! How … when did this happen??'

'One month ago.'

'But … but how … all of a sudden?'

'I'm sorry, there is nothing more I can say. Goodbye, Ricky.' Kaamiya's voice was choked, she was too distraught to speak.

As the receiver clicked, Ricky stared blankly into the distance, searching for answers, grappling with the loss of his beloved Rhea. Had she committed suicide, ashamed of what she had done in Rishikesh? Could Rhea have overdosed on marijuana? Was that even possible? Or, had she got hooked to some other, more dangerous drug that had eventually consumed her? Had her mother, perhaps, murdered her for bringing dishonour to the family?

A blood-curdling cry, part howl, part wail, emanated from deep inside the distraught young man. The terrible outburst of anguish reverberated through Casa Kumar, rattling the Rajasthani latticed windows and almost causing the plaster on the ersatz Michelangelo mural to crack.

The incessant rapping on his bedroom door brought Ricky

back to his senses. He unlocked the door to find his anxious parents standing outside.

'Jaanoo, are you okay? What has happened? Why are you shouting like this?'

Ricky looked at his mother and fell into her arms, weeping uncontrollably. 'Rhea is dead, Mamma, my Rhea is dead!'

'What nonsense are you babbling, Ricky boy? Rhea isn't dead,' snorted Kapil.

'She is, Papa, Aunty Kaamiya told me so!' sobbed Ricky.

'You really ought not to take everything my melodramatic mum says so seriously, Ricky.'

Ricky looked up from his mother's shoulder, where he had buried his head, to find Rhea standing there, in the flesh, looking resplendent in a blue silk sari.

'Rhea! You're ... alive?'

'Yes, very much so! So, my mum told you I was dead, huh?'

'Yes. She said you died a month ago, and then hung up on me,' said Ricky, reeling with shock and attempting to wipe away his tears.

'Oh, you poor boy, I'm so sorry ... but you know what a demented drama queen my mum can be! Well, I suppose, in a sense I have been dead to her since I walked out of home a month ago.'

'But where have you been? And why didn't you call?'

'I ... I needed time to clear my head, Ricky. I realized I couldn't lead a cloistered existence in Antwerp any more. Besides, my mum was driving me crazy with all her ranting and moaning. So I spoke with my dad, and we decided the best thing for me to do was to go back to working with Babaji.'

'You ... you've been with Babaji all this while?' Ricky was baffled.

'Yes. I knew I couldn't abandon his project after having

caused so much embarrassment at the launch. I needed to make amends for my foolishness and Babaji was gracious enough to take me back. I'm now officially the national coordinator for Project Pavitra.'

'But … but … I was with Babaji just a couple of days ago!'

'I know, he told me. I was away in Indore when you visited the ashram. And since I was scheduled to fly into Mumbai today for a meeting with some donors, Babaji said I should come over to your house in the evening. He said you had something important to tell me?'

Manju Kumar realized it would be prudent for Kapil and her to withdraw at this point. 'Ricky, jaanoo, why don't you take Rhea to your room and make her comfortable. Your papa and I will go to bed now. Goodnight, you two.' Saying this, she hastily bundled her perplexed husband away before he started asking any awkward questions.

Ricky nodded at his mother in gratitude as he led Rhea inside the bedroom and bolted the door. Grabbing her faultless face with both hands, he began to smother her with kisses.

Rhea exclaimed, 'Hey, what do you think you're doing? You know we can't possibly …'

'Yes, we can, Rhea! Yes, we can!' said Ricky, excitedly, as he pounced on her again.

'But how … all of a sudden?'

'It's a miracle, Rhea—but I finally got conclusive DNA evidence this evening that Kapil Kumar is not my natural father after all!' exulted Ricky. 'I'm Babaji's son, Rhea, I'm Babaji's son!'

Rhea was stunned. 'Oh my god! So, this is what Babaji meant when he told me to remain patient and never compromise? That's why I could never allow myself to go through anything serious with Tarun—because deep down I knew we were meant to be! But, how come …'

'Listen, stop talking, will you? I've waited far too long for this moment!' said Ricky, as he threw Rhea on the bed and started to unravel the swathes of silk she was wrapped in. Unfastening her bra and gazing in rapture at the magnificent breasts he was about to ravish, Ricky remembered his biological father's prophetic words.

'When the time is right, she will appear just as suddenly as she disappeared.'

The universe had taken its time teasing, tormenting and testing him, but ultimately it had proved equitable and rewarded Ricky with the true love of his life.

'Fuck, fuck, fuckity fuck!' Ricky shouted triumphantly, as he pulled off his pyjamas and clambered atop his giggling soul-mate. 'Fuck, fuck, fuckity fuck!'

Manju Kumar reddened when she heard Ricky's frenzied war cry, but her husband, yesteryear's superstar Kapil Kumar, grinned proudly. His once wimpy son had finally proved a chip off the old cock.

EPILOGUE

Amanda Hardy sat at her computer, putting the final touches to her debut novel. It was a rambunctious tale of two warring young men, both born into wealth and privilege, who had loved, lost, and sometimes loved again.

Their lives intersected and collided intermittently across different cities around the globe.

Their trials and tribulations were both laughable and lamentable.

They were poor little rich kids who were also lost souls, desperately trying to find themselves.

They had both suffered for the sins of their fathers but found it in their hearts, finally, to forgive them.

They were chalk and cheese but, ultimately, kindred spirits.

Amanda was going to regale her readers with this thinly veiled exposé of the foibles and shenanigans of the high and mighty. She meant to hold a mirror up to the strutting peacocks who regularly appeared on the society pages and occasionally made it to the front page for entirely the wrong reasons.

Amanda had a tentative title in mind for this delightfully scurrilous tome.

She intended to call her novel *Scandal Point*.

ACKNOWLEDGEMENTS

Grateful thanks to Nonita Kalra, for believing.
Ash Chandler, sounding board and soul brother.
My family, for reasons innumerable.
Sidharth Bhatia, Shefalee Vasudev, Alex Kuruvilla, Seema and Jaideep Mehrotra, Jerome Marell, Shunali Shroff, Chinmayee Manjunath, Deepanita Singh, Anita Shirodkar, Sujata Assomull Sippy, Ravina Raj Kohli, Zubin Shroff and Ashwin Mushran for their generosity and friendship.
Shruti Debi, agent extraordinaire.
V.K. Karthika, for her implicit faith and impeccable taste.
Thanks also the indefatigable team at Harper Collins India.